Freedom in My Love

By the same author

The Lady and the Luddite
The Major's Minion

Freedom in My Love

Linden Salter

ROBERT HALE · LONDON

ISBN 0 7090 7054 3

Robert Hale Limited
Clerkenwell House
Clerkenwell Green
London EC1R 0HT

2 4 6 8 10 9 7 5 3 1

Typeset in 11/14pt Palatino by
Derek Doyle & Associates, Liverpool.
Printed in Great Britain by
St Edmundsbury Press, Bury St Edmunds, Suffolk.
Bound by Woolnough Bookbinding Ltd.

To my mother, Mary Salter,
with thanks

Acknowledgements

I thank my family and friends who read and commented on early drafts: Brian Salter-Duke, Michal Salter-Duke, Chris Salter, Mary Salter, Sue Carpenter, Meaghan Duggan, Linda Broemel and Diane C. Sheats for their invaluable information and advice.

I am also grateful for the help of the Deafness Association of the Northern Territory, members of the Republic of Pemberley at http://www.pemberley.com, and the Northern Territory Writers' Centre and Department of Arts and Museums.

If I have freedom in my love,
And in my soul am free;
Angels alone that soar above
Enjoy such liberty.

To Althea, from Prison

by Richard Lovelace (1618–1657)

Chapter 1

I SHALL not cry out, I vowed. She would not want me to cry out. She was parted from me by ten years and an ocean, and she could not know this was happening, or even that I was still alive. She would want me to bear without a sound the lash of this man who wasn't worthy to sweep the road in front of her.

I was tied to the whipping post, arms spread wide on the crossbar, back bared. Before me I could see dismayed black faces drawn up in a half-circle to watch this example of terror. I'd been forced to whip all too many of them, but they knew their lives would be even worse when another slave-driver was chosen from among them or bought from outside to replace me. I had stood between them and our owner for seven years; I would not stand so again.

I felt the warm sun of the South Carolina Christmastide weather on my back where in a moment the whip would strike; I smelt the stench of the swamp and the plantation. Behind me, I heard the voice of my owner; though I had to call him 'Massa' to his face, in my mind I refused to recognize his mastership merely because the law made me his property.

'Listen hard, if you got God's good English enough to understand me,' he roared to my fellow slaves. 'There's Caesar on the post; you'll be there too if you disobey me. I could get a high price for him – as much as any two of the rest of you niggers together – but I scorn the lure of money when I deliver justice. Two of you, Olakunde and Sarah, dared to try to run away, but

11

by God's providence they were caught, and they told who'd helped them.'

Of course they had told; I didn't blame them. Sarah had been strung up from a branch by her wrists, pregnant as she was, and lashed until she or Olakunde talked. Their loyalty to me had earned her ten stripes before Olakunde broke.

'I swore to them that they'd be whipped no more if they told me, and I won't imperil my immortal soul by breaking my word to a nigger. But Caesar – I trusted him as I never trusted a nigger before, but Satan found a place in his soul to tempt him to betray me. He'll feel the Lord's wrath and mine. When my arm's tired, I got three sons to continue justice. He won't come down until he's dead.'

I didn't fear death. Ahead of me I saw a lot of misery and little joy; I wasn't going to miss much. And she wouldn't grieve that I was no longer in this world; I'd been out of her world for ten years. Though I couldn't see it, I could almost feel his arm raised for the first blow. Then, suddenly, I heard the voice of his youngest son. 'No, Pa.'

'You try to stop my justice, Luke? Why?'

'Pa, it'd be – wrong.'

'Wrong? You gambler, you wastrel, you fornicator! You dare to tell me what's wrong when I see three half-breeds of your unnatural begetting in front of me? If your mother, God rest her soul, hadn't been the pure woman she was, I'd say you were none of mine. Get out of the way of my justice!'

The first blow fell, filling me with an unendurable agony that had to be endured. I waited for the second, trying to think of her through the pain.

But it didn't come. Instead I heard the sounds of a scuffle behind me, and then the old man's voice raised to a fury that none of us had ever heard even in him. 'You raise your hand against your father? You – you—' Then he gave a great cry, and there was silence.

'My God, Luke,' came the voice of the eldest, Matthew. 'See what you've done! You've driven him into an apoplexy!'

'He's not dead,' cried Mark. 'Quick, call a doctor.'

Then the whispered voice of the old man, desperately getting the words out. 'And a lawyer. Bring a lawyer.' I heard the sounds of him being carried into the house, and I saw the rest of the slaves being sent back to work.

I hung there the rest of the day, without water, the insects maddening the wound on my back, until night fell. Under cover of darkness, black hands untied me and black shoulders supported me back to our quarters. After seven years of being their driver, I was one of them again.

I joined in the subdued talk in Gullah, the half-English that had developed between people with no language in common except that of our owners, almost incomprehensible to outsiders. I waved away Olakunde's apology, saying that I'd have broken earlier than he had, and that he should have spared Sarah those stripes. They had rejoiced when she'd told him she was carrying his child, but their joy had changed to despair when old man Smith had decided to make a quick profit by selling her as a wet nurse. They'd tried to escape together, but they'd failed. Now their punishment was to be sold separately to owners as far apart as the old man could find. Punishment enough, as I knew; I'd gone through ten years of it. I saw in Sarah and Olakunde what my love and I had once been to each other; that's why I'd helped them run. My love and I had once done the same, and we had ended in the same failure.

Old man Smith would have been gratified if he'd known how much everyone except me wanted him to live. Appalling though he was, most of the other owners in the district were even worse. His Bible told him that fornication was a sin, so he kept away from slave women and tried to get his sons to do the same (a failure in Luke's case). He made sure that we always had Sundays off. He never ordered a whipping without what he thought was good reason, and though there were all too many good reasons, these didn't include bloody-mindedness and the pleasure of hearing people scream. While other slave owners would inflict hundreds of lashes, old man Smith abided by

Deuteronomy 25:3, and forty was the most he'd order – though forty lashes with a bull whip would flay the skin off the back. Either from his faith in the Bible or from his desire not to destroy his belongings, he had never before ordered a slave to be whipped to death. His sentence on me was a measure of his fury because he had trusted me and believed that I was his faithful slave; he wanted to show by terrible example that even his most expensive item of property was not immune.

If he died now, his property would be broken up and slaves divided with little regard for family ties. Matthew and Mark were their father's sons, and we could expect no better treatment from them. Even the hope of going to Luke was destroyed by the news that the lawyer had been and gone while old man Smith was still conscious enough to change his Will and disinherit his youngest son.

Luke was not exactly our friend – there could be no friendship between a black slave and a white owner – but in dreams of bloody rebellion, everyone agreed that he should be spared. All of the many slave women he'd had were willing; he relied on charm and generosity rather than force, and the rest of us had conspired to keep his misdeeds from his father unless there was a brown baby in evidence against him. He'd undoubtedly have wasted his substance in riotous living, but until then life would have been more endurable. Now we didn't have even that to console us.

So we talked, and worried about a future over which we had no control, and then we slept. I lay on my belly to spare my wound, dreaming – as I'd dreamt every night for ten years – of Althea.

Once I had been a page boy in an aristocratic household in Grosvenor Square: one of many page boys in England chosen for the blackness of our skins to set off the whiteness of the fashionable ladies we served. I was a slave, with a silver collar round my neck to mark my bondage, but I was as well fed and petted as Pompey, the little black spaniel who wore a collar that

matched mine and whose care was one of my duties. Those
duties were many: attending Lady Mountford at any time of the
day or night, carrying all the things she might need, calling a
sedan for her, and otherwise standing immobile in my gaudy
livery as evidence of the Mountfords' wealth and fashion. But
they were, on the whole, duties I enjoyed and tried to be good at.
When I failed, I was beaten rather than whipped, and could
sometimes get away with a mere reproach. It had not been a bad
life; I was far better off than many of the English children I saw
starving on the streets or sweeping our chimneys.

I have only confused memories of the time before I was a
page. I don't know where I was born, or when; I don't know who
my parents were, what they named me, or why I was taken from
them. But I have no memory of a long sea journey, so I might
have been born in England; some time around 1750, it must have
been.

Althea was the only child of Lady Mountford's sister, a
woman who had married for riches as Lady Mountford had
married for rank. But a contagious brain fever had robbed
Althea of her parents and her hearing in one blow. She was nine
at the time; I was probably a year or so older. Lord and Lady
Mountford took no more account of me listening to their conversation than they did of Pompey, so I knew that they regarded as
a chore the task of looking after their deaf orphaned niece, but
were consoled by the thought that her hand and her consider-
able inheritance would become one day the property of their
son, George.

One day soon after she arrived, I heard the sound of sobbing
coming from her room. It wasn't my place to do anything, but I
couldn't pass by. I knocked – there was no answer, of course –
and went in. She was lying with her face buried in her pillow,
weeping bitterly. She couldn't hear me; only when I knelt by her
bedside and lightly touched her shoulder did she lift her head
and look at me. 'Can I help?' I asked. It didn't matter that she
couldn't understand me; I was the first person since the death of
her parents and the loss of her hearing to show human

sympathy. She wept on my shoulder, sobbing out her miseries, and I put my arms round her and said comforting words that she couldn't hear.

That's how it started. In the eyes of the world I was a black slave and she was an English heiress, but in our own eyes we were children who were happy only when we were together. She learnt to read my lips long before she learnt to read anyone else's, so I was appointed as her interpreter, a duty which suited us both very well. George Mountford showed no sign of thinking of her as a prospective wife, but treated her with the indifference and contempt that was to be expected from an Etonian towards a deaf girl-cousin.

An expensive governess arrived: Miss Campbell, who knew the ways of Mr Braidwood, founder of a college for the deaf and dumb in Edinburgh. Very intelligent and well-educated, she spoke the finest English I've ever heard; only when she was relaxed and comfortable did any trace of her Scottish accent appear. She taught Althea how to manage in a hearing world; and she taught me to read. She might have lost her position if it had been discovered, but her evangelical conscience told her that all God's children should be able to read His word. Ever since, when I read the Bible, God speaks to me in her pure, clear, careful voice.

One day we took a discreet walk to the church and I was baptized. I didn't want to be called Caesar, a name bestowed on me by my owners; I wanted to choose my own name. There was a line from the Old Testament, *The Lord spake unto Joshua the son of Nun*, which I heard as 'the son of none'. I was the son of none, too. To God, Althea, Miss Campbell and myself, I became Joshua.

For years, Althea and I were as happy a pair of children as could be found anywhere in London. With her courage and quick wit, she learnt to let her deafness trouble her no more than my slavery troubled me. If we thought of the future at all, we planned that she would set up her household, with places for Pompey, Miss Campbell and me, and we would continue more or less as we were.

It was a foolish dream of childhood. Perhaps Miss Campbell could have warned us, if we'd let her know. And when the years started to turn Althea into a woman and me into a man, perhaps the feelings for each other that were developing should have warned us too, but we suppressed them. Happiness is hard to give up.

We were forced to. I was getting much too big to be a page; I was already taller than Lady Mountford and would soon overtop her husband. My voice broke – to Althea's delight, since she could hear deep voices better than high ones. Lady Mountford seemed to forgive me for growing, once I'd seen off a couple of footpads who tried to rob her late one night (if you're a well-dressed black boy in London and you want to survive, you learn to fight). I assumed that I'd become a footman; there were plenty of black servingmen in London, and I had an ambition to reach the towering heights of butler.

Then came Miss Campbell's departure; Althea and I put on faces of congratulation at her marriage to Mr Macleod, a Presbyterian minister, and her return to Edinburgh, but with each other we confessed our dismay. The last straw was a trivial incident: I let Pompey free of his leash and he caused an accident that embarrassed the Mountfords.

A day or two later, Althea came to me with the dreadful news. Through a window she had read the lips of Lord and Lady Mountford as they were having a serious and private conversation. 'Oh, Joshua!' she cried. 'They're going to have Pompey destroyed, they're going to send me to school to learn how to be a fit wife for George, and they're going to sell you!'

We made a fantastic, childish plan: we would run away to Scotland, which had different laws from England. Under Scottish law we'd heard there was no slavery, and I would be free. Under Scottish law we'd heard it was possible for people even as young as we were to get married; we would become husband and wife, and she would be out of the Mountfords' guardianship. Then we would go to Miss Campbell and her new husband in Edinburgh and beg them to help us to earn our

17

livings until Althea came of age and could control her fortune.

Fantastic, childish – even more so as we took Pompey with us – and yet it nearly worked. In hindsight I marvel at the qualities in us that took us across the border to Gretna Green, the first place in Scotland, well known as a place for eloping couples to marry. I knelt down and ceremonially kissed the soil that made me a free man. Then we went straight to the blacksmith's to have him take off my silver collar: I would not wear this expensive mark of bondage a moment longer than I had to.

It was many hours into the long Scottish night of late autumn, and the blacksmith and his journeymen were packing up, so he was reluctant, but he agreed when I explained that he could keep the collar. We had to use signs as much as speech to communicate: Miss Campbell's slight Scottish accent and even her husband's stronger one hadn't prepared me to understand his thick brogue, and Althea couldn't follow a word.

Correctly assuming that we were eloping, he did his best to explain Scottish marriage laws while he took my collar off, and I translated for Althea.

'He says anyone can perform the ceremony – it doesn't need to be a priest.'

'That's good.'

'We don't need to have lived here three weeks as we would in England.'

'That's very good.'

'We're old enough to marry.'

'That's wonderful!'

'But we need to be sixteen to do it without the consent of our parents or guardians.'

'That's not good at all.'

My size and deep voice meant that I could easily pass for sixteen (I had no guardians now the Mountfords were no longer my owners), but Althea could not. She took off her diamond bracelet and put it next to my silver collar where it now lay on the anvil. 'Does this prove that I have the consent of my guardians?'

There was a brief conversation between the blacksmith and the journeymen, of which I could follow about one word in two. Then he turned to Althea and spoke very clearly and loudly; thick though his accent was, she could understand him. 'Do – ye – want – tae – wed – this – man?'

'Oh, yes!'

'An' ye want tae wed her?' he asked me.

'Yes.'

'Then – I – shall – marry – ye.' He picked up my collar and her bracelet, and put them in the pocket of his apron.

We turned to each other, relieved and smiling. I didn't listen to anything more he said, until there was a noise loud enough even for Althea to hear as he hit the anvil with his hammer to attract our attention. Then he made it very clear that a proper ceremony couldn't be performed until the morning, so that his family, friends and journeymen could partake of the marriage feast, for which we would pay. Althea's ear-rings would have to go the way of her bracelet.

We took a room in a nearby inn – Gretna Green is used to supplying the needs of runaway couples – and we celebrated. Soon Pompey curled up before the fire, and Althea made ready for bed. As before on our journey when we'd slept in the same place, I turned my back for decency's sake.

'You won't have to do that tomorrow,' I heard her say. 'We'll be husband and wife.'

I nodded: there was no point in my saying anything to her when she couldn't see my lips.

'You're sure you want to marry me?'

I caught the uncertainty in her voice, so I put my hand over my eyes to preserve her modesty and turned to face her. 'Of course I do. You've helped me to get my freedom; the least I can do is help you to get yours.'

She said nothing, and I heard the sound of her getting into her bed. 'You can open your eyes now,' she said as she wrapped the covers round her to keep out the cold. Soon I heard her quiet breathing.

19

I was too excited by my freedom to sleep – my neck felt light now the collar had gone – and for an hour I sat by the fire rejoicing. Then I shifted Pompey from the hearth, unrolled the blanket where I intended to sleep, prepared myself for bed, and put out all the candles except the one by her bedside. Just before I blew that out too, I took a look at her to make sure she was comfortable. I saw her golden hair spread out on her pillow, the freckles that she so disliked on her nose and cheeks, and her lips parted in sleep.

At last I knew the truth: I was in love with her. Our marriage on the morrow would not be merely a contrivance to save her from the Mountfords' plans: it was something I wanted from the depths of my being, far more important to me than my freedom. And I knew, from that moment on, there would never be any space in my heart for any woman but her. Her eyes opened, and I saw in them that she felt the same for me. She held out her arms to me, I leant towards her, and we kissed. We started our journey as boy and girl; we finished it as man and woman.

Before dawn the Mountfords found us; they'd guessed where we would come. We were literally pulled from each other's arms and carried back to England. Lord and Lady Mountford drove off with Althea (and Pompey); I was trussed up and left to George. From the border to the wharf at Liverpool, the only time he stopped punching and kicking me was when he was too tired to continue. I was lucky that we hadn't managed to get married, he said; if we had, the best way to get her out of it would have been to make her a widow.

I didn't feel lucky. I was sold to the first slave trader who offered for me; as it happened, he was sailing direct for Charleston. If he'd been going on the other two sides of the infamous triangle, via the coast of West Africa to take on more slaves, I doubt if I'd have survived; to endure the Middle Passage in the hold of a slaver you need a will to live, and I had none. I was sold to a half-literate rice grower in South Carolina, whom I would have turned away from the door in Grosvenor Square.

Straight from the cold English climate to the heat of a South

Carolina rice plantation newly cleared from the swamp and still alive with biting insects and venomous snakes, I was almost as shocked and despairing as any African off a slave ship. Only my determination that I would return to Althea had kept me alive then – that, and my contempt for the man who was my new owner. Between him and his sons they couldn't summon as much learning as I'd picked up as a page boy. He read the Bible, went to church every Sunday, prayed to God, claimed to be Christian, and would have a fellow human beaten to the bone.

What use to me then were my skills? The ones I'd been taught – care of silks, how to dress and powder hair, the best way to summon a sedan chair – were as irrelevant as the ones I'd picked up from civilization's table, all the books I'd read surreptitiously. The other slaves were either born into their condition and accustomed to the work, or they had been torn from Africa and were at least accustomed to the climate. They had their own society, their own religion and belief: it was not mine. The only skill I had that saved me from being the lowest of the low was my ability to fight.

But eventually I learnt the language of the plantation and the ways of the slave quarters. I learnt the yearly cycle: clearing the ground, digging the dykes, sowing the rice, flooding the fields, pulling the weeds, harvesting the crop, and threshing and polishing the grains. I learnt to work in the heat of the sun knee-deep in mud with my back aching from bending, and I learnt to work efficiently so that my day's task was over soon enough to give me an hour or two to myself.

Life became – no, I won't say tolerable, because it wasn't. But it was at least less intolerable than at first. Sometimes I could even satisfy my hunger to read: there were newspapers that were supposed to be used for our bedding. I stole a Bible, and found a discreet place to read it. Any other book would have brought me a whipping, but I risked it on the chance that my God-fearing owner might be embarrassed to punish someone for reading this one. Not that I believed in it any more; my faith was soon worn away by the example of my new Christian

21

owner, so different from Miss Campbell. But there were good stories, and promises of vengeance on the oppressors.

Then old man Smith gave me a task that spared me some of the backbreaking work in the fields: the care of the dogs. The other slaves feared and hated those fierce hounds, but I like dogs. Even these could appreciate a scratch behind the ears and a pat on the back, and I'd taken care to make friends with them in case they were ever used to hunt me down. Those big vicious brutes were as different from pampered little Pompey as I was from the pampered page boy I'd once been. I'd been turned into a big vicious brute too.

Three years after I arrived, an outbreak of smallpox carried off Mrs Smith and a quarter of the slaves; I was immune, thanks to Lady Mountford's insistence on having her household variolated against it. I was made slave-driver in the place of the Yoruba man who'd previously held the position. I was bigger and stronger than those born on plantations and fed slave rations all their lives, and I knew the ways of the white man better than the Africans who'd been brought in to replace the losses, so I was given the whip of office.

And I used it. For seven years I used it. I never inflicted a stroke that I wasn't ordered to, but I inflicted every one of those that I was. I still had the occasional whipping myself, but never so badly that I couldn't pick up the whip afterwards and carry out our owner's orders on someone else. Last thing Saturday, so the victim had Sunday to recover, old man Smith would assemble us and order the punishments that he'd decided – twenty for missing a weed in the field, thirty for not obeying an order instantly, forty for what he considered insolence – and I would carry them out. I worked on every trick I could to make the torture less: hitting the post before the body, which part of the back could endure most pain, how to make a lot of noise and merely raise the skin until the last few strokes when I'd draw enough blood to satisfy our owner.

I had to hide my contempt for him and my hatred of what he made me do. I had to be fawning and abject towards him so that

he'd think of me as his good and faithful servant rather than
what I really was: a man forced to be his property, who loathed
him and all he stood for. And to the other slaves I had to become
the toughest man on the plantation; they had to know that,
though I might seem brutal, I could have been a lot more brutal
if I'd chosen. I had very little space to make my life and theirs a
fraction less abominable than it could have been, but I used
every inch of it. It cost me my self-regard, and it would have cost
me my spirit if I had not had my dreams. Only in dreams could
I be what I wanted to be: not Caesar the slave and slave-driver,
alternately grovelling and vicious, but Joshua, a man who loved
a woman a world away.

I became known as a good driver; good in the eyes of both
slave and owner. I could calculate to a nicety how much work to
do that would leave us a few hours to ourselves without being
assigned to other tasks; I helped the Africans out of their despair
on their arrival and showed them how to survive; I settled
disputes among the slaves with calm logic, kind words, or
strong fists.

Most of the time I got away with show and threats – I could
flick the whip so close to a body that the slave could feel the
wind and know that an inch to one side would have taken the
skin off. But sometimes threats weren't enough. One night, two
big Africans that I'd flogged the month before decided to take
their revenge on me rather than our owner. Nobody interfered
either way; I was on my own against them. But for sheer bloody
savagery, the streets of London are a better school of fighting
than the forests of Africa; though I was bruised and reeling at the
end of it, I was still on my feet with all my teeth, and they
weren't. I could have had the skins flayed off their backs if I'd
reported it; I did not. One of them was Olakunde, who became
the nearest I had to a friend (I couldn't let any man – or any
woman – get really close to me in case I had to flog them one
day). The other ran away six months later and was caught and
brought back – as a corpse, luckily for him.

Miserable as our lot was, with men turned old before they

23

were forty, with women seeing half their children dead before their first birthdays, with the whips, the snakes and the back-breaking work, it could have been worse. That ran like a refrain through our lives. Old man Smith could have been even more brutal; a lot of slave owners were. When the work was hardest in the heat of the summer, at least the whites fled the conditions and left us alone most of the time so long as we did the work we had to. In what passed for winter in South Carolina they came back, and at least we didn't have to work so hard. Above all, everyone knew that any other slave-driver would have been worse than I was, and they knew that I made our lives as bearable as I could. There were few runaways; though I never informed on them, I never helped them escape – until Olakunde and Sarah reminded me of what I'd once had.

I nursed three longings: for revenge on the powerful white world in general, and in particular on old man Smith, and on the Mountfords who had brought me up and then sold me; for my freedom; and, even more than those, for Althea: to share with her once more what we'd had for a few hours.

A stupid dream: even if the impossible happened and we met again, she would be a fashionable lady, in all likelihood married to George Mountford, and I'd be a black slave. But it kept me alive when I had nothing else, and that night I dreamt of her as I'd done for ten years.

Chapter 2

OLD man Smith died in the early hours of the morning. Until the funeral and the reading of his Will we had a unique holiday. Nobody came to assign us tasks, and I wasn't going to fill their place as I'd have done before. The only thing they did was secure our quarters so we couldn't escape. Usually our days off were filled with singing and dancing as we used up our energy in purposes that were all our own, with tunes from Europe marrying rhythms from Africa to produce a music that belonged entirely to us. But celebrations were not in order now, so everyone quietly did what they wanted. People caught up with work that they chose to do, mothers played with their children, lovers enjoyed each other's bodies not exhausted from work, and the rest of us luxuriated in the rare bliss of idleness. There was no point in making plans: we had no control of our destinies. The best we could do was enjoy the moment and try not to worry about the future.

For quiet entertainment we told stories. African tales mixed with those from the Bible; we didn't care what the origin was, just so long as it was a good yarn. My reading in England had given me a stock of tales that the others didn't know, so the tricky tortoise and Daniel in the lions' den were joined by Puss in Boots. It was the first story I had learnt to read aloud; I remembered as I told it to the slaves in the quarters how Althea had intently watched my lips, her own moving in sympathy when I stumbled over a word, and her applause when I finished: 'You can read, Joshua! You can read!'

Too soon our holiday was over and the future began. We were all assembled in front of Matthew and Mark. Olakunde was despatched to Jamaica, and Sarah to Virginia, which was better than the other way round. He knew that he'd probably have hell in the West Indies, but he could take comfort that she would have a privileged position in the less vicious conditions of Virginia – there was even a chance that she'd be well fed enough to have milk to give their own child with what would be left over after the white woman's baby had taken its fill.

The rest of us waited for our fate to be decided as we were divided between the two half-properties. The brothers had been brought up to respect marriage, so husbands and wives were kept together with their small children. Even those who were parted from those they loved knew that the properties were close enough that visits were possible. It could have been worse.

At the end, when the rest of the slaves had been allotted to one or the other, I was still left standing. Matthew looked at me with hatred. 'As for you, you're Luke's. You deserve each other.' Their father, in his notion of Christian forgiveness on his deathbed, had left me to him as his only inheritance.

Between that moment and the moment I stood before my new owner in the room he'd grudgingly been allowed to keep, my plan came to me. It was the story of Puss in Boots that did it: the third son left with only a clever cat who passed him off as a lord and won him a fortune. I didn't have time to fill in the details, only the outlines and the way to begin. Luke, the amiable forni-cator and gambler – he might agree to play the part. And what could I lose in trying?

It didn't start well; Luke glared at me with loathing. A bottle of rum was half empty on his table, and his breath reeked of it. Usually he took care of his appearance, but now his chin was unshaven, his fair hair was lank with sweat, and he'd obviously been sleeping in the same clothes for days. 'It's your fault, you nigger rat. If it wasn't for you I'd have my share of Pa's money. What got into me to save your goddamn black skin?' He grabbed his whip and started to raise it. 'I'll flog you half to death, and I'll sell the rest for what I can get!'

For ten years I had waited for a chance as good as this; I must not lose it. 'I suggest that you reconsider,' I said; and the accent that came from my mouth was not the half-English of a South Carolina slave, but the finest, most aristocratic English I could contrive.

His hand stayed in mid-air; he blinked. I seized my small moment of grace. 'You might get four hundred dollars for me – though somewhat less if I'm badly beaten. On the other hand, I could make you extremely rich.'

'What?' He stared at me as if indeed I were a cat that had suddenly started to speak to him. His eyes told him one thing about me; his ears told him something utterly different. I could see perplexity in his face; would his upbringing and his eyes defeat his ambition and his ears? Curiosity came to my rescue. 'How?' He lowered his arm, but he did not put the whip down.

'Before I was sold here, I was page boy to an English lady. I know about the English aristocracy; I grew up watching them. I can show you how to make them accept you as one of their own, and you can make a fortune from them.'

He raised the whip again. 'Don't spin me your yarns, nigger.'

I was about to lose him. 'You consider that a South Carolina rice grower's son isn't as good as an English nobleman?'

'Of course he is, you—' He broke off, looked at me thoughtfully, and put the whip down on the table. 'I'm listening, boy.'

'In London there are beautiful, high-born ladies with husbands who neglect them, just waiting for someone like you to pleasure them. There are brothels with women who make the best of the ones in Charleston look like half-dollar whores. There are gambling clubs where they play for stakes that could buy up your father's property a hundred times.'

'I'm still listening.'

'You could marry an earl's daughter. You could sneer at all

those rich merchants in Charleston who try to keep you away from their women. It will take a quick wit, courage, and the ability to bluff.' He had the last two, certainly, and he could convince himself that he had the first. 'I know the rules of the game; all you'd have to do is play the cards right.'

'But I ain't got no cards!'

'You have some. You can ride and shoot better than any man in South Carolina – the English lords will like that. You have charm and good looks – and the English ladies will like that. You can learn their manners, a man with a mind like yours.' At least, I hoped he could.

'Nope. I couldn't do it. Learning ain't my style.'

'If I didn't have a black skin I could pass as one of them myself. You think you can't learn what I've learnt?'

'Course I could, nigger. But I'm a good patriotic American. Ain't right for me to desert my country when like as not we'll be fighting against the goddamn British for our liberty and independence within the year.'

I had my own fight for liberty and independence to worry about. 'You think that a good patriotic American shouldn't cheat the British ruling classes and take money from them that might otherwise go to keeping America a colony?'

He sat down and poured himself a slug of rum. 'Keep talking, boy. I don't believe you, but it's a goddamn fine story.' Then he looked at me suspiciously. 'What's in it for you?'

'I would become the superior manservant of an English gentleman, a condition vastly better than being a slave on a South Carolina plantation. And I am grateful to you for preventing me being whipped to death.' This was true. I would not tell him my other reasons, but I had no objection to doing him a good turn in the process.

'What kind of English gentleman?'

'Perhaps you could be a duke's illegitimate son, who has made his fortune in the Americas.'

'Which duke?'

'You don't reveal your father's sin.'

He smiled. 'I like it. Being a bastard won't spoil my chances?'

'Not when balanced against your enormous fortune.'

'I ain't got no enormous fortune!'

'You will be believed to have; perhaps you own a gold mine. Who will know otherwise, sir?'

'What's this *sir*, boy?' he said, angered. 'You call me *Master*!'

I took the first step in his education – and my freedom. 'An English gentleman is addressed as *sir* by his servants. And he does not call them *boy* or *nigger*.' Though white men thought *boy* was less of an insult than *nigger*, I always found it even more galling. I was, after all, black; I was not a boy.

'Hmm.' He gulped down the rum. 'Then what do I call you?'

'You call me by my name.'

'Caesar, then?'

'No, sir.' I wanted never to be Caesar again, and I would not tell him what I called myself. 'I shall be Fortescue.' I had once admired a butler of that name.

'Forty-skew? What the hell kind of a name is that?'

'It's a very proper name for a superior English servant.' I chanced another step. I picked up pen and paper, and wrote the name. 'That's how it's spelt.'

He put down his rum and looked at me slowly. 'You can read and write? I didn't know that.'

'I have taken good care to keep it hidden over the past ten years, sir. A slave who can read and write is regarded with suspicion and fear.'

'And I got reason to ree-gard you with suspicion and fear, boy. How do I know that you won't run away just as soon as we get there?'

'You don't, sir – any more than you know that I won't run away here. But I will need you just as much as you will need me. That's the best reason for trust.'

He poured himself more rum – I was impressed with the quantity he could hold and still talk. 'Hell, boy, what have I got to lose?'

In all conscience I had to tell him – he would have found out

29

anyway. 'Well, sir, there is your life. Fraud is a hanging offence in England.'

'You think I'm a coward?' he snarled.

'Indeed no, sir. I merely mention it so you may take precautions.'

'I ain't made no decision, boy. I'm too drunk to think straight right now.'

My freedom and perhaps my life depended on impressing him with my knowledge. 'Very wise, if I may say, sir. The Ancient Greek historian Herodotus recounted how the Persians would make a decision once when they were sober and again when they were drunk; if it was the same decision, they'd act upon it.'

Another glass went down his throat. 'I like your Persians.' He stood up unsteadily, went to the window and pissed out. It could have been worse: he might have used the fireplace. 'I'm going to bed. And you sleep right here on the floor. You is my property, remember that, nigger.'

The room was uncarpeted, so I lay belly-down on the bare wooden floor to spare the wound on my back, ignoring my owner's drunken mutterings as I tried to sleep, but the best I could do was stop myself twitching with hope that I was on my way to the things that I had desired for so long.

Suddenly I heard his voice clearly, though he wasn't talking to me. 'Ma, forgive me for killing Pa, please. I didn't mean to. Forgive me for not being sorry he's dead. He's there with you in Heaven, now. He's happy.'

I doubted that, and not only because I didn't believe in Heaven. Mrs Smith had been a kind-hearted woman, who'd done what little she could to soften her husband's brutality; I wouldn't have survived those first years without her. Perhaps that strange impulse in Luke that had saved my life came from her; it didn't come from his father – who was certainly not in Heaven with her.

'I miss you, Ma,' he continued. 'I wish you was here, telling me a story in bed the way you used to.' Then he spoke to me. 'Boy, you awake?'

'Yes, sir.'

'You can spin a fine yarn. Spin me one now, until I get to sleep.'

So I sat up in the dark, and I told him the story I wanted him to hear.

Once upon a time, *I began*, there was a miller who had three sons. When he died, he left his mill to his first son and his donkey to his second, but all he left for the third son was a cat. The miller's son was just about to skin the cat and sell its fur, when the cat said to him, 'Follow my plan, master, and you can become very rich.'

The miller's son was surprised to hear the cat speak, but he thought that he didn't have much to lose, so he agreed to do what the cat suggested.

'First, master, buy me a pair of boots,' said the cat. With the last of his money, the miller's son bought the cat some boots, and the cat looked at himself in the mirror and thought he was magnificent.

Next day, the cat set off in his new boots with a sack and some vegetable peelings to a rabbit warren. He propped open the sack, put the peelings inside, and lay down and pretended to be dead. It wasn't long before a couple of young rabbits were lured into the sack. Instantly the cat jumped up and trapped them.

Then he set off to the palace and went to see the king. He made a low and polished bow, and said, 'Sire, these fine rabbits are a gift from my master, the Marquis of Carabas.'

The king had never heard of the Marquis of Carabas – which was not surprising, since the cat had just invented him. But he accepted the rabbits, and said, 'Tell your master that I thank him.'

Another day, the cat waited in a cornfield until he caught a couple of game birds, which again he took to the king as a present from his master, the Marquis of Carabas. This went on for some time, and the king began to have a strong curiosity to see this Marquis who sent him such fine game.

One day, the cat overheard the king's servants saying that the

31

king would be taking a drive along the river with his daughter, who was the most beautiful princess in the world. Quickly the cat ran to the miller's son. 'If you do what I say, master, your fortune is made.'

So the miller's son went for a swim in the river. The cat hid his clothes under a rock and waited for the king's coach. Then he ran out and stopped the coach. 'Help! Help!' he cried. 'My master, the Marquis of Carabas, is drowning.'

The king stopped the coach and ordered the coachmen to go and rescue the Marquis. They pulled him naked out of the river, and wrapped him in a blanket. The king was very pleased to see the Marquis. So was his daughter, because the miller's son was a charming and good-looking young man, and soon she began to fall in love with him.

The cat ran ahead of the coach and came to a fine meadow where reapers were working. He looked as fierce as he could and said to the reapers, 'When the king's coach passes, you must tell him that this meadow belongs to the Marquis of Carabas. If you don't, I'll have you all chopped into mincemeat.' The reapers were frightened, and agreed to do what the cat told them. The cat played the same trick at a beautiful forest and at a rich corn-field, so when the king came along and asked who owned all this property, he was told it belonged to the Marquis of Carabas. The king was very impressed.

The cat came to a great castle which was owned by a fierce ogre. The ogre invited him in, and they began to talk. After a while, the cat said, 'I have heard far and wide of your great power. People have told me that you can turn yourself into a lion. I can't believe that.'

The ogre instantly changed into a roaring, fierce lion, and frightened the cat so much that he ran up the curtains (which was not easy in his boots). Then the ogre turned back again. 'Are you satisfied, cat?'

The cat came down. 'Oh, that is wonderful!' he exclaimed. 'But perhaps not so wonderful as it could be, since you and the lion are the same size. Could you turn yourself into something

32

much smaller, like a mouse?' The ogre was a fool, and did so. At once, the cat caught him and ate him up.

When the king's coach arrived at the castle, there was the cat waiting for him. 'Welcome to the castle of my master, the Marquis of Carabas,' he cried. So the king and the princess and all the courtiers went inside, and they were amazed at the magnificence of the castle. The king saw that his daughter was falling in love with the young man, and decided to make the Marquis of Carabas his son-in-law on that very day.

So the miller's son married the princess, the cat was made into a great lord, and they all lived happily ever after.

Luke woke late, muttering and reaching for the coffee I brought him. For half an hour he lay in bed unspeaking, and I knew better than to disturb him. Then he sat up. 'Right, boy, I'm sober. And it looks as good to me now as it did last night when I was drunk.'

I managed not to show my exultation. 'Then we shall be on our way, sir?'

'Yes, boy, this afternoon. Go pack your belongings, then come pack mine.'

I made my way to the slaves' quarters for the last time. There was an air of insecurity and loss among the slaves; I could tell them nothing, only that I was leaving. I kept my stony face as well as I could, because my happiness would rub salt in their wounds. I packed the few belongings I'd accumulated over ten years: my knife and my best clothes were all that was worth carrying. But there were two more things: my Bible and my whip. I wrapped them in an old rag of a shirt together with a stone, then went to the river that supplied water to the fields. I stood for a moment amid the mosquitoes and the cypress, then hurled the bundle into the middle of the river. I'd need neither of them in my new life.

I packed Luke's bags and we set off, me carrying his belongings as well as my own. 'One thing you ain't thought of, boy,' he said as we walked. 'We got to get to England, and it's mighty far to swim.'

'There are ships, sir.'

'And they want passage money, and I ain't got more 'n ten dollars to call my own.' I had assumed without thinking that all white men were rich, at least enough to pay for our passage. 'So, boy, I'm going to make us what we'll need. You come with me, now, and follow my lead.'

He wouldn't tell me where. For a fearful hour, as we walked to what passed for a town in those parts, I thought that he might take me to the slave market and sell me; I was the only property he had. I kept telling myself that he needed me, and that he'd talked of 'our passage'.

We arrived at Jamestown, the centre of the district; muddy streets, rotting buildings and garish signs proclaimed civilization. He headed straight for the tavern, pushed the door open and went in. I would have stayed outside, but he waved to me to follow. There weren't many customers in the middle of the afternoon, only a few thirsty travellers and a card game that seemed to go on continuously. 'No niggers allowed in here, Luke,' said the tavern owner. 'You should know that.'

'I see Bill Carter there with his dog, and Crazy Jake with his basket of snakes, and I don't hear you complaining about them bringing their livestock in here.'

'Dogs is dogs and niggers is niggers.'

Luke walked over to the card game and pulled out a chair to join in. 'And this nigger is my stake.' The rat! The treacherous, reckless fool! The gratitude I felt for him saving my life disappeared at that moment. But there was nothing I could do except play along with him, trusting in his gambler's instinct.

'Sorry about your Pa, Luke,' came some voices. 'Sorry about what happened after.'

'Maybe it's done me a good turn. I'm fixing to find out right now.' He gestured at me. 'See this nigger? He's all I got in the world. I'm going to leave this room either without him, or with him and enough to set me up where I'm going. What'll you stake me for him? My Pa refused offers for five hundred dollars for him.'

'Should have taken it, your Pa. Then he'd be alive today,' said a surly voice. 'That nigger is trouble. He ain't worth nothing.'

'Aw, come on! He's learnt his lesson. He won't go helping no slaves escape again, will you, Caesar?'

'Oh, no, Massa,' I said in the accents of the plantation, grovelling with all my might. 'Caesar no help no runway no mo'.' Indeed I would not; from that moment on, if there were a chance of escape I had every intention of taking it myself.

The gamblers stood up to inspect me; they opened my mouth to look at my teeth, they stripped me almost naked to examine my skin, they prodded and poked my muscles. And I took it obediently.

'I'll stake you three hundred on him,' said Bill Carter, the worst slave owner in the district. 'Big strong nigger like that; he'll be worth more 'n that once I've beaten obedience into him.'

At that moment I wished that I believed in a god I could pray to, and regretted throwing the Bible away. As Luke gambled for my freedom and his fortune, I wanted to vomit every time he lost and shout for joy every time he won. But I stood watching, trying to keep as impassive as I'd been for many hours standing in elegant card rooms in Grosvenor Square. I was no gambler myself – my life held risks enough without wanting to add to them – but I knew gamblers' faces; I could tell the slight twitch of joy or despair that all but the most hardened gamblers showed when they looked at their cards.

Luke, it seemed, was a hardened gambler; nothing disturbed his expression of calm. At first he played for smallish stakes – though even the smallest loss would mean that he couldn't redeem me, and I was destined for a life on the worst plantation in the district.

I didn't even know the rules of the game. They called it Poque; I gathered that one of them, French Charlie, had brought it with him from New Orleans, though judging by his losses and expressions of disgust they'd made changes to the rules. As I watched I realized it was close kin to the game of Commerce which I knew quite well, except that it was played with five cards rather than three. One card was dealt face down, one face up to each player; bets were taken, then there was one more card and one more round of bets, and so on until each player had four cards showing and one concealed.

After some fifteen minutes by the tavern clock, though it seemed a lifetime to me, as if by unspoken agreement the stakes started to rise. Forty, sixty dollars were wagered. Luke was ahead, and I hoped desperately that he'd stop; he had enough to cover our passage money with some to spare. Perhaps he was wondering about it himself, but no sign crossed his face as he stayed at the table for the next deal.

It began. In front of him face up was the king of diamonds; he lifted his concealed card only enough to see it. It seemed to satisfy him, and he joined in the betting. There were two more rounds of cards and wagers, which gave him the ace and ten of diamonds, and Bill Carter the queens of clubs and hearts. Several men pushed their cards away before the fifth was dealt; French Charlie, more talkative than the rest, exclaimed, 'At best I shall get a pair – only a fool goes on a pair when the stakes are so high.' His glance happened to rest on me; he must have seen my anguished confusion and took pity on me. He stood up and joined me. 'You don't understand, do you, boy?'

'Not much, Massa Charlie.' By that time the fifth round of cards was being dealt: French Charlie gave a gasp at Bill Carter's second four; but at Luke's card he exclaimed, 'The jack of diamonds!' Then he explained: 'You see, boy, if your master has the queen of diamonds, he is unbeatable. If he has the queen of spades or another diamond, he still has a good hand. Anything else is worthless.'

'I'll go to eighty,' said Luke; all but one player threw their hands in.

Only Bill Carter stayed, two pairs showing. 'Your eighty, and raise you.'

Beside me the merciful Frenchman continued, 'If Carter has a four or a queen to match one of his pairs, he will win unless your master has the queen of diamonds. If he has anything else, then he will still win if your master does not have the queen of spades or a diamond.'

Carter was sweating: 'Shut your big French mouth!' he snarled. Luke was as calm as ever – but was there a slight, almost unnoticeable air of confidence about him as he raised the stakes again? Carter looked at him, looked at the cards, looked at the money beside him. For a second his fingers drummed on the table; he stopped drumming and raised again. Luke raised him; he was near his limit. There was complete silence in the room; even the dog seemed to stop scratching. And then, with a foul oath, Carter pushed his cards away.

'Ah!' exclaimed the Frenchman. 'He has folded.' And so, almost, did I. I slumped with relief as Luke collected all the money in front of him.

'Now, Luke, show us what you had,' came the cry.

'You know I don't reveal my cards.'

'Won't do no harm to show your style if you ain't going to play here no more.'

He stood up and pocketed the money. 'So long as I get to keep it – it's going to be my lucky card.' Curiosity made them agree. He picked it up but kept it concealed as he walked towards the door, pulling me with him. 'I reckon a man's got to know the signs,' he drawled, still calmly smiling. 'And I reckon it'd be plain ungrateful not to follow a sign as clear as getting dealt the king of diamonds for me, and this one—' he said, drawing out the suspense '—for my stake,' he finished as he turned it round.

It was the king of spades.

There was uproar. '*Mon dieu*! He went on a pair!'

'Beaten by a miserable goddamn pair!'

He gave a great roar of laughter. 'Come on!' he cried to me. I couldn't move, I was so shocked at what he'd done; he had to drag me out. 'Fortescue, we're on our way!'

Chapter 3

HE was seasick; I wasn't. It's just one of those chances of nature; nothing to be proud or ashamed of, or to make you feel superior or inferior – rather like the colour of your skin.

Nevertheless, I enjoyed a quiet feeling of superiority as I cared for him in his wretchedness: holding the bucket, cleaning him off, and making him drink even if he couldn't eat. I was considerate and patient, and only occasionally did I say something like this: 'You'll feel better soon, sir.'

'I'm going to die.'

'Oh, no, sir. Nobody dies of seasickness. Except—'

'Except what?'

'Well, sir, on the Middle Passage, many of them do die when they're chained up so they can't get to the bucket, and they have to piss and shit and vomit where they lie, and they get cleaned out once a day – and not as often as that when the weather is foul, so that there are hundreds of people lying in each other's filth for days or weeks on end—' I stopped; he needed the bucket again.

We were in the smallest cabin on the ship; only one bed, which he took, leaving me to hang up a hammock at night – a mistake on his part which I didn't correct. While he was retching in misery, I was enjoying myself more than I'd done in ten years, and would have done even if I hadn't had the pleasure of the contrast between my hopes on this voyage and my despair on my last.

Though everyone else complained about the ship's food, I'd been living on slave rations and I thought it was perfectly edible.

Though the crew made it clear that they resented my superior status as a passenger, and I heard the word *nigger* many times, they couldn't actually beat me and I could ignore them. I was free to walk on deck, enjoying the blue of the sea and sky, the creak of the rigging, the perfect wind, taking an interest in everything around me, knowing that every hour took me further from South Carolina and closer to Althea. I was as happy as the dolphins that danced in our wake.

And I could read! We had bought a box of books in Charleston; it had been easy to find instructions on etiquette and nobility in that town of socially ambitious merchants and their families. We had gone round the bookshop and I'd indicated one after another; if he protested, I'd murmur, 'An English gentleman would know this, sir,' and hand *Clarissa* to the shopman. Now I found a quiet, sunny place on deck, and read my old friends such as *Gulliver's Travels*, and met new ones like *Tom Jones*, that Miss Campbell had kept out of Althea's way.

Best – by far the best – of all to my spirits was this little item in the Peerage:

George James Mountford, Baron Mountford, of Mountford Park, Hertfordshire and Grosvenor Square, London . . . He has issue, George Henry, b. 4 May, 1745; m. 8 July, 1770, Charlotte, daughter of Thomas, Lord Winterton . . .

Althea hadn't been forced to marry George! I couldn't search for her directly, since her parents were commoners and wouldn't appear anywhere; but if she'd married into the peerage or the baronetage, that would be recorded. So I spent an hour every day working my way through those mighty tomes looking for her, hoping all the while I wouldn't find her. I was far too happy to ask myself what right I had to expect an English heiress to wait ten years for a black slave.

Luke recovered from his seasickness, and my holiday was over. I had about six or eight weeks remaining, more or less depending on the weather and the speed of our voyage, to turn a half-literate son of a South Carolina rice planter into an English gentleman; there was no time to waste. His lessons began.

'. . . duke, marquis, earl, viscount, baron; those are the lords. The eldest son may take a courtesy title lower than his father's. Then there are the commoners: baronet, knight, esquire. Now the wives: duchess, marchioness – wait for it, not an earless, a – a – countess! . . .'

'. . . a dollar is worth four shillings and sixpence. There are twelve pence or pennies in a shilling, twenty shillings in a pound, twenty-one shillings in a guinea . . .'

'. . . Beauchamp is pronounced "Beecham". Beaufort is pronounced "Bofort". Beaulieu is pronounced "Bewly". Goddamn it, why can't the English spell their own names properly?'

Eventually he rebelled. Throwing the Peerage down with disgust, he cried, 'Now I know why you was the best slave-driver in South Carolina! Well, you ain't got no whip now, Fortescue. You is still my property for all your flash ways. And you ain't going to make me speak like no English lord.'

'I preferred to use persuasion; I never used the whip unless I was ordered.'

'Ain't no way you can persuade me to copy some high-born British bastard. I'm too good an American.'

I thought for a moment. 'You are right, sir. But can I persuade you to copy Benjamin Franklin? Is he a good enough American to take as your model?'

'I ain't never met him.'

'I have.'

That impressed him more than anything else I'd said. 'You have?'

'Only a couple of times, sir, when he was in London representing the interests of the American colonies, but Mr Franklin is not an easy man to forget. He once gave me sixpence for running an errand.'

'You still got it?'

'Had I known you would one day like to see it, sir, I would doubtless have kept it. As it was, I spent it on a spinning top.'

'Ain't no way – there isn't any way that I'd spend sixpence from Ben Franklin on no – on a spinning top.'

'Oh, very good, sir! You're starting to sound like him already!'

He looked at the Peerage again, sighed, then pushed it away. 'Ain't it – isn't it better we commenced to work on our story?'

'Yes, sir; I was awaiting your decision.'

'Let's start with my name. Who am I?'

'Luke Fitzgeorge would be an admirable name.'

'Not something flash, like Lucius? From my experience of the swells in Charleston, that'd be a good name.'

'Forget your experience of the swells in Charleston, sir.' I gave a visible shudder. 'Or rather, remember them and do the exact opposite on all occasions. The higher you are, the less need you have to be flash.'

'And I'm high, am I?'

'Your father is.'

'How high?'

'As high as you can imagine, with a name like Fitzgeorge.'

'Why?'

'As well as being a perfectly good name in its own right, Fitz something can imply that you are the illegitimate son of someone of that name.'

He understood me. 'No! I ain't – I am not going to pass myself off as the son of King goddamn George!'

'Very well, sir,' I sighed. 'Besides, though you Americans call him a tyrant, his private life is one of exemplary dullness and it might not be believed. Fitzjames, then; your father could be any one of a dozen dukes with that name.'

'Luke Fitzjames; James Fitzluke. It Fitz, Fortescue.'

'Very comical, sir.'

'So, I was brought up in England. As a gentleman?'

'In the manner appropriate to a nobleman's bastard: well, but discreetly.'

'Where?'

41

'You don't reveal that, sir, any more than you reveal your father's name.'

'And then I went to America. When?'

'Ten years ago. That's long enough to account for any Americanisms, and that was when I was shipped out; it will cover the gaps in my knowledge.'

'I found a gold mine, did I? Where?'

'Is there anywhere in the continent with which you are familiar?'

'Only South Carolina.'

'A gold mine in South Carolina is implausible. The Mississippi it must be.'

'Is there gold in the Mississippi?'

'Who knows? The English certainly won't.'

'But I ain't been – I isn't been – *Damn*! I haven't been to the Mississippi.'

I reached into the box of books and passed him one. 'It's the account of someone who has; badly written and unpublished outside America, but most informative. There is little chance of anyone in England having read it.'

'You think of everything, Fortescue.'

'I do my best, sir.'

A sailor was to be flogged. Passengers did not have to watch, but I wasn't going to miss the sight of a white man on both ends of the whip. And the man on the receiving end had spat on my foot, a few days into the voyage. I could have beaten hell out of him, but I'd had enough of brutality – I never wanted to hit anyone again. I merely loomed over him and smiled at him (or at least bared my teeth), thanked him for starting to clean my shoes, and suggested that he finish the job on his knees.

I lounged comfortably on deck, watching that white man suffer, taking an expert interest. The whip was divided into nine lengths to be both more painful and less deadly than the bull whip I'd been forced to use; a hundred lashes with a bull whip would have been a death sentence. I saw that the man at the other end of the whip wasn't using the tricks to lessen the pain that I'd done; this was as bad as he could make it.

I walked away, sickened. Not with what was happening: I'd seen worse – I'd done worse. I was sickened with myself for my initial pleasure at it. Skins may be black or white, but blood is always red.

Luke was growing a beard; there might come a time when he would need to change his appearance in a hurry. He left the cabin only long enough to get exercise and stop speculation about the mysterious passenger who never showed himself. The rest of the time, he studied.

Not so much from books: 'Book learning ain't – isn't my style.' But I would serve him ships' biscuits and skilly as though they were part of a fashionable dinner, while he engaged in polite conversation with the Duchess of Doorknob on his right and Lady Bedworthy on his left.

In the evenings we played the card games he would have to know ('It's a pack of cards including a knave, sir, not a deck of cards including a jack.') He was familiar with many games, or at least variations of them, and the pirated copy of the work of Mr Hoyle that we'd bought in Charleston told him the way they were played in London. The games that were new to him I won at first, but he soon overtook me, and by the time the voyage ended I owed him more than fifty thousand imaginary pounds. 'I hope all the gamblers I meet are as bad as you, Fortescue.'

'The word is *gamester*, and they won't be. In an exclusive gentlemen's club, twenty or thirty thousand pounds can be won and lost in an evening. They aren't places for bad gamesters.'

'Twenty or thirty thousand! I gotta – I must get in there!'

'It will take time, sir, and caution. You will need an introduction before you get into White's.'

'Why that one rather than the others?'

'White's is a Tory club. I assume you prefer to fleece Tories rather than Whigs.'

'Do I?'

Did the man have no idea of the world outside South Carolina? 'Because the Whigs have sometimes been known to support the American cause, sir,' I explained patiently. One or two of them had also been known to denounce slavery, but there was no need to tell him that. 'Take money from Tories, and you may plume yourself on your patriotism as you count the gold.'

'Well, yee-hah!' he laughed. 'I'm doing my duty as a good American!'

Dancing was a problem; there was no room in our cramped cabin for me to show him anything more than the correct behaviour towards his partner, and it took imagination on both our parts to turn a six-foot-tall black man into a fair maiden; I simpered manfully. But he knew many of the steps already: 'The Sir Roger de Coverley is much the same as the Virginia reel, sir, except that you take off your spurs and you don't shout, "Yee-hah!".'

By the time the sky turned grey and the sea turned green as we approached land, and I'd discovered that Althea had married neither into the peerage nor the first half of the baronetage, Luke had made remarkable progress. He said 'ain't' only when he was excited, he pronounced '-th' and '-ng' without effort, and his conversational manners were excellent; he'd always had charm. Then he said something which made me realize that we'd missed the most important lesson of all. 'When I'm claiming to be the son of a duke and the owner of a gold mine—'

'No, no, no, no, sir. You don't claim anything of the sort!'

'Excuse me, I didn't quite catch what you meant, Fortescue,' he said politely. 'I thought that was the whole point of the game.'

'Sir, when you wanted everyone to think you held the Queen of Diamonds, did you say, "Hey, fellahs, I'm holding the Queen of Diamonds"?'

'No, but how will they know?'

'I tell them. The miller's son never claimed he was the Marquis of Carabas, did he? He left it to Puss in Boots.'

He scratched his beard reflectively. 'You're right, Fortescue. If a man came to me in South Carolina and looked me straight in the eye with his hand on a stack of Bibles claiming to be the

Marquis of Carabas, I'd have him tarred and feathered. But if you came to me and said, "Hey, Massa, dat man, he a big lord", I'd believe you straight away. People are fools everywhere, aren't they?'

'Not everywhere, sir; don't underestimate the British ruling classes. But everywhere there are people who are rich, greedy and stupid. They're your quarry. In fact, sir, if you are ever asked whether you're the son of a duke and own a gold mine, you should deny it. It's more convincing, and it's safer for you if things go wrong and you're charged with fraud.'

'So I can say, "My goodness, I did my best to deny the story. I don't know how it spread around. It's all the fault of my man Fortescue".'

'Exactly.'

'But what happens to my man Fortescue?'

'I take off my livery, and I run. In England, they're no better than they are in South Carolina at telling one black face from another.'

'So you don't think you will be recognized after ten years away?'

'No, except for—' Except for Althea; she would know me at once. 'Except perhaps for the people in the household where I grew up. But what if they do? Caesar the page returns as the manservant of an English gentleman who has spent ten years in America; nothing remarkable in that.'

For the first time he showed interest in me rather than in the knowledge I carried. 'What was it like when you were a page, Fortescue?'

I told him about life at the Mountfords, mentioning Althea as little as possible. 'These Mountfords, they treated you pretty well. I guess you don't want me to fleece them, do you?'

'They treated me well, they made me admire them, they allowed me the hope of becoming a superior English manservant. And then they sold me to the first slave trader who made them an offer. Mr Fitzjames, I hope you take them for every penny they own.'

45

*

I found her.

>...m. 8 May, 1768 Althea, d. of Charles Freeman Esq., of Bristol ..

The world didn't really change at that moment. The wind was just as strong, the sea was just as green, the gulls were just as loud as they'd been before, but something inside me vanished like water poured on dry sand.

I looked again at the entry to find out more about the baronet who had been her husband for nearly seven years.

>Sir Bertrand Verity, of Galbury Hall, Galston, Warwickshire, and South Audley Street, London. Born 22 April 1741.

I'd never heard of him. But I knew Galston. On the road to Scotland, there was a barn where we'd sheltered one night on our flight north in the last days of our childhood. I wondered if she ever went there. Of course she would remember it; there was nothing wrong with her memory. But how? As an embarrassing reminder of a youthful escapade, or as it was to me?

I recalled every wooden beam, every cobweb, every bale. Pompey running around failing to catch anything. The taste of caraway in the seed cake we bought for our supper. The smell of hay and wet dog. Althea, sitting with her back to the window so the dim grey autumn light fell on my face, her golden hair like a halo round her shadowed form. The childish game we played to pass the time:

>I love my love with an A because she is Adorable. I hate her because she is Absurd. She eats Apples and her name is Althea.

>Ilove my love with a J because he is Jolly. I hate him because he is Jealous. He eats Jam and his name is Joshua.

46

Oh, yes, Althea, I'm jealous. Forgive me for not being jolly.

For the first time in ten years she became something other than a dream and a memory. She was a baronet's wife: Lady Verity. For the first time I thought of what could happen when we met, because now there was a chance that we might. I would cut off my hand rather than bring her any harm. But if I did what I most wanted to, then I would bring her more harm than her worst enemy. Lady Verity kissing a nigger: what a juicy piece of gossip that would be!

I closed the book with a snap, then dropped it over the side.

'Hey, Fortescue, what are you doing?' Luke cried, coming up to me on his morning's walk about the deck. 'That was the Baronetage!'

'Don't worry about it. Baronets aren't important.'

At last, the English coast. Blustery spring weather sped us up the Channel, amid all the other ships, naval and merchant, from Britain, France, Spain, The Netherlands. I had waited more than ten years for this; I contained my feelings and remained an impassive superior manservant, but all the other passengers pointed excitedly to every landmark we passed. We had all become very nautical, and referred to the coastline on our 'port' rather than on 'the left'; if the worst happened and we had to run, Luke and I would easily find places, no questions asked, as deckhands on a convenient outward-bound ship.

Then, up the Thames, filthy and stinking even at the estuary from the refuse of the world's largest city. We made slow progress up the river, it was so crammed with other shipping. But at last the first smoky whiff of London, the smell of my childhood, that I hadn't had in my nose for more than ten years.

We waited many hours for a place at the wharf, amid so many masts that it was like a forest in midwinter when the leaves were shed. I pointed out the great buildings, as though Luke were a guest and I was proudly displaying my home: perhaps I was. 'See, that's the Tower of London, there's St Paul's Cathedral, and that's the Monument: it was built to commemorate the Great Fire of London.'

'What fire?'

'Oh, more than a hundred years ago; it burnt down most of the old city, and it had to be rebuilt. Apart from The Tower, almost everything you see is new.'

'A hundred years old and you call it new?'

Bags were packed and farewells were said. We let the others disembark ahead of us; Luke was trying to count all the ships (he'd thought Charleston was busy, but he'd never seen anything like this), then he gave up and tried to count the church steeples, which was almost as difficult. I was content listening to the cockney voices of the watermen, my natural accent. Not the clipped aristocratic tones of the Mountfords, which I used as Fortescue, and certainly not plantation Gullah, but this: the voice of the London streets and servants' halls.

I carried our bags down the gangplank behind Luke, and my feet touched solid English land. I couldn't help it; my legs gave way and I fell to the ground, almost embracing it with happiness and relief.

'What's the matter, Fortescue? Get up,' Luke said, giving me a kick: a gentle one, but still a kick. 'Pick up those bags.'

I'd planned to do this later, well away from the ship; I had bitter experience of what could happen at such a moment. But everything rebelled at hiding it a moment longer. I stood up, dusted myself down, and said in my London voice, 'Pick 'em up yourself. I'm not your property any more. I'm a free man.'

'What? Since when?'

'Since I set foot on English soil. There's no slavery in England any longer, as you'd know if you bothered to take any notice of the world outside your stinking South Carolina swamp.'

'What you talkin' about, nigger?'

'Three years ago, *Smith*, the highest court in the land ruled that nobody in England could be forced out of the country against their will into slavery. It's called the Somerset Decision. It was even in the Charleston newspapers that your father gave us because he was too bloody mean to pay for decent bedding. You can read about it in any library – if you know what one of those is.'

He grabbed my collar. 'I don't give a shit about no fancy English law. I'm American. An' if I shout out, the good Americans behind you on that ship will come and drag you on board and take you back in chains.'

I grabbed his collar and lifted him far more easily than he could lift me. 'Well, I'm English. And if I shout out to the good Englishmen behind you on the wharf that a Yankee rebel is trying to kidnap me into slavery, which one of us do you think will end up in chains?'

I wasn't sure which way good Englishmen would go when faced with that choice, but I'd learnt something from him too: how to bluff on a poor hand.

For a moment we stood nose to nose. Then I said mildly, 'Shall we put each other down before we attract so much attention that it might ruin our plan?'

My bluff worked. He let me go, as I did him, then he exclaimed, 'What goddamn plan? You just gone and ruined it yourself!'

'No, I haven't. It's still a good plan, and I'd be happy to go ahead with it if you still want to. If you say no, I'll just walk away whistling into London with nothing but my freedom, and you can get back on board with the money that you won on my body and go back to your home with Charleston as the height of your ambition. Or you could say yes, and together we'll take on the British ruling classes. But as equal partners, not as master and slave.'

He looked at the ship where he'd spent more than two months in a cramped cabin stuffing his head with knowledge that would be useless to him the moment he went back on board. He looked around him at London, bigger, richer and more exciting than anything he'd ever imagined. Then he gave a great roar of laughter that made him very hard to dislike. 'If you think I'm going back to confess that I've been outsmarted by a nigger, you is much mistook.'

'The word is Negro, Black or African.'

'A damned British Black, too,' he said, in his best English accent. 'I don't know which is more humiliating.' He put out his hand. 'Shake on it, partner.'

I took it. 'My name is Joshua.'

'Delighted to know you, Joshua.'

'The pleasure is all mine, Luke.'

Chapter 4

W<small>E</small> took lodgings in St Giles, the poor area close to the rich squares of Mayfair; they were cheap, convenient, and not too verminous. We would spend a few weeks finding out the lie of the land and getting our bearings (we were still very nautical in our speech). We tossed for choice of beds, and we unpacked our own bags. Luke had to be reminded that this was the way to do things now we were partners, but he only needed to be told once.

'The next thing we do, Josh, is find a whorehouse. I've been stuck in a cabin for more than two months with only you for company, and frankly, you aren't to my taste. You snore too much.'

'Take my advice, Luke. Wear a cundum. English prostitutes service men from everywhere on earth, and you could pick up something very unpleasant.'

'What's a cundum?'

This was not a part of his education that I'd thought of. 'Well, it's – er – it's a tube of animal gut, sewn at one end and tied on at the other. It stops infection.' I slipped an imaginary one over my finger.

'Tied on to what?'

'What do you think? Use your imagination, for God's sake.'

'Oh, I get you! Doesn't it take away the pleasure?'

'I don't know, I've never used one. I wasn't much more than a boy when I was shipped out; none of this is from my practical experience, only servants' hall gossip. The best thing to do would be to find a good brothel – not whorehouse, by the way – and get the women to show you what to do.'

'Find me a good brothel, Josh.'

'Very well; I'll go and buy a book and see what's recommended.'

'You can buy books about brothels?' he asked, awestruck. 'If this is civilization, I like it.' I went out; it took me about two minutes to find one. He leafed through it, his mouth open. 'This is the kind of book learning for me. Look at this one: "Meg Blossom: tall and graceful, with rich golden hair both on her head and in a more intimate place. Her white skin and vermilion tipp'd globes are sure to please the most discerning customer." Vermilion tipp'd globes, eh? Here's one for you: "Sable Sue: with gleaming black skin, she promises all the heat of her African birthplace." Let's get at 'em, Josh!'

'You go and have a good time. I'm not interested.'

'You're not? What's the matter with you? Who are you saving it for?'

A good question. I had been faithful to her in the spirit, but not in the flesh: pleasures on the plantation were too few to refuse those available. But here, in England, where she could be only a few miles away— 'I have other pleasures I've been looking forward to; and for more than ten years, not two months.'

So we went to Covent Garden, where he found Meg Blossom of the vermilion tipp'd globes, and I went to the theatre and watched *Hamlet*, and we both had a good time in our different ways.

Next day we began our exploration. I needed it almost as much as he did; London had changed in ten years, getting both smaller and bigger. Smaller, because all the buildings I remembered seemed to have shrunk since I had grown; and bigger, because the open spaces where Althea and I had played as children were now covered with houses. I stood in the middle of an elegant square on the spot where I had once climbed a tree to fetch apples for her, and though the buildings were very fine, I mourned for the fields.

Fashions had changed too. Ten years ago, the macaroni style had led to fashionable young men wearing clothes that were extravagant enough, but the years had made them even more extreme, and now the macaronis were unbelievable. Gaudy embroidered silk coats and breeches, high heels that made them mince and totter, and hair three feet high, with an absurdly small hat clinging to the top like a fried egg on a rock. My mouth fell open as wide as Luke's as I watched them.

'Am I going to have to dress like that?' he asked, horrified.

I bent down and picked up a pigeon feather from the pavement. I put it in his hat and said, 'Now all you need is a pony.'

He looked puzzled, then laughed as I started to whistle the familiar tune. Arm in arm we strolled into High Holborn singing:

> Yankee doodle went to town, riding on a pony,
> Stuck a feather in his cap and called it macaroni.

We stayed arm in arm otherwise we would have been separated by the crush of people; even two big strong young men like us had difficulty making headway. Not that he wanted to; he was content to gaze into the shops. Tea, toys, tobacco; silks, sultanas, swords; gloves, glassware, globes: there were things to be bought that he'd never seen or even knew existed. I let him stare while I watched a superbly dressed black footman tip a crossing sweeper for cleaning horse droppings out of his way across the road; I was taking in all the details of his livery so I could use him as a model.

'Josh, look at that! Shit!' Luke exclaimed as he turned to see what I was looking at.

'The word is *filth*.'

'I don't mean that. I mean – Jesus, I've just seen a white man sweep the road for a black man. I don't think we're in South Carolina, Josh.'

We spent hours with pawnbrokers and rag dealers looking for

suitable clothes. The accoutrements of an English gentleman were well beyond our rapidly decreasing stock of money – we would take a leaf out of the book of Puss in Boots to solve that problem – but we could put together the makings of a livery for me. I was trying on a resplendent sky-blue jacket with gold frogging when Luke said, 'Look at these', holding up a pair of knee-length boots.

'Boots aren't part of a livery. It should be white stockings and shoes with silver buckles.'

'Humour me, Josh: "First, master, buy me a pair of boots". Try them. If they fit, we take it as a sign.'

Feeling more like Cinderella than Puss in Boots, I pulled them on. Fine black leather, strong stitching: someone must have been badly down on his luck when he pawned these. They fitted me well, apart from the wear of another man's tread which would be sorted out with a few days' walking in them.

'Am I allowed to be eccentric and have my manservant dressed in boots?'

'I think you are. I bow to your superior judgement about reading the signs.'

While he went out on his own for the first time the next day, I spent the time cleaning, polishing, repairing, letting out and taking in, my page's skills coming back to me as I worked. It had been a problem to find clothes big enough to fit me, but footmen are often chosen for their height and fine physiques; in the richest households, their main task is to stand around looking magnificent.

And magnificent I looked. While Luke told me about what he'd seen that day, I dressed myself. The blue jacket went over a green and gold striped waistcoat and a plain white shirt; dark red breeches tucked into my gleaming black boots, which looked unusual rather than out of place. Yards of gold trimming, bright brass buttons and a shoulder knot finished me off. The only thing I didn't like was the powdered white wig; as a page I'd worn my own hair under a turban, but the wig was more suitable for an upper servant, and it would make me less recognizable. It looked deliberately artificial against my skin, as if to make a black man in these clothes look slightly comical. 'There,' I said as I peacocked in front of the mirror. 'What do you think?'

'And you said the aristocracy don't go in for flash stuff. I have to shade my eyes just to look at you!' He continued talking about what he'd seen that day, asking me questions often far out of my knowledge. He'd spent some time watching the army parade, and was beginning to realize that if it came to a war, the Americans weren't going to have it as easily as he'd believed.

'Something else, Josh.' He was uneasy. 'I saw a black man and a white woman walk down the street arm in arm, and nobody but me took any notice.'

'Why should they?'

'Well—'

'There are ten black men in England to every black woman. What are they supposed to do for wives if they can't marry Englishwomen?'

'You mean they might have been married?' This shocked him even more than the thought that they might not. 'And nobody thinks any the worse of her? Her family wouldn't raise objections?'

'I've been called nigger in England too, plenty of times. If an Englishwoman wants to marry a black man, yes, her family will counsel her against it. But the English take much more notice of rank than of race. If she's only a servingmaid and he's in a good line of work – owns a shop, say – then they might think that she's doing very well for herself.'

'What about the children?'

'You should know. You've fathered at least three such children yourself.'

'That's different.'

'Why?'

'It just seems – wrong, unnatural.'

'More wrong and unnatural than letting your own children grow up as slaves to be treated as property?'

He didn't say anything.

'If it makes you feel easier, Luke, consider that perhaps she was his godmother rather than his wife.'

'Would you do it?'

'What, walk down the street with my godmother on my arm? Done it dozens of times.' Althea and I always wore Miss Campbell out on our walks, and she often welcomed my support on the way home.

'You know what I mean. Would you – do you want to – you know – with a white woman?'

Oh, yes. 'I'm not going to ravish the fair white womanhood of England, if that's what you're thinking. But if I'm in love with an Englishwoman, and she's in love with me, we are not going to take into account your sensibilities.' He was uncomfortable, so I seemed to change the subject. 'Luke, as part of your education you must see at least one play by Shakespeare.'

'He's good, is he?'

'The best in the world. There's one tomorrow. We'll go.'

It was, of course, *Othello*, the tragic love of a black man and a white woman. Luke recognized that I'd played a trick on him once it started, but he laughed good-naturedly and allowed himself to be sucked into Shakespeare's genius, nearly two hundred years old and still magical. He blew his nose when Desdemona died.

'Powerful writer, that Shakespeare,' he agreed as we walked home together, my arm firmly in his to guide him away from the feminine distractions that were so plainly on offer. 'Just one thing wrong.'

'Yes?' I said, bristling and ready for another argument.

'Why does he have to write in such old-fashioned language?'

There were still yawning gaps in his education.

It was time for Puss in Boots to spread the word about the Marquis of Carabas. Dressed in my livery, I hung around the coffee shops and inns around Fleet Street where the hack writers and journalists went, waiting for a chance to strike up a conversation. After a couple of days I found myself surrounded by half a dozen journalists who thought it would be good sport to make this superior black servant roaring drunk. All I needed to do was act naturally as they poured gin down me, and concentrate on remembering the story rather than the truth.

' 'S a shame, a crying shame,' I mumbled. 'If his father had only married his mother, he'd be Marquis of—' I broke off, putting my finger to my lips. 'Oh. Mussn't say. 'S a secret.'

'Come on,' cried the journalists. 'We're all friends here. You can trust us.'

'No. He trusts me. He's a great man. Did I tell you he saved my life?'

'Yes, three times already.'

'He's brave. Did I tell you how he wrestled an alligator?'

'Four times.'

'And lived among Indians?'

'Five times. Tell us something new. Tell us why he's coming back to England. To see what he can get from his father, eh?'

' 'S other way round. He doesn't need money. Might even give it to the family. He's rich.'

'How rich?'

'Very rich. Found a gold mine.'

'A gold mine, you say? A big one?'

'Big. Bigger 'n a mountain. Bigger 'n a big mountain.'

'Where's this mountain of gold?'

' 'S not a mountain. 'S a mine. Mines are underground, mountains are on top. Everybody knows that.'

'Where's the mine, then?'

'Mishi— Mippi—' I took a deep breath. 'Missy-pissy.'

'What's his name?'

'Mussn't say. 'S a secret. He knows I can keep a secret.'

And with that I collapsed on to the table.

I groaned and retched the next morning, and thoroughly hated Luke as he exulted over the item in the newspaper. 'You did it! Listen to this, Josh:

One of the highest in the land may have cause to rejoice in,

57

rather than regret, his youthful indis— indics—'

'Indiscretion.'

'—his youthful indiscretion. The result of his sin now returns bearing a mountain of gold. After wrestling Indians and living among alligators, the high-born bastard has found gold in the Mississippi, and promises to share it with his noble father. We cannot condone the nobleman's fault, and we hope that the young man will find better uses for his fortune than rewarding the sins of the father.'

I went round to the tavern, grabbed the throat of the man from the newspaper that had printed the story, and threatened to punch his eyes out for betraying my secret. The other journalists held me, picked me up and threw me out. I was dusting myself down when one of them came out and helped me to clean myself off. 'I'm sorry that happened,' he said. 'I'm not like the others. You can trust me; my newspaper hasn't published your story.' (The fact that he worked for a weekly journal that wasn't due out for two days might have something to do with it, of course.) 'Come with me, old man. Let me buy you a drink to make up for it.'

'Oh, no. Strong drink is a snare!'

'Well, let's go to a coffee house. You can tell me your troubles.'

I went, and told him how badly I felt that I'd betrayed the trust of Mr Fitzjames who'd sent me ahead to prepare things for him, and why Mr Fitzjames was grateful to his father for giving him the upbringing of a gentleman, and then I bored him with stories about life on the Mississippi.

By the end of the week, all London was speculating about the mysterious Mr Fitzjames and his mountain of Mississippi gold. Soon the miller's son would go for a swim and emerge as the Marquis of Carabas.

'You want me to swim in the Thames? Josh, I'd be dead of putrid fever before they pulled me out!'

'No. You get assaulted by footpads, who rob you of all your clothes and all your papers; then you are taken into the household of a nobleman to recover.'

'Which nobleman?'

'This one.' I opened the page of the Peerage to our victim. 'Earl Winterton. He has a house on Park Lane; it would be natural to seek help there if you were attacked in Hyde Park. He's a friend of Lord Mountford. One of his daughters married George Mountford. And he has three other daughters unmarried.' Winterton would have been perfect even if he and his connections had been complete strangers to me. I told myself that I was setting Luke on to him to put me in a better position to take my revenge on the Mountfords, and it had nothing to do with increasing my chances of meeting Althea.

I could not decide whether to tell her I was back. Sometimes I thought that I should not: if her feelings for me were the same as they once were, she'd be torn between love and duty; if they had changed, I'd be at best an acute embarrassment to her, and at worst a danger if my reappearance somehow revived the story of our elopement and spread the gossip of what Lady Verity had once done. But sometimes I thought that I should: I had never deceived her in my life, and I did not want to do so now. The Althea I knew would have wanted the truth even if she loved me no longer; I did not know what Lady Verity would want.

'Earl's daughters and still unmarried?' said Luke. 'What's the matter with them? Henrietta, born 1752. Maria, born 1758 and Louisa born 1760. Oh, Maria and Louisa might not be out yet.' I was pleased with both of us; he'd mastered the intricacies of coming out enough to be able to work it out for himself.

'I don't remember much about Maria and Louisa except that they were pretty, silly little girls. Maria's coming out this season; there'll be balls, dinner parties, all sorts of opportunities to meet people if you're a friend of the family.'

'What about Henrietta? She must have a hump and a squint to be still unmarried at twenty-three.'

'No, she's tolerable from what I recall.'

'Then what's wrong with her?'

'In a word, she was a bitch.' She'd often been sent to play with Althea, and would sit disapproving of Althea's high spirits, with her mouth tight and her lips barely moving as she spoke: unattractive at the best of times, but downright rude when talking to a deaf person. A tattle-tale, too. 'Mama, Althea's playing with Caesar and won't let me join in the game.'

'They won't remember you?'

'What, somebody else's black page from ten years ago? They barely remember the names of their own servants.'

'They don't seem a very likeable family.'

'You want to fleece people you like? Whenever you have scruples about deceiving your hosts, the Wintertons will give you plenty of cause to tell yourself they deserve it.'

We went for a walk in Hyde Park, dressed plainly to be inconspicuous, to seek a good spot for him to be assaulted. It was a pleasant, warm April day with a gentle breeze; once we found the place we needed, we succumbed to temptation and continued to stroll about the Park. We put the occasion to good use: we would agree on a passing stranger, then deduce what we could about him or her from the appearance alone. Where we disagreed, we would try to settle the matter, perhaps by eavesdropping on their conversation. I was more often right than Luke, but he beat me twice: once when I was misled by my ten-year-old knowledge of fashion to mistake a lady's maid in her mistress's cast-off clothes, and the other when his eye for a military bearing detected an off-duty soldier. 'What about that one, Luke? The man walking towards us on the other side of the carriageway with that black dog?'

'Footman,' he said instantly. 'He's wearing a shoulder knot.'

'He'll lose his position soon, the way he's walking the dog without a leash. Spaniels are the most foolish creatures in the world, always causing accidents.'

'No, look at the way it's wheezing and hobbling along. That one's far too old to cause any trouble.'

He was wrong. The breeze must have carried my smell to the dog; he lifted his nose and sniffed. Then he gave a sudden bark of excitement, and with all his remaining energy dashed across the carriageway towards me, yapping delightedly. He caught the footman by surprise. 'Pompey, come back this minute!'

But it was no use: he ran straight under the wheels of a passing carriage. I ran to him and knelt beside him. It was the end: even a younger dog couldn't survive such injuries. While the coachman and the footman argued about whose fault it was, I lifted him as gently as I could and carried him off the carriageway.

'Oh, Pompey, you stupid dog: all nose and no brain. How did you manage to live as long as this?' His eyes opened and he tried to lick my face. His little stubby tail gave one wag, then another, then stopped wagging for ever.

I sat on the grass, cradling him in my arms, ignoring the hubbub around me. After all I'd endured without shedding a tear, I was unmanned by the death of an ancient spaniel. 'What's the matter, Josh?' I heard Luke's voice.

'Bloody English weather. I've caught a cold,' I croaked, blowing my nose.

'How am I going to break the news?' cried the footman, wringing his hands. I knew what he felt: I had committed the same offence many years ago. I emptied the pockets of my coat, then took it off and wrapped it round Pompey's old, broken body. It was a last service for him, and it was also for his owners, whoever they were. They had cared for him in his old age – perhaps they were even the people who had saved him from being destroyed by the Mountfords. They would grieve for him as I did; I would spare them the sight of him so torn and mangled. 'What can I tell my lady?' the footman continued to wail.

I stood up and gave Pompey to him. 'You can tell her the truth – it might save your position,' I said, trying to keep the crack out of my voice. 'Say that he died quickly, in the arms of an old friend.'

'Thank you, sir, I shall. It's not my position that I worry about: my lady wouldn't turn me off for an accident. But it will comfort her, I hope.' He looked down at the dog in his arms and sighed, 'You were always a nuisance, Pompey. Why did Lady Verity love you so much?'

I felt as though he'd kicked me in the belly. Damn! Why hadn't I thought of that? Who else would love that stupid dog so much? I turned away before he could see my expression. But Luke caught it instead. 'You haven't caught a cold, Josh,' he said, as we walked back to our lodgings. 'That was your dog when you were a page, wasn't it?'

'Yes,' I said, thankful that he could guess no more, and thankful also that I could keep my voice steady and my face impassive.

'Cheer up, man. There are worse ways for a dog of that age to go than quickly, in the arms of an old friend.'

'I know.'

'She'll know it too, this Lady what's her name? – Verily?'

'Verity. Wife of Sir Bertrand Verity, baronet.'

'You know her?'

'She was Miss Freeman, the Mountfords' ward.'

'She was one of those who sold you?'

'She did everything in her power to try to stop it. But she was only a child; what power does a child have?'

'She'll recognize you?'

'Yes.'

'You should keep out of her way, then.'

'I should.'

My decision had been made for me: she would know as soon as the footman described me and gave her my message. I didn't know whether I was more dismayed or overjoyed.

When I was a page I'd lacked time to mix much with the community of black Londoners, but now I did. I told Luke that the best way of spreading a rumour and picking up gossip was through servants' halls, but really it was because I wanted to

62

find out how large numbers of black people behaved in freedom.

The answer: nervously, tiptoeing round the fringes, finding a place for themselves in a world that wasn't made for them, aware that they could still be kidnapped and sold into slavery across the Atlantic: illegal, but unstoppable. Many were doing well: some had simply changed from slave to servant and had kept their old positions, while others were publicans, watermen, musicians – black military bandsmen were very popular. But others had paid a price for freedom: after the Somerset decision they had been thrown out on the streets to starve, or had run with no job to go to. They were forbidden by law to take up apprenticeships or seek relief from the parish, so many were forced to turn to the resources of the destitute: begging, prostitution, and crime. Yet there was no longing for the old days; every one of them knew that it was better to starve in freedom than live in slavery.

The community was not entirely black. There were plenty of English wives and a few English husbands, and their children: young people with brown skins and cockney accents. Others who were welcome were the small but growing number of Abolitionists. In general they were prim Evangelicals and Quakers, driven by conscience to work to end the abomination of slavery, and they seemed out of place in the rakish world of musicians and whores. But that was the point: they were the ones who were out of place. Uncomfortable though they felt, they knew it was nothing compared with the experience of those round them. They were good Christians, a world away from the Bible-bearing barbarian who would have flogged me to death.

I spread my story about Mr Fitzjames; there were a few who recognized me as Caesar the page, but Luke and I had worked out a story to account for how I had turned into Fortescue. I didn't like deceiving them, but seven years as a slave-driver toughens the tenderest conscience.

I also picked up a lot of gossip. Lord Mountford had suffered a stroke a few years back, depriving him of his speech and the use of one side of his body, but otherwise he was perfectly healthy; he could live for ten years or more. No revenge I'd planned could match that living death.

While he was kept alive in Mountford Park, their country estate, Lady Mountford was still in their town house in Grosvenor Square. She was living quite openly with a cavalry officer some ten years her junior, a younger son of a viscount. Nobody thought anything of it; it was assumed that they'd marry when her husband died, but in the meantime they were a recognized couple, invited to the same occasions and treated more or less as man and wife.

George Mountford was the head of the family in everything but name. One day he'd gain the title and move to the House of Lords, but now he was happy in the Commons, one of the most bloody-minded of all Tories, in favour of hanging every poacher, pickpocket, rebel American, and publisher of seditious libels that could be caught. I thought he hadn't changed, but I was surprised to hear that he had developed some redeeming graces. He visited his sick father regularly, he was polite to his mother's lover, and he didn't rack every penny out of the Mountford estate tenants. In the old days Lady Mountford had been obliged to find other positions for at least two maids to keep them out of his way, but now I heard from his stable lad that his servants were well treated – so long as they knew their place.

I hadn't known my place. I still didn't. I wondered if I ever would.

One day I set out to call on some Abolitionists, both black and white; they had promised to introduce me to Mr Granville Sharp, who was more responsible than any other single person for the Somerset decision and other law cases that had set us free in England. Now he and other Abolitionists were concentrating their efforts on making the slave trade illegal; though they loathed slavery in all its forms, the Middle Passage was the worst hell of all, and they thought that owners in the Americas would treat their slaves better if they couldn't replace them so cheaply from the womb of Africa.

The place they used as an office was in the crypt of a Presbyterian church. I recalled Mr Macleod, the Presbyterian minister who had married Miss Campbell and taken her away to Edinburgh, and I wondered what would have happened if she'd stayed. To my disappointment Mr Sharp had an appointment elsewhere, but I reflected that he was better employed on such work than being thanked by yet one more black person, which was all I wanted to do.

As I was leaving, another door opened and a woman's voice said, 'I'll find a place for him.' It stopped me dead. They were the pure, clear, careful tones of the Voice of God.

I tiptoed towards her as she faced into the room, my finger to my lips warning the people inside not to tell her; this was one of the very few places in the world where a big black man could do this to a small white woman and get away with it. I covered her eyes with my hands and said, 'Good morning, Miss Campbell.'

She gave a jump and said, 'I've been Mrs Macleod for nearly eleven years.'

'I know. I came to your wedding.'

She took my hands from her eyes and turned round to look at me. 'Joshua!' she cried, delighted. 'What a fine tall fellow you've turned into. I thank God you're alive – and so well!' She turned back into the room to introduce me. 'This is my godson Joshua.'

'And never was there a fairy godmother who waved her wand to such advantage. Mrs Macleod taught me to read.'

'Joshua, I think you're old enough to call me Fiona. You're certainly big enough.' A tall sandy-haired man of about forty held out his hand to me. 'You remember David, my husband.' These were Christians who believed in using Christian names whenever possible.

'I trust she taught you to read the Bible,' he said.

'Of course. It's been my comfort these past ten years.' It was true, after all.

After a few moments' conversation, she said, 'I'll leave you to your business, David. My big strong godson will take me home, won't you?'

'It would be a great pleasure.'

We went to find a hackney, and she took my arm; I wished Luke could see us. I didn't want to lie to her; fortunately she'd worked with enough former slaves to know not to press me when I said that I didn't want to talk about the past ten years. As we were driven to Clapham where she lived, a village south of the river within an easy distance of London, she told me about her own life.

Her husband was minister in another of the churches that served the large Scottish community in London. She was not Presbyterian, but love overcame the barriers (how I wished my love and I were separated by a barrier only that small), and they could spend hours discussing such matters as whether human free will was compatible with divine omnipotence – which wasn't my taste in conversational topics but suited them. They had one daughter and two sons, all now at school – she was not someone who believed education was only for boys.

'Now I have time to do the work of God in finding employment for those who don't wish to be idle,' she said. 'I combine helping the Deaf and the Negro.' She trained out-of-work black people to act as attendants for the elderly who were losing their hearing. 'If a man has a clear deep voice and a good character, he's excellent: wide lips are easier to understand. The best of them I train as teachers of the deaf.' She looked at me sadly. 'I would have trained you. You already knew a lot from watching me. Oh, Joshua, why didn't you ask me for help?'

'I was going to be sold.'

'I could have persuaded the Mountfords not to do it. Even if I couldn't, David and I would have found the money to buy your freedom. Why did you two go off like that? It was madness, madness!'

'We were only children, Fiona.'

'Children eloping?' She shook her head. 'If only I'd known. It would have saved so much pain.'

I bit my lip. 'Pain for her?'

'Yes, Joshua. Pain for her. That's why I came back to London. I had a desperate letter from Lady Mountford, begging me to help. They feared for her life; they thought it might be a recurrence of brain fever. By the time she was out of danger David had found a place here, and we stayed.'

I put my head in my hands. I'd nearly killed her. 'She told you about it?'

'No. All that I know I heard from Lady Mountford. Althea never mentions it. She never mentions you. She avoids mentioning you, Joshua.'

I couldn't speak.

'The Mountfords hid the scandal well. I had to know the truth because I was looking after her, but the servants were told— Are you willing to confirm this for her sake if anyone recognizes you?'

'Of course.'

'So was I; even David doesn't know. The story was that she ran away with Pompey to stop him being destroyed, and took you along for protection. Everyone knew how you were always getting beaten for following her into scrapes.'

'That's much the way we presented ourselves on our journey. It's not so far from the truth.' Until our last night.

'An irresponsible childish escapade, not the sort of story that anyone wanted spread around, but nothing very serious. All the servants liked Althea so they kept it quiet. I don't think her husband knows.'

'What's he like?' I had to know.

'He's a typical Tory country squire. Not a bad man: he treats her well. I think she could have done better, but he has a big booming voice; that's why she chose him out of all the other offers that were made to her.'

'Is she happy?'

'She is – content. Sometimes she's happy; after the Somerset decision there was an enormous celebration, with every Negro and Abolitionist in London dancing through the night. We were all happy; there was no regard for skin or rank, and she was twirling round the room with a big boxer and a beggar off the streets. She can't hear the music, but she knows the steps. She often comes to the Abolitionist office; she says she's going to make the cause fashionable as well as moral.' She put her hand on my knee. 'Stay away from there. Stay away from her. It will do her no good to meet you. I'll have to keep this a secret from her.'

'It's too late. She already knows about me.' I told her about Pompey's death.

She sighed. 'That dog saved her life, I think. She wouldn't let him go when she was ill, so she was allowed to keep him. Perhaps it's for the best in her grief at his death to know that you're alive and free. But that's all the good you can do her, Joshua. I wish you'd leave London.'

'I can't. I have a task to do.'

'You still love her, don't you?'

'Yes.'

'As you love her, stay away from her. Try to forget her. You can only hurt her worse.'

I had met her dog; I had met her governess. It would be difficult to avoid meeting her, especially if our plan succeeded and Luke was installed in a household so closely connected with her relations. I tried to persuade him to choose another victim, but he only stared at me in surprise. 'Why, Josh? The Wintertons are perfect.' I couldn't deny it.

Fiona had urged me to go to Scotland; she'd recommend me for a place with Mr Braidwood at his college for the deaf in Edinburgh, where I could earn my living and get further training. But I knew what it would mean to Luke if I abandoned him now; he had lost his inheritance in saving my life. Strange irony: when I'd been his slave I'd lost all sense of obligation to him when he'd staked me in that poker game, but now we were equal partners I could not desert him.

All I could do was keep watch for Althea and try to keep out of her way. Useless of Fiona to tell me to forget her: if I hadn't done so in a South Carolina swamp, I certainly could not do so in London, where almost every street brought back a memory. *Here* was the park where we'd played with the top that I'd bought with Benjamin Franklin's sixpence; *here* was the alleyway down which Pompey had chased a cat, causing the accident that had provoked the Mountfords to get rid of him and me; and *here* was the road we'd first taken on our flight to Scotland.

Did she remember them too?

It was time to set the Marquis of Carabas on his way. We spent the day checking that we had everything perfect, and I trimmed his hair and shaved him.

'Leave me a drooping moustache, Josh. It'll hide the scar on my upper lip.'

'What scar on your upper lip?'

'The one they'll put in my description if we ever have to run for it.'

At midnight we set off for Hyde Park. We had an uncomfortable time hiding from the eyes of passing watchmen, but eventually everything was quiet, and it was time to move. Luke stripped off everything except the finely made cast-off shirt we'd bought for the purpose at a pawnbroker, and we hid his clothes behind a bush – some beggar would be lucky in the morning. I rolled on the ground to look as if I'd been in a fight and set my wig carefully awry.

'Time to go, Josh,' he said, holding out his hand to shake mine.

'One more thing. I'm sorry about this, but you need a real injury; there are some things that you can't fake.'

He didn't say anything for a moment, then asked quietly, 'Why didn't you mention this before?'

'I didn't want to worry you. If I didn't know that you were a brave man, I'd have done it to you without warning. You know I'm right.'

He shrugged. 'Yes, you're right.'

I produced my knife.

'You think of everything, Fortescue.'

'I do my best, sir.'

'What injuries do you have in mind?'

'A blow on the head, and a knife wound to the right arm; it will prevent you being asked to write for a few weeks at least.' I hadn't been able to do anything about his illiterate scrawl.

He held up his arm as if he were fending off a knife attack. 'You're going to enjoy this, Josh, aren't you?'

'No. I spent seven years inflicting pain on your father's orders and hated every blow. But I learnt how to make injuries seem worse than they really are.'

'Get on with it,' he said, gritting his teeth.

With a swift, precise stroke I slashed his arm up to the hand, then I punched him hard enough on the temple to give him a bruise and me bloody knuckles. He made not a sound, but staggered as he fell to the ground. 'Go, man, now!'

I ran over the road, throwing the knife into the gutter, and hammered on the Wintertons' door; I knocked and knocked until lights started to show inside. The door opened.

'Help! Help! My master, Mr Fitzjames, has been attacked!'

Chapter 5

Luke sat up in bed, his eyes closed, a compress on his brow and a dressing on his arm, doing splendid work of not quite hiding his pain. The doctor had gone; Lord Winterton remained, looking just as I remembered him except even fatter and more florid – it was a surprise that an apoplexy hadn't taken him off years ago.

Luke sighed. 'Everything taken, Fortescue?'

'Everything, sir,' I lamented. 'Your clothes, your bags, your money, your papers, your go— your samples: everything!'

'You warned me against walking round the Park at night, Fortescue. I guess I underestimated English footpads; they're better fighters than the Indians. How many were there?'

'Eight – ten – a dozen!'

'Don't exaggerate. There weren't more than six. I'm glad to see you landed a blow. I hope it hurts him as much as this blow hurts me.'

'I'm sure it does, sir.'

He looked up at Winterton gratefully. 'I must thank you, my lord, for showing such hospitality. You are a truly good man.'

This was undoubtedly the best thing anyone had ever said about Winterton. He waved the compliment away. 'Not at all, not at all. It is an honour to be able to help Mr Fitzjames. All London has been talking about you for a week.'

Luke put on a pained expression. 'You see what you've done,

71

Fortescue? Even Lord Winterton has heard that – that foolish story.'

'I'm sorry, sir. I don't know how it slipped out.'

Luke looked at Winterton again. 'May I ask you, my lord, to deny it on all possible occasions? I shall do so myself. It is the gossip of a servant. I'd dismiss him for it if he hadn't done me good service in the past.'

Winterton glared at me. 'I'd dismiss you, if you were mine!'

'I have chided him enough, my lord. He knows his fault.'

'Oh, I do, I do, sir,' I grovelled.

'And what do I do now? It'll be months before I can get anything from Charleston – even if I could write! Even if those damned rebels don't start their insurrection!'

'Mr Fitzjames, please feel free to accept the hospitality of my house, at least until you recover from your wounds.'

'I hate to do it, my lord; it is such an imposition.'

'Not at all, not at all.'

'Thank you; you show true charity to a poor stranger.' He closed his eyes, apparently tired.

Winterton accepted the hint. 'I'll leave you to the care of your man.' Then to me: 'I hope you show that you are worthy of his forgiveness.'

'I'll do my best, my lord.'

'I'll have the housekeeper arrange a bed for you in the servants' rooms while your master is staying with us.'

As he left Luke murmured quietly, 'Alligators, indeed. Exaggerating as usual, Fortescue. There was only one.'

I was proud of the boy.

I was the only black servant in the household; apart from the French cook, all the others were British. I shared a room with three menservants; they obviously resented it, and gave every impression that they expected me to perform a cannibal dance or ravish the housemaids. I could have loomed threateningly, but I was tired of being tough; I could have ignored it, but I was tired of being insulted. So I took the only other choice open to me: I set out to please. I was helpful, polite and efficient, and by mid-afternoon the next day I overheard one of them say, 'Oh, he's not so bad for a nigger.' I counted it as a triumph.

All the servants wanted to know about Mr Fitzjames; I told a few stories of the alligators-and-Indians variety, but refused to be drawn further. 'I nearly lost my position because of my loose tongue,' I said. 'I give thanks to providence that I didn't reveal the name of his father.' Cajoling from the groom, brandy from the butler and flirtatious glances from the scullery maid could get no more out of me.

Luke stayed in bed for a day, reviewing etiquette with me until he had it perfectly, and that evening he came down to dinner. Though his borrowed clothes fitted him badly, he looked very handsome, even dashing, with his arm in a sling and a patch over the eye that had turned red. In deference to the state of his health, it was only a quiet family dinner, for which we were both grateful.

Lady Winterton was a faded and sickly woman: no surprise, since she'd borne eleven children. Seven survived, but only four were still living under the family roof: the three unmarried girls, Henrietta, Maria and Louisa, and the youngest, William, a boy of thirteen.

I stood behind Luke's chair, serving him and cutting up his food. He was almost perfect, with only a slight hesitation about the cutlery that could be explained by his need to eat with his left hand. He was perfect, too, in his treatment of the family: deferential to Lord Winterton, solicitous to her ladyship, charming with no sign of undue interest with the daughters, and accepting young William's incipient hero-worship with good grace. When the ladies left the room, and William's request to remain was rebuffed, I was allowed to stay: 'In case I need his assistance,' Luke said. I stood motionless and invisible as I'd been taught to do many years before, and I watched him perform.

He admired the port: 'It's a long time since I've drunk anything as fine,' and the conversation was general for a while. Then he said, 'Lord Winterton, you have been so generous with me, I have no hesitation in asking for your advice.'

'Of course, Fitzjames.'

'Where would you advise me to find a way of earning my living for the next few months, until I can expect a return from Charleston?'

'Earn your living? I won't hear of such a thing! A man of your condition?'

'I must do something. I learnt many skills in America; I can ride a horse even with one hand, for example.'

'You could not—' Winterton paused. 'I've read the stories. You could not ask your father for help?'

'You must not believe everything in the papers. They did not report the matter at all accurately. My father is dead.'

'I'm sorry to hear it.' He was obviously crossing off his mental list all the living dukes and trying to recall the ones that had died in the past few years.

'Thank you, my lord. I don't think the rest of the family knows of my existence. I had planned to return with my fortune and proof of my identity. Those footpads did me a very ill turn. The money they are welcome to, but they took all my papers as well, and they are irreplaceable this side of the Atlantic. Fortunately I have certified copies in a bank in Charleston, but it will take four or five months, perhaps more, before they arrive. I do not wish to appear before the present head of the family as a nameless, penniless beggar.'

'Your sentiments do you credit.'

'Thank you. But otherwise my credit stands at naught.'

Winterton eyed him speculatively. 'Would you accept a small loan, Fitzjames? Just to tide you over a few months?'

'It is most generous of you, my lord. But I couldn't accept it. Unless—'

'Unless?'

'I know what an unsecured loan to a man with no credit costs in interest. I can't possibly accept your offer unless you allow me to repay you double.' He held up his hand to quell a non existent protest. 'I insist. I will not be moved on this.'

Rich, greedy and stupid Lord Winterton hesitated only a moment. 'That would be more than generous. Would a thousand pounds be enough?'

'It would be most kind.'

'Hmm. That's only two hundred or so a month, and you must buy new clothes and such like. What about two?'

'I bow to your knowledge of what a gentleman needs.'

'Well, let's make it a gentleman's currency: two thousand guineas.'

'Two thousand guineas, Josh! Two thousand goddamn guineas!' he whispered excitedly as I helped him get ready for bed. 'That's – what, two thousand one hundred pounds! Around nine thousand dollars!'

'Nine thousand, three hundred and thirty-three and a third.'

'Thank you, Josh.'

'You could take it and run.'

'What, now? You're joking!'

'You'll have to find four thousand guineas in four or five months.'

'I'm a South Carolina gambling man. I'll raise it in a month.'

'Think, Luke. This is more or less what your share of the inheritance was worth. It could set you up for life with almost no risk.'

'With the rest of the season ahead of me, with two thousand guineas in my pocket, with all those pretty girls and all those fat pigeons ripe for plucking? Oh, no, Josh. I'm not running now. In any case, I'd only have half that money; the other half's yours.'

'I don't want it. Give me a hundred pounds and keep the two thousand; that's more than enough to get me to Scotland.'

'What's in Scotland for you?'

'Safety. A position.' No chance of meeting Althea.

'Doing what?'

'I've met my godmother. She thinks I could become a teacher; she'll recommend me to a college in Edinburgh.'

'I guess seven years as a slave-driver is good practice for

becoming a teacher, Josh. I know you're good. What's your godmother like?'

'She's a fine Christian woman, very well educated. Not your kind at all.'

'She taught you about obligations, I guess?'

I knew what was coming. 'She did.'

'The way I look at it, the trick you played on me about getting your freedom cancels out the one I played on you putting you up as a stake. All that learning you gave me; we both know it was for your sake as well as mine. But after all that, there's one more thing you owe me, Josh; you owe me your life.'

'Yes, I do.'

'Give me a few months, that's all I ask. There's no risk – he doesn't expect payment until then. If I find as the time draws near that I won't be able to pay, we'll have good warning. Until the end of August, Josh, and we'll call it evens.'

'Very well, Luke. Until the end of August.'

Next morning, Lord Winterton escorted Luke, with me in attendance, to his bank, where he arranged for the transfer of two thousand one hundred pounds into the account of a complete stranger whom he had picked up off the streets. I sometimes wonder how the British ruling classes manage to stay ruling.

Next we went to his tailor, who was happy to give credit to Mr Fitzjames when vouched for by Lord Winterton. Luke lost his head. Silks, satins, laces, linens spread out in glorious profusion in front of him; he was like a boy who'd been let into a pastrycook's shop and told to help himself. I had to give a very loud cough to stop him decking himself out in an array of red and gold that only needed a shoulder knot to be indistinguishable from a footman's livery.

'I think your man is right, Fitzjames,' Lord Winterton said, having heard my cough. 'I understand now why you don't dismiss him.'

'Thank you, my lord. I've lived in America too long.'

Makers of hats, canes, shoes, and watches were equally glad

to give him credit, and soon he was fitted out to the satisfaction of both himself and his patron. Only on one occasion did they disagree. 'The moustache, Fitzjames. It's not the thing.'

'I'll shave if I must, my lord, but it will reveal an ugly scar.'

'Best keep it on, then. How did you come by it?'

Any other man might have come up with something about alligators or Indians, but I was beginning to realize the depth of Luke's talent. He gave a rueful laugh, and said, 'Nothing very adventurous, my lord, I'm afraid; a mere tavern brawl. A lady's honour was at stake, you see.'

'I'm sorry you came by it in such a cause.'

'Don't feel sorry for me, but you might feel sorry for the other man.'

That night it was another family dinner party, but a larger one, with all of the Winterton children in attendance. There was the heir, Viscount Hargreaves, and his wife; Rodney Winterton, a grown younger son; and Lady Charlotte with her husband – George Mountford.

'Is he likely to recognize you?' Luke asked, as I was helping him to dress.

'I doubt it. I've changed a lot since the last time he saw me. Quite a lot.'

There was something in my tone that made him ask, 'And when was that?'

'When I lay tied up on the wharf at Liverpool at his feet, bruised and bleeding from the beating he'd given me.'

'So you don't want me to go easy on him?'

'Not at all.'

There were too many at the table for the conversation to be general, so Luke confined himself to entertaining the eldest and the youngest daughters either side of him. Louisa was a pretty, silly girl, envious of Maria who was coming out that season, and easy for him to amuse. Charlotte, George Mountford's wife, was more of a challenge. She had a pinched, wary look, and from time to time gave glances across the table to her husband to ensure she had his approval. But Luke's charm worked on her, as it did on every other woman I'd seen him with, and soon she was smiling and talking freely. At the end of the second course he said something that made her burst out laughing. George Mountford looked up and gave a slight warning cough. Instantly her laughter stopped, and she said barely a word until the ladies left the room.

That could have been Althea. I gave thanks to whatever had spared her.

The ladies and young William retired, and the gentlemen turned to their port and brandy; I and another footman remained in attendance. It soon became clear to me that George Mountford was, as they say, needling Luke. Or rather, he was trying to, since at first his points simply bounced off. Luke didn't understand the poisonous English art of not quite being rude to people. His parents were married, so Mountford's excessive stress on words like 'illegitimate' caused no wounds. The conversation turned to a man of loose habits and Mountford said, 'And he fathered a fine crop of bastards.' Then he turned to Luke and said, 'My apologies, Fitzjames; I forgot your condition.' But Luke accepted this as a genuine apology; in South Carolina, if someone insulted you, you knew you were being insulted.

When the conversation inevitably turned to America, Luke was too busy controlling himself to take any notice of Mountford's darts. This was the one area of politics where he knew more than these ignorant, hang 'em and flog 'em Tories, but he could not reveal his strongly held views. I knew he was boiling inside, but he sat with his calm gambler's face, saying nothing until Rodney Winterton asked him directly, 'Fitzjames, you've been very quiet, but you must know the sentiments in America. What do you think: will there be war?'

'Yes,' he said bluntly. 'Gentlemen, I've listened to you, and I've listened to conversations on the other side of the Atlantic, and you are as far away from them in views as you are in miles. I can't see any chance of reconciliation.'

'Why? What do they say?'

'That King George is a tyrant; that the British parliament imposes taxes on Americans without giving them any representation; that time after time the British have passed laws for the benefit of people on a small island rather than those on a great continent; that trade has been stifled and regulated to benefit Britain, not America; that a Standing Army has been imposed on Americans in peace time that is subject to no American law or consent; and that American legislatures have been suspended for passing laws that benefit their citizens but not the British. That's what they say.'

I had never heard him speak so well. But it didn't impress his hosts. 'I believe you're in sympathy with the rebels, Fitzjames,' said Mountford.

'There is no man in America who is not in sympathy with them.' (Well, there were, but they were black and didn't count.) 'For some, their loyalty to the British crown will outweigh their sympathies – and I'm one of them, of course,' he added without blushing. 'But most will take up arms and fight for their liberty. I'm sorry if my plain speaking has offended you, especially as I'm a guest in the family, but you ought to know what you're facing.'

'No offence taken,' said Winterton. 'We're English, damn it; free speech is our birthright.' (Well, so long as it is spoken by a duke's son with a gold mine.)

Luke again sat quietly while they scorned the possibility of a rabble of farmers and shopkeepers standing up against the might of the British Army, and they sneered at the capabilities of American generals; scorn and sneer which Mountford contrived to reflect on Luke himself, that at last began to get through Luke's skin; I saw his lips tightening with effort not to reply in strong South Carolina style. Mountford must have sensed he was drawing blood, and his jibes became more open. Perhaps that was what caused Luke to make a minor slip. Forgetting that peers are not usually addressed by their rank, but simply as Lord So-and-so, he said, 'What do you think, Viscount Hargreaves?'

It was a small error which men with better manners would have ignored, but Mountford seized his chance. 'I see that your years in America have made you forget your breeding, Fitzjames.' Then, when Luke appeared to give nothing more than a rueful shrug, he added, 'Or rather, your half-breeding.'

Luke couldn't ignore that one. Turning to Lord Winterton, he said, 'As Mountford says, I've been a long time in America and I have forgotten things. Was that an insult? Of course, when my hand gets better I could show him what I have learnt there – about shooting, for example.'

There was a silence. Then Winterton said, 'I'm sure no insult was meant, Fitzjames. Was there, George?'

Mountford said nothing for a moment; everyone waited. 'No insult was meant, Fitzjames.'

'And no insult will be taken, Mountford,' he replied with a smile.

As he was preparing for bed, Luke said, 'Josh, I really do not like the Honourable George Mountford. I don't like him at all. Did you see the way he treated his wife?'

'Perhaps that's why he was attacking you; for committing the crime of making his wife laugh. I didn't much like her when she was a girl, but nobody deserves that treatment.'

'Maybe I should have challenged him. But I think I'll wait until my hand's better; I'm quite sure that an opportunity will arise.'

The Macleods had invited me to dinner, and one day when Luke was taken by Rodney Winterton to his club, I accepted. After the pompous formality of the Wintertons, and the rigid order and sly insults of their servants' hall, it was a joy.

I discovered that David Macleod had a dry wit beneath an austere manner, and their three children were a pleasure to be with. Freckle-faced and sandy-haired like their father, with their mother's fine features, they were shy and polite at first, but they soon became lively without being boisterous, and showed that they had inherited the full measure of both parents' intelligence.

Eager – too eager – to learn, Janet, the oldest, a girl of nine, wanted to know about my experiences as a slave.

'Well – er—' I said, looking to her mother for help.

'Janet, people who have been slaves often have things they don't want to talk about,' she said gently. 'It's very bad being a slave.'

'Well, if we can't hear about it, how can we know how bad it is?' Janet said with ruthless childhood logic. 'Will you tell us about one of your friends, then?'

'I don't think I can tell you anything that's fit for children to hear.'

'If it's the truth,' said their father, 'it's fit for children to hear.'

'Well, once upon a time,' I began, 'there was a boy called Olakunde; about your age, Janet. He lived with his mother and father and brothers and sisters in a beautiful village in Africa. Then one terrible day he and his sister were kidnapped by a band of slavers from the next village. They were tied up and taken far away from their home. They had to walk a long, long time, with all the other people who had been taken as slaves, until they came to the sea. Olakunde had never seen the sea; he thought it went on till the end of the world. He had never seen white people before, and they were so cruel to him that he thought they were going to eat him. He and his sister were sold to different people, and he never saw her again.' I spared them the horrors of the Middle Passage as much as I could and still tell the truth, but the two younger children were sobbing by the time Olakunde got to Charleston, and Janet was sitting white-faced, her freckles standing out against her skin.

I stopped: making children cry is not to my taste. But Janet said, 'Go on. We should know this.' She reminded me of Althea at the same age. The boys nodded through their tears, following their big sister's lead.

'Well, Olakunde was washed to make him look presentable for market, then he was marched off the ship on shore and put in a large yard with the rest of the slaves. None of them knew what was to happen. Then the gates were thrown open and in rushed a lot of people who wanted to buy slaves; they were all shouting and grabbing the healthiest-looking slaves, and Olakunde was very frightened and confused, especially when they started to poke and pry all over him to see if he had any diseases. Unfortunately he wasn't well, so he was one of the last to be sold. He was bought by an old lady who didn't have much money so she couldn't afford one of the better slaves, and she didn't know the tricks that the traders use to make the slaves look healthy.' I shouldn't have said that, I thought, and tried to hurry on to the next stage. 'Anyway, she—'

Janet was too quick-witted for me. 'What tricks, Joshua?'

'They—' I looked at their parents. 'I'm sorry, I didn't mean to tell them this. You're Abolitionists: you must know what happens to a slave with dysentery.'

Their father nodded grimly and helped me out. 'The slave traders try to conceal it by stopping the flux.'

Janet didn't understand, so her mother explained. 'They stop his anus with tar,' then said it again in words a child would know. 'They put tar up his bum, so he doesn't soil himself all the time.'

There was silence; the boys were so shocked they stopped sobbing. 'They did that to Olakunde?' Janet whispered.

'Yes, I'm afraid they did,' I said. 'But listen to the rest of the story: life became better for him after that.' It couldn't have become any worse. 'The old lady took him home, and although she was angry that she'd been cheated, she didn't take it out on Olakunde. She called in a doctor, and she fed him up properly, and he soon became healthy again.' Making the best of a bad investment. 'He stayed with her for several years, and he quickly learnt to speak English.' She'd had him beaten if he didn't progress fast enough to suit her. 'He didn't have to work any harder for her than many servants do in London.' Up at five, working all day with barely time for meals, and to bed at ten if he was lucky or midnight if he was not. 'She fed him as well as she fed herself, and he grew up into a big strong man, almost as big as me.' Once he'd learnt to rummage through rubbish heaps to satisfy a growing boy's hunger that an old lady's portion of food could not. 'He was sorry when she died.' He'd come to know her ways. 'Then he was sold to the plantation I was on, which was the property of one of the best slave owners in the district, and there he met a woman called Sarah and fell in love with her, and she fell in love with him, and they lived happily,' I said, finishing on as cheerful a note as possible.

'But that's not fair!' Janet cried. 'Why do they do it?'

'Well, the heathen Africans do it because if they don't they won't be able to get any guns and their neighbours will capture them and turn them into slaves. And the Christian white people do it for money.'

'That's not Christian! I want to stop it!'

'You can help your mother and father, who are doing their best, and if you ever hear any of your friends talking about how slaves are happy, tell them Olakunde's story so they can learn better.'

'That's not enough. I want to do more!'

'I'm afraid that there isn't much more that a child can do,' said her father.

Fiona and I looked at each other, remembering a child who'd tried to save just one slave, and failed.

But children can cheer up very quickly, and soon we were all laughing in a noisy game of Speculation; the Macleods had no objection to card games if they weren't played for money. I rapidly lost all my fish, and would have lost them even sooner if Janet had not let me win at one point, as though to do what she could to make up for my past sufferings. She was very like Althea.

'Luke's right,' I laughed at the end. 'I'm the world's worst card player.'

'This is your Mr Fitzjames?' asked Fiona. 'What's he like?'

'It's not my secret, Fiona.'

'Even in the wilds of Clapham we all want to know about him. Would he care to dine here?' I didn't say anything for a moment. 'Or would our hospitality be beneath his touch?'

'No, no; any man of good sense would appreciate your hospitality, and I've known him bed down in a hovel with nothing but beans and river water inside him. But – well, he's a gamester; he's not a good Christian by any means.'

David protested. 'Surely you know that we wouldn't thrust the Bible down a guest's throat!'

Janet looked at me beseechingly. 'Please, Joshua.'

'Well,' I said, infuriatingly adult. 'We'll see.'

They had to be content with that, and soon Fiona took the children off to bed. David poured me a glass of whisky; it was the first time I'd tried it. 'What happened to Olakunde afterwards?' he asked. 'You didn't finish your tale for the sake of the children, but I'd like to know.'

'Sarah became pregnant and was going to be sold as a wet nurse. So they ran away together, but they were caught. Sarah was strung up by her wrists from a tree and whipped until they confessed who helped them; I can't blame them for revealing that it was me. They weren't punished any further, except that they were sold to places more than a thousand miles apart. But my owner was so angry with me that he was going to have me flogged to death. Luke stopped that; it cost him dearly. That's why I won't betray his trust.'

'You said he was not a good Christian? He seems something like it to me.'

If there's a hell and old man Smith is in it, I thought, I hope he can hear that testimony. 'I'll invite him.'

He accepted. My fears were groundless: the meeting between my two very different kinds of friends was a great success. He responded to their unforced goodness, and they responded to his easy charm. 'Ma'am,' he said to Fiona, 'Josh told me that if I wanted a model for my speech I should look no further than you, because you speak the purest English in the world. May I take his advice?'

He had the gift of being liked in any society, from the English nobility to the plantation slaves. He could use it unscrupulously, when getting a woman into his bed or two thousand guineas out of Lord Winterton, but here he wanted nothing from the Macleods but their good opinion: he had it.

After dinner, he taught everyone how to play Poque. He won all our fish the first time, but after we distributed them for a second round, Janet, showing the utmost composure and calculation of the odds, completely routed him. He fell to one knee before her. 'Miss Janet, will you be my partner for life? Together we could take on the world.' She giggled in triumph.

On the way home, he sighed. 'Josh, I've just been beaten at my own game by a nine-year-old girl brought up in a family that doesn't approve of gambling. I guess you were right: English gamesters aren't going to be so easy as I thought.'

'The family's Scottish.'

'English, Scottish, what's the difference?'

'Don't let them hear you say that. The Scots have fought the English even more than the French have: the last time was only thirty years ago. England and Scotland – and Wales too – are all part of Great Britain now, but the Scots have a different legal system, almost a different language. If you think David Macleod has a strong accent, you should hear what they're like in Scotland: it's as different from what we're speaking now as plantation Gullah.'

'You've been there?'

'Once. Very briefly.' Two hours too briefly.

'Where?'

'Just over the border. A place called Gretna Green.'

'That's where all the runaway couples go to, isn't it? Why?'

'It's much easier to be married there: the laws are different from England.'

He laughed. 'Maybe I'll find myself an heiress to elope with! It all sounds a great adventure, dashing off with her family in hot pursuit. Can you imagine it?'

'Yes, Luke. I can imagine it.'

Luke decided that it was time to move out; two weeks of the Wintertons were enough for anyone. He had everything he wanted out of them: money and an introduction to society. Winterton would sponsor him for membership of the more respectable clubs, and the two elder sons for the more rakish ones. He tried to leave at the next dinner. 'I'm imposing on you when you have Lady Maria's coming out ball next week.' But they wouldn't hear of it, and he was forced to agree to another two weeks, by which time his hand would be healed.

'He wants me for one of his daughters, Josh,' he said later.

'Do you want any of them?'

'Louisa's too young, Maria can think of nothing but her season, and Henrietta – you said it, Josh: she's a bitch.' She had taken the responsibility for most of the preparation for her sister's ball on her own shoulders, and as she harried the house-maids and fussed the footmen I realized that she had missed her vocation: she would fetch a good price in South Carolina as a slave-driver.

So far I had managed to avoid Althea by going the other way in the street whenever I saw someone who could be her; as I seemed to see her everywhere I looked, this entailed a good deal of hiding behind walls. When Luke was invited to dine at the Mountfords, I pleaded that I was far too likely to be recognized there, and was let off attending him. But she would be at the ball; I didn't need to overhear Maria and her mother talking over the guest list and saying, 'Oh, Sir Bertrand and Lady Verity, of course', to know that. All the servants were required to attend and help; indeed, several more had been hired for the occasion.

The afternoon before the ball I procured some alum water and sent a message to Luke that I was unwell. Downing the foul-tasting liquid, I soon began to produce evidence of my claim. Luke came up to see me; his arm was out of a sling, probably too early, but he wasn't going to miss his chance of dancing tonight. 'I'm sorry to see you so ill, Fortescue,' he said. 'I shall miss your help in getting ready.'

'I'm sorry, sir, but I don't think—' I broke off, grabbing the chamber pot just in time and producing enough to convince him. He backed out hastily.

I lay in bed listening to the music until the ball was over, knowing she and I were under the same roof, feeling sick to my gut and sick to my heart.

Two days later, I showed Luke around the rooms I had found in Bond Street above a jeweller's shop; just right for a bachelor in his condition, he agreed. The rooms had only just been left by their former occupant, and would need a few days of preparation for us. Luke and the landlord were discussing what was needed when it began to rain.

'Ah, that's one item I haven't equipped myself with,' Luke said. 'Fortescue, go out and buy a – what's-it-called? – an umbrella.'

I was returning with my purchase held over my head when a sedan chair stopped a few yards in front of me outside the jeweller's shop. Out of it emerged a lady in a hairpiece so high that she had to kneel on the floor of the chair rather than sit. As she clambered out in a very ungraceful fashion, her high heels showed beneath her silk dress, enormously wide with its side panniers. I smiled to myself, wondering what Althea thought about such a ridiculous fashion. The lady stood up, thanked the sedan carriers, and turned in my direction.

She stopped, motionless.

So did I.

Some time later – seconds, minutes, hours, I don't know – she said, 'I have the strangest feeling, as though the rest of the world has suddenly disappeared.'

'The world is still here,' I said, my joy at being only yards away from her swamped by my fear of what it could lead to.

And the world intruded. Luke came up saying, 'Ah, Fortescue, there you are.' I didn't look at him – I couldn't turn my eyes away from her – and he must have followed my gaze. 'Will you introduce me, Fortescue?'

It's not the part of a servant to perform introductions, but I did it anyway. 'Lady Verity, may I introduce Mr—' The words stuck in my mouth; I could not give even this simple lie to her.

'Fitzjames, ma'am. I see you know my man Fortescue.'

Still looking at me, she said, 'I learnt Pompey was dead. And then I learnt you were alive.'

'May I offer my condolences about your dog, ma'am?' Luke said. 'I was there when it happened. As Fortescue said, he died quickly.'

At last she turned to him; she couldn't have taken in a word he'd said until that moment. 'Thank you, sir,' she said: a useful phrase at any time. She turned back to me, her eyebrows raised in the gesture that I knew asked for help.

I silently mouthed the words, 'Mr Fitzjames.'

'Mr Fitzjames,' she said, smiling at him. 'I believe you are staying with Lord and Lady Winterton. We must have missed each other at Lady Maria's ball.'

'How uncivil of me, keeping a beautiful woman standing in the rain,' he said, not knowing that she couldn't understand him as he turned away from her to take the umbrella. He held it above her three-foot-high hair and five-foot-wide skirt, and she laughed at the failure of this attempt to keep her dry.

'These fashions are not made for this weather, Mr Fitzjames. If you will excuse me, I'll complete my errand in the shop. I hope we shall meet again.'

'What a charming woman,' he said as we walked away. 'The Mountfords' ward, I remember you saying.'

'Yes. Fiona Macleod used to be her governess.'

He kept on talking; I took no notice of him, this man who had saved me from being flogged to death. At that moment, I wished that he hadn't.

Chapter 6

Next day I was summoned with a message that Lady Winterton had a visitor who wanted to see me. This time I was prepared, so I could calmly enter the drawing room and acknowledge her presence as a good servant should.

'Lady Verity has been telling me that you were helpful to her when her dog was killed, Fortescue,' said Lady Winterton. 'She has come to thank you and to return your coat. She has asked for a few moments in private with you, so that you can tell her more about it.' I could see from Althea's tightening lip how much she resented the way that Lady Winterton was speaking for her as though she were dumb as well as deaf.

'Very good, my lady.'

Lady Winterton stood up and turned her back to Althea. 'Fortescue, Lady Verity is deaf. She can understand you if you speak loudly and clearly. You will say nothing to distress her; she was very attached to her dog.'

As soon as the door closed behind her, I said, 'She was telling me how to speak to a deaf person, and that I shouldn't distress you about Pompey.'

'Thank you, Joshua. You remember how I hate it when people do that, as though they can't even take the trouble to hide the fact that they're keeping a secret from me.'

I remember the smell of your hair, the touch of your lips— 'I remember, Lady Verity.'

'Oh, Joshua! Call me what you used to call me, at least in private.'

For more than ten years I've called you my love: I still do. 'Very well – Althea.'

'And stop standing there like a stuffed bear and come and sit here and talk to me,' she said, patting the place beside her on the sofa.

'You know I can't do that. I'm supposed to be a servant.' I couldn't have sat close to her in any case: those panniers took up most of the space.

'Mysterious Mr Fitzjames's sinister sable servitor, who follows him like a shadow. There are almost as many speculations about you as there are about him. I wondered if it was you; I kept my eyes open for you at Lady Maria's ball, but I didn't see you.'

'I must try not to be so sinister-looking.'

'But how is it that you're in his service?'

'Althea, it's his secret as well as mine. I can't lie to you, but if I tell you, you must keep it secret too, and not let him know that I've told you.'

'I'm good at keeping secrets. Who is he really? Who is his father?'

'His father was a South Carolina rice grower, who left me to Luke as his only inheritance. I persuaded him to come to England to try his luck here.'

She looked at my boots and burst out laughing. 'He's the Marquis of Carabas and you're Puss in Boots!'

'Exactly.'

'And the mysterious assault in Hyde Park: "Help, help, my master, the Marquis of Carabas, is drowning!" Oh, that's funny! That's the funniest thing I've heard for a long time!' She was laughing so much that tears were running down her face. 'Everyone's heard that his father is dead and the rest of the family don't know of his existence. So everyone is looking at him, wondering if it's they who'll benefit from his mountain of gold, and all the girls are concerned about falling in love with him in case he turns out to be their half-brother!' I was laughing with her; it felt very good.

She stopped laughing and wiped her eyes; she looked up at me. 'What does he know about us?'

'That you were the ward where I was a page. He doesn't know about – afterwards.'

'That's how we'll keep it, shall we?'

'Yes. That would be best.'

She stood up and started to leave. 'You've been in London all this time and haven't called to see me. I think that's most unfriendly of you. In fact, I think you've been avoiding me.' I nodded. 'Why?'

'I thought – I thought that it would do you no good if we met.'

'You were wrong.' I held the door open for her, and as she left, I heard her say to Lady Winterton, 'Thank you for permitting me to hear Fortescue's story. Meeting him has done me a lot of good.'

Of course it would be best, I told myself that night as I lay in bed, ignoring the snores of the three men in the room with me. She will treat me as a childhood playmate, someone for whom she had a regard many years ago and is pleased to see alive and free. We shall behave as if we'd done something sensible ten years ago, such as asking Fiona Macleod for help instead of embarking on our mad adventure. Of course that's the right thing to do.

But I wanted more, so much more. I'd thought that I couldn't love her more than I'd done, but I was wrong. Seeing her and hearing her made my desire for her even greater, adding new, fresh memories to the old ones. For ten years I'd loved her memory in defiance of the tribulations of my life; now I loved her all over again for what she was.

I should be happy, I told myself. Think what Olakunde is suffering at this moment, still in chains and separated from Sarah by a thousand miles. But the contemplation of someone else's misery doesn't make one's own easier to bear in the slightest.

I tried to contemplate my advantages over what I had been

last Christmas. I was free. I had friends. My whip was the other side of the Atlantic. If anyone beat me to death it would be a crime, not mere destruction of property. Soon I could be trained in a worthwhile career. Indeed, I had a choice, since I might stay with Luke now there was no need for me to flee to Scotland to avoid her.

I must think of those things, not the memory of her voice as she'd been dragged out of the room in Gretna Green crying, 'Joshua, I'll love you forever.' I shouldn't have felt so bitterly disappointed when I'd searched through my coat that she'd returned and found no hidden note from her. I must try not to hope that she was hiding the same sort of feelings that I was. Far better for her if she were not, if she had come to regard what we did as one of those foolish things one does as a child. She must not love me.

And I must learn, somehow, not to love her.

In the morning, after the other servants had left for their duties and before Luke awoke to bring me to mine, I took pen and paper and began to write. I needed a reminder of what would be said about us if Althea felt for me what I felt for her, and if we acted upon it.

Lovely woman of high station has stooped to the folly of embracing a servant in the past, and will doubtless do so again, lamentable and wicked though it is. None, however, has stooped so far nor shown such folly as the beautiful and fashionable Lady V—— in her choice of paramour: the sinister sable servitor of the mysterious Mr F——. Deaf alike to the voices of honour, prudence, wisdom, morality and nature, she now lies, as Shakespeare puts it, 'in the gross clasps of a lascivious Moor'.

Once it was engraved in my memory I burnt it; the last thing I wanted was for anyone else to read it. It did nothing whatever to lessen my love, but it did strengthen my resolve not to do anything about it.

*

A couple of days later Luke and I moved out of the Wintertons' with a sigh of relief and set up in Bond Street. I retrieved our boxes from the place we'd stored them during our stay in Park Lane, and we spread things out comfortably. My own room, small as it was as befitting a servant, gave me great pleasure; it was the first time in my life I'd had a room of my own. I put the books on the single shelf and surveyed my ten-volume library with satisfaction.

Then I went to Luke and gave him two guineas. 'What's this, Josh?'

'Equal shares of the profits. I've taken four guineas in bribes from Lord Winterton, Lord Hargreaves, and George Mountford, for which they have learnt that you do own a gold mine, you are the son of a duke, but that either I don't know or won't say which one. The other two got away with a guinea, but the dishonourable George had to pay two for the privilege.'

Supper was my treat; these were my first earnings as a free man. I bought a large meat pie and a jug of porter to try to give him a taste for English beer (a failure). Over supper, we worked out the details of what I would say in future to anyone who tried to bribe me, and planned what to do on the morrow. He would go to one of the clubs; he had played quietly and steadily until now, earning himself fifty guineas and a reputation as someone to be sought out as a partner.

But I had to go and see Fiona Macleod to explain what had happened with Althea. She sighed. 'Well, perhaps she does know her own good better than I do. I don't need to tell you that things must be left at that, do I, Joshua?'

'No, you don't. I'm relieved, I must say. I have an obligation to stay with Luke until the end of August; I'd have spent the next few months ducking round pillars if it hadn't happened.'

'And after that?'

'I don't know; I'll decide nearer the time. I might stay with him, or I might take up your offer of training to teach the deaf, if I may.'

'Of course you may. If you like, you can start now. I'll lend you a book and you can read it at your leisure.' I agreed. 'Althea lost her hearing when she'd already learnt English,' she said. 'She can manage by reading lips. But children born deaf find it almost impossible to learn to speak that way. Abbé de l'Epee in Paris has set up a fine school to teach people sign language: here's the book. Take it away and learn the signs and the way the system works. You must learn their language if you want to teach them.'

I did, and in my spare moments worked my way through it. Luke came in from the club as I was doing so, and I explained. 'Let me take a look at that book,' he said, and he thumbed through it thoughtfully. Then he looked up. 'Josh, do you have strong objections to cheating at cards?'

'It depends who you're cheating.'

'The English aristocracy?'

'No objection whatever.'

'Because sometimes it would be very useful indeed, if you happened to be passing behind a man who's holding his cards in a way that you can see them, for you to find a way to let me know what they are.'

'I shudder at the thought of what Fiona would say if she found out what we were using her book for.'

As it happened, the book wasn't very useful for our purpose: the signs were intended to be seen, not concealed, and the good Abbé had neglected to create signs for use by gamesters. We had to design our own system. It took some time to refine it, but with industry and perseverance that would have won us applause from David Macleod in any other cause we had the system working.

'Fortescue, fetch me a drink,' he said, scratching his right ear with his left little finger and frowning.

'You want to know if the player opposite is holding the ace of spades.'

'Good.' He looked at me rubbing my left eye with four fingers of my right hand and smiling. 'The player on my left is holding four low clubs.'

'Damn. The player on your right.'

'Smiling is my left, your right. Have we got it?'

At last we had it perfect. 'Luke, there's one player whom I'm not going to help you cheat: a very good one, someone who's already beaten you.'

'Who's that?' he asked, concerned.

'If you want to win any fish from Janet Macleod, you're on your own.'

Now there was no need for me to avoid Althea, we were often in the same room: Mr Fitzjames and Lady Verity were part of the same circle and were frequently invited to the same occasion.

She behaved towards me just as she should: agreeable and civil to a valued former servant. She gave neither me nor anyone else any sign that there could be more than that between us – and neither did I. I was filled with desire for her every moment that we were together; if love gave out a radiance I could have done service as a lighthouse, but not a gleam of it escaped me, and I saw nothing of the kind from her. No smile or flush at a passing comment that might have provoked a memory, no significant glances between us. The single exception to this would occur if I happened to be close at hand when she was having difficulty with a conversation; she would glance at me with her eyebrows slightly raised, and I would silently mouth the words she hadn't understood. If anyone noticed, it was readily explainable: I was the first person whose lips she had learnt to read, and this had always been one of my duties.

I hated her husband before I knew him; this changed to contempt when I first saw him. A big, beefy, red-faced man, with an enormous voice. Of no more than moderate wit – perhaps even less – I doubt if he'd had an original idea in his life. He was content to parrot those of others, or rather to broadcast them loudly. But my contempt changed as I saw how he treated her: not just as any man should treat his wife, but with a tactful consideration for her deafness that surprised me in such a boor. He instinctively took a position with a light on his face as Fiona

Macleod and I would. She'd direct a flash of raised eyebrow to him asking for help if he was at hand, and he'd silently mouth the words as I would have done. I saw no sign of passion or love between them, but long-married couples rarely show such signs in public. I saw regard and good manners, and I knew how she could be content as his wife; after all, she didn't have to hear his inanities.

One evening she was placed next to Luke at dinner; I stood behind them, ready for his orders. I watched her as they conversed – how well I knew that intent look as she concentrated on reading his lips. I could tell when she hadn't understood him: she wore a slightly blank smile, and she stopped nodding her monstrous headdress, with flowers, feathers, beads and shells adorning its curls of false powdered hair. I wondered if she realized that she was signalling her incomprehension to anyone in the room who understood the sign. I waited for her glance of appeal for help, but she sent me none. The worst moments were when Luke indicated that I should fetch him something. I'd serve him, and her too if she asked, with my arm only an inch away from her, aching with the struggle not to move it that extra inch so I could touch her.

That night as I helped him ready for bed, he gave a whistle of appreciation. 'What a fascinating woman, Lady Verity! She's not exactly beautiful, but she made me feel as if I was the only person in the world when I was talking to her. What is she doing with that oaf of a husband? Did you hear him, Josh? Of course you heard him. I'm surprised we couldn't hear him in South Carolina!'

At last I found control of myself enough to reply. 'It's part of his attraction.' He looked puzzled. 'She's deaf, Luke.'

'No! She can't be! She has such a beautiful voice!'

'Deaf isn't necessarily dumb; and remember, Fiona Macleod used to be her governess. Why be surprised that she·speaks well?'

'But she was dancing with me!'

'She can't hear the music, but she knows the steps. That's why she made you feel important; she was concentrating hard on reading your lips. She can barely hear her own voice; she certainly couldn't hear yours.'

'That poor woman!'

'Don't pity her. She hates that.'

'Can I admire her, then? What courage she has!'

'Yes, you can admire her.'

He shook his head in amazement. 'She's wonderful! She was following my conversation so well!' I didn't disillusion him; she worked hard to make people believe that. 'Can she hear any sound at all?'

'If her hearing hasn't changed in ten years, she can hear very loud noises. Thunder, a hammer on an anvil – and, I imagine, her husband. Before you despise him, I must tell you that she was destined to marry George Mountford.'

'Well, he's better than the dishonourable George, I'll give him that. How did she escape such a fate?'

'I don't know. It was after I – after I was sold. But I'm thankful to whatever it was that prevented it.'

'You seem to have known her well.'

Oh, yes. 'She always found me easy to understand. When she and Fiona needed a servant, I was always chosen. That's why Fiona says it'll be easy for me to learn how to become a teacher of the deaf; I watched their lessons together, and I already know what to do to help deaf people understand me.'

'What should I do?'

'Make sure your face is in the light and don't cover your mouth. Speak clearly, but Don't-Exaggerate-Your-Lip-Movements-Like-This,' I said, showing him what not to do. 'Don't raise your voice; unless you can speak as loudly as Sir Bertrand does naturally, or as Fiona Macleod does by training, it won't make any difference to her and it just makes you seem angry – she has only enough hearing that a big voice in a quiet room helps her to read lips. You could do worse than copy what her husband does, by the way; he's not quite such a fool as he appears. It's a shame about your moustache, though; it doesn't help.'

'I'm stuck with it, or I'd shave it off. She'd be worth the sacrifice.'

'She's a married woman, Luke.'

'That makes it easier to get to know her: if I pay attentions to a single woman everyone asks my intentions. I thought she was fascinating before, Josh, but now I know what it costs her – I've never met a woman like her in my life!'

Except for the strain of loving Althea and having to conceal it – and that was a big exception – I was enjoying myself, and Luke had an even better time. No ducal family dared offend him in case it turned out to be theirs for whom the mountain of gold was intended. His good looks, single state and agreeable manner would have won him approval in any case, and most evenings he had more invitations than he could attend. Usually I went with him. I couldn't go into the exclusive clubs, and I wouldn't go into the brothels, but otherwise I followed him like a shadow, as the newspapers said, and was accepted as part of his air of mystery; I earned a pretty income in bribes.

It was all working perfectly; we heard many jokes about Robinson Crusoe and Man Friday, but not a whisper about the Marquis of Carabas and Puss in Boots. Speculations flew about us, some of them even true: he had indeed saved my life (though not from being eaten by an alligator), and he had, in a sense, won me in a card game. The one about being bound together in a Satanic pact made us laugh, though the one about us being Sodomitical lovers made us embarrassed.

Luke set out to give evidence to the contrary and would often return home groaning with satisfaction. I could have provided similar evidence if I'd chosen: I was astonished by the number of offers I received, several from well-born ladies. Some wanted to know Mr Fitzjames's secret; others wanted to know whether it was true what everybody says about black men. Tempted though I often was, I didn't satisfy their curiosity.

Luke was a good enough card player in any case to make money. With my information as well, he was ahead of the target if he intended to repay Lord Winterton's loan. It wasn't always possible: the best gamesters kept their cards concealed, but there were plenty incautious or drunk enough that I could learn what Luke needed. It may seem strange that someone dressed as spectacularly as I should be invisible, but the English upper classes never look at servants unless they cause annoyance.

We tried to live as moderately as we could – we need never pay for dinner – but there are many expenses involved in maintaining the life of an English gentleman. He looked at the first bill, and exclaimed in surprise and dismay, 'What do I do with this, Josh?'

'If you want to behave like an English gentleman, you'll throw it in the fire. If you want to behave like an honest man, you'll pay it.'

He put it in a drawer. 'I'll keep my choices open.'

When Luke didn't need me, I spent time with the London black community making friends. They were as curious as anyone else about Mr Fitzjames, but accepted my reticence with good humour. Many of them had had worse experiences than I, and we trod carefully around each other's pain. It was good to be a free black man among other free black men.

At other times I dined with the Macleods, and Luke would too, when he'd had enough of dissipation. In the true meaning of good company – agreeable, well-informed, hospitable – they were by far the best we knew, and he enjoyed pitting his wits against Janet Macleod for fish just as much as he did against the gamesters in White's for hundreds of guineas.

But I wished he wasn't so taken with Althea. I had come to the stage where the pleasure of being in the same room with her outweighed the pain it caused me. But not when I saw Luke exert his charm on her. Perhaps that little smile and sparkling eye she gave him was caused by her glee at knowing who he really was – it was the same expression as when she read the lips of someone speculating about him – but perhaps it wasn't. I was much less jealous of Sir Bertrand than I had expected to be; he gave her a comfortable life, and that won some regard from me.

But Luke? I'd seen him with women before.

He wished to know her more, and that meant getting to know Sir Bertrand. At first Luke treated him with contempt: 'I tell you, Josh, if he's an example of British Members of Parliament, then American independence is a certainty.' But a liking grew between them; on the really important matters in life – horses and guns – they had much in common. When Sir Bertrand learnt that Luke relied on hiring a hack, he offered free run of his stables, generosity which Luke accepted with as much intention of enjoying a ride together as of saving money. The hunting season was months away, so guns had to be confined to the shooting gallery, but it was clear they'd both enjoyed the match. 'He's not a bad sort for a Tory,' Luke decided. 'And you were right, Josh: he treats Lady Verity well.'

Sir Bertrand and Lady Verity requested the pleasure of Mr Fitzjames's company at the theatre one night, and she made it clear that there would be no objection to him bringing his manservant.

'What can she get out of a play, Josh?' Luke asked as we were getting ready.

'She'll arrange to have a copy of the playscript in front of her, with a small light to let her read it. She can still enjoy it.'

'What a wonderful woman!'

I fetched and carried for the party, which included three other people, and otherwise stood silently and unobtrusively. It was a comedy, simple-minded enough for Sir Bertrand's bray to boom out frequently. About half-way through, between the acts, she put her hand to her forehead and said, 'Bertrand, it's a little stuffy. Would you mind if I went home?' He offered to take her, but she refused. 'No, you're enjoying it so much, I won't drag you away. Mr Fitzjames, may I ask for the services of your man to escort me home?' There were a few protests, but nothing she couldn't wave away, and soon we were sitting in the coach together; she showed no sign of a headache.

'Neatly done, Althea.' There was a small lantern fixed in the carriage for the purpose of illuminating someone's lips.

'Yes, I think so too,' she said, pleased with herself. 'I wanted to ask you something, Joshua. I'm worried. I think – well, I think you may harbour some ill-feelings towards the Mountfords.'

'After what they did to us? Yes, I harbour ill-feelings.'

'I've been thinking about what we did; I've had a long time to think about it. Watching Janet Macleod growing up just like me, I've thought about her. In a few years' time when she's thirteen, if she does what I did, I'll try to stop her.' I didn't say anything. 'Joshua, would you try to stop her too?'

I pictured it: the Macleods, frantic about their daughter, begging me for help. 'Yes, I would,' I said slowly. 'But that doesn't alter the fact that the Mountfords sold me.'

'We might have stopped them, but we never even tried. They were going to have Pompey destroyed, but they changed their minds when they saw how much I needed him.'

'I'll spare you the details of what George Mountford did to me on the journey to the slave ship at Liverpool, but it wasn't pleasant. Althea, if you insist I'll try to forget it, but it'll be hard.'

'Oh, George!' she said with loathing. 'Do what you like to George, so long as it isn't anything that will bring much grief to his mother. If you need my help, just ask. In fact, I shall be most annoyed if I find you've done something and you've left me out.' Then she closed her eyes and went to sleep, and I indulged in the pleasure of silently looking at her all the way home.

I wondered how to convince Luke to spare the Mountfords without telling him the reason, but soon after he said, 'Josh, I fear I'm going to disoblige you about Lord and Lady Mountford. I've just been having a conversation with Lady Verity, and it's pretty clear that she holds them in high regard.'

Clever, clever Althea. 'So you want to go easy on them? Oh, very well, just so long as you don't expect me to forgive the dishonourable George.'

'Oh, George!' he said. 'She doesn't like him at all. I don't think she'll worry about what we do to him.'

I'd tried to avoid Lady Mountford, but in that circle it was inevitable that I'd sometimes attend an occasion where she was present with her cavalry officer. She hadn't recognized me so far. But one dinner, perhaps because it was held in a house where I'd often attended her in the past and I happened to be standing in the same spot as Caesar the page had once done, I saw her glance brush over me; she looked back startled, then appalled. I don't know what excuse she gave to the hosts, but soon we were alone in a small private room. 'Caesar, you must leave London at once,' she said with no preliminaries.

'Lady Mountford, I'm no longer your slave Caesar. I'm Fortescue, a free man in the service of Mr Fitzjames. I'll stay as long as he wants me and as long as I want to stay.' I enjoyed saying that.

'I'll pay you to go. Name your price.'

'Do you think you can match what Mr Fitzjames can give me?'

She bit her lip. 'Caesar, Fortescue, whatever you call yourself, if you have any regard for Lady Verity's happiness, you will leave. Please, I beg you.'

I looked down at her from my ten-inch advantage in height, and saw that she did care for Althea, and I remembered Althea's words. This was enough revenge for me, this moment when I claimed my freedom to her and she begged to me. 'Lady Mountford, Lady Verity already knows I'm here; I tried to avoid her, because I feared the same consequences as you do. But there was a chance meeting in the street and she knew me at once. She treats me as she ought to do: as a former page boy in the household where she grew up, one for whom she had a regard in those days, and is pleased to see alive and free. In other words, she treats me as if we'd all done what we should have done all those years ago: as if she and I hadn't run away to stop you from selling me. If you don't believe me, just watch her. If you see any sign of anything more from her, then come and ask me again. Yes, I have a regard for her happiness; I'll do what I can to ensure it.'

She looked at me and nodded to herself. 'You were a good page boy; you served me well. I was right to try to stop what I saw growing between the two of you, but I did it in the wrong way. We did badly by each other, you and I. If you will forgive me, I shall forgive you.'

'I forgive you, Lady Mountford.'

'Then let it be as she wants: as if we had all behaved properly. I shall not tell anyone about this, and neither will you.'

I lay in bed that night reflecting on all that had passed between us – the years of my childhood and the admiration I'd had for her and her husband, the hatred I'd felt all the years after they'd sold me, and our meeting that evening. I laughed: I was running out of people to be revenged upon. Old man Smith dead, Lord Mountford dead in life, Lady Mountford forgiven. There was only George Mountford left; I would not show mercy to him.

Chapter 7

IRETURNED from seeing a lady discreetly out of our rooms to find Luke lying stretched out in his bed wearing nothing but a contented smile. 'Josh, is there one of the seven deadly sins we haven't committed in the past two months?' he asked, scratching himself. 'You're the Bible scholar: tell me.'

'They aren't listed in the Bible, but I know them anyway.'

'There's lust, I remember that one.'

'I haven't committed it.' Except in my heart.

'Your loss, Josh. But since you're so virtuous we'll just look at my sinful ways. What are the others?'

'Gluttony.'

'Done that one: I don't think I can stare another roast goose in the face.'

'Avarice.'

'Over one thousand guineas so far.'

'Envy.'

'I've envied plenty. Sir Bertrand Verity, for one.'

'Wrath.'

'Have I been wrathful? I can't remember.'

'You called me a clumsy goddamn nigger when I burnt your waistcoat.'

'Should I have called you a clumsy goddamn Negro?'

'A clumsy great oaf would have been better.'

'Wrath, then. What are the other two?'

'Pride and sloth.'

'I'm very proud of what I've done: a poor South Carolina boy passing myself off as the son of a duke.'

'But I don't think anyone can accuse you of sloth.'

'Hear that, Pa?' he said addressing the ceiling, though I thought the floor was a more likely direction. 'Your little boy isn't guilty of sloth. And do you know something, Pa? I don't give a damn what you think.' He looked back at me. 'I've met good people here: people who make me ashamed of my deception.'

'You aren't deceiving the Macleods about anything that matters to them. They don't care whether you're the son of a duke with a mountain of gold.'

'I know, and that's why I can be easy with them. But Lady Verity – it would matter to her.' I should have told him then that he wasn't deceiving her, and that it had given her the biggest laugh she'd had for a long time. But that would have meant also explaining to him why I couldn't tell lies to her. I could tell lies to him, and so I did.

One night in the card room, I became aware of George Mountford's eyes on me as I was scratching my left ear with my left ring finger and smiling to indicate that Rodney Winterton on Luke's left held the King of Hearts. I converted the scratch into a cough, and wished we'd arranged a signal to cover this. I saw Mountford, who wasn't playing at that moment, go to Mr Winterton and whisper in his ear. Winterton looked startled, then watched us; I was immobile by that time, but unfortunately Luke kept on frowning and scratching his left eye with the knuckles of his right hand to ask how many clubs were held by Sir Bertrand Verity opposite him. (Out of regard for his wife Luke wouldn't cheat him, but he had no objection to helping him win when they were partners).

'Damn it!' cried Winterton, throwing his cards on the table. 'I wouldn't have believed it if I hadn't seen it with my own eyes.'

'What's the matter?' boomed Sir Bertrand.

'Fitzjames is cheating! He's exchanging signals with his man!'

There was an awful silence. Calmly, Luke addressed his partner. 'I've been in this difficulty before, Sir Bertrand. Is Mr Winterton calling me out?'

'Yes, I damned well am! Name your seconds.'

'Sir Bertrand?' Luke asked; the other man nodded.

'And the other?'

'Fortescue, of course.'

This produced even more outrage than the original accusation. 'That's an insult, Fitzjames!'

'If Fortescue is enough my man to help me cheat at cards, then he's enough my man to be my second. You may, of course, take advantage of my resolution to withdraw your challenge.'

Winterton would have none of that, and named his own: his brother, Lord Hargreaves, and Mountford, who accepted with an unpleasant smile.

'Get me out of this, Josh,' said Luke when we were home. 'I don't want to kill him. Is there any way I can avoid it without seeming to accept his charge?'

'You could choose swords.'

'Damn it, I don't want him to kill me either! I've never picked up a sword in my life. What are my choices with pistols?'

'You could shoot to kill, to wound, or to miss as if by accident. Or you could delope – fire in the air. To some extent it'd be taken as an admission of guilt, unfortunately. The dishonourable George put him up to this, you know.'

'We must do something about him once this is over. Too much of a coward to call me out himself, but he has no objection to making young Winterton his catspaw.' He rubbed his moustache. 'I don't want to wound him any more than kill him, but I don't want to appear a bad shot. He's not going to withdraw, is he?'

'No, he's not. It would make him seem like a coward. But I do have another idea, one that will allow both of you to prove your courage, and will show off your marksmanship.' I told him what it was.

'You think of everything, Fortescue,' he said.

'I do my best, sir.'

Next day I called on Sir Bertrand, torn between hoping that Althea would be there and hoping that she wouldn't be. He was unsure how to treat a fellow second who was a servant, and his voice boomed out to cover up his indecision. 'His seconds won't see you, Fortescue. The arrangements must go through me.'

'Very understandable, Sir Bertrand.'

'What are Fitzjames's conditions?'

'Pistols, one shot each, at the longest possible distance.'

'Hmm. That gives the advantage to the better marksman. Mr Winterton's no more than a tolerable shot. It might seem unsporting of Fitzjames.'

'He is aware of that, Sir Bertrand, which is why he will allow the other man to provide the weapons and set all the other conditions.'

'Good, good. That would even things up. Leave it with me, Fortescue, I'll make the arrangements.'

As I was leaving, she was coming in. 'Good morning, Fortescue,' she said pleasantly. 'Have you an errand to me?'

'No, my lady. A matter of business with Sir Bertrand.'

'I hope it is settled satisfactorily,' she said, and passed on.

There was a stray dog in the road. I resisted the urge to kick it. It wasn't the dog's fault that I was bleeding inside.

If I'd had any doubts of Luke's courage, they would have been dispelled that day. He gave not a sign that he'd face death on the morrow, not even to me, and he made three plain girls smile and blush with his compliments that evening at the ball he was invited to.

As we drove through the early dawn in Sir Bertrand's carriage, Luke said, 'Sir Bertrand, I could shoot young Winterton through the heart if I wanted to. But will you support me in a plan which might allow both of us to emerge with honour and skins intact?'

'Of course!'

'Fortescue has his instructions.' Ha! It was my bloody plan.

We arrived at St George's Fields; Winterton arrived a few

minutes later with his seconds and a doctor. A few final words between Mountford and Sir Bertrand settled it that neither man would draw back at this stage. Luke and Winterton stood back to back, then paced out the distance. They turned.

'On the count of three, you will aim and fire,' said Sir Bertrand. 'One.'

This was the dangerous time for Luke: this was when he would prove his courage to everyone.

'Two.'

If Winterton turned out to be a more than tolerable shot, Luke would at best be wounded, perhaps killed.

'Three.'

But Winterton knew that he was facing a first-rate shot; his only hope was to shoot faster. His hand moved instantly and he fired. Luke hadn't moved his hand. He stood calmly unwounded; the hurried shot had missed completely.

'Gad!' came the exclamations. Luke had proved his courage, certainly; but now he had the other man at his mercy. Winterton turned green, knowing that he must face an excellent marksman with all the time he needed to aim.

I walked over to him, carrying what was needed on a salver. 'Mr Fitzjames's compliments, sir. He asks you to hold this out at whatever distance you please.' He blinked, then picked up the Ace of Hearts.

Sir Bertrand's roar of laughter must have been heard in Clapham. 'Oh, good man, Fitzjames! Shoot him through the heart, eh?'

The colour came back into Winterton's cheeks. He wasn't being asked to face certain death, but nobody could doubt his courage if he held out the card at that distance for a man with a pistol he'd never fired before. 'Anything I should know about this pistol, Winterton?' Luke called. 'Aims high or something?'

'I wouldn't have given it to you unless it was perfect,' he replied, holding the card out at arm's length, then, with a show of bravado, drawing it in so his forearm was vertical. 'Ready when you are, Fitzjames.'

Luke aimed and fired in one movement. Before I even heard the sound of the pistol, the card had a half moon cut out of the edge. 'Aims a little to the left,' said Luke. 'I'd get that seen to if I were you.'

There was a burst of relieved laughter from everyone except Mountford. Backs were clapped all round, including mine and the doctor's, and everyone went off to breakfast – which I served rather than ate, of course.

The story was too good to keep quiet, and within days it joined the alligators and Indians in the tales about Mr Fitzjames. Luke had shown cool courage, a nice regard for the other man's honour, and superb marksmanship. This proved that he couldn't possibly cheat at cards. The English gentleman has some strange logic.

Lady Mountford was 'At Home' with her cavalry officer. It was a smallish party: only a couple of dozen. Luke was invited, as were the Veritys. I had a suspicion that this was so Lady Mountford could watch how Althea behaved when I was in the room: impeccably, of course. Sir Bertrand was absent, having been called away on urgent government business, and when he burst into the room with horror on his face, we learnt what it was.

'Dreadful news has just arrived from America!' he cried. 'The British army has been defeated at Lexington and Concord!'

I was pouring coffee for Luke and two or three other people, for which I was grateful. I saw a whoop of joy just about to form on his lips, and I hastily tipped hot coffee into his lap. 'You clumsy nig— great oaf!' he yelled.

'I am very sorry, Mr Fitzjames. My hands were shaking – I was so appalled at the dreadful news. Please forgive me.'

'I'll consider it, Fortescue, after I see what damage you've done.' He excused himself; he wanted to change his clothes and get some treatment for the scald.

'Did it have to be that hot, Josh?' he said when the apothecary left. 'I'm going to have difficulty walking for a week.'

'Congratulate me on my aim. Three inches higher and it'd be something much more important than walking that you'd have difficulty with.'

'You were right. An English gentleman doesn't shout "Yee-hah!" at the news of a British defeat.'

'It's more than that. I don't know how long the news has taken to get here; it must be six to eight weeks at least. By now your entire fictitious fortune could be in rebel hands.'

'Damn! So it could be. I should be devastated, shouldn't I? Well, at least it'll give me an excuse not to pay old Winterton back.'

'And what will all those ducal families do when they know that there's no chance of your mountain of gold until the hostilities are over?'

'What are we going to do, Josh?'

'You're going to get some rest. Tomorrow I'll get the newspapers to find out more, and we'll work something out. That scald will give you an excuse not to see anyone until we have.'

'You think of everything, Fortescue.'

'I do my best, sir.'

In the morning we pored over the reports; Luke could express his elation in private. 'Listen to this, Josh: "They were attacked from all quarters from where any cover was to be found". Good boys! Attack from all quarters! "The whole country was assembled in arms with surprising expedition, and several thousand were assembled about the town threatening an attack and getting up artillery". I wish I'd been there!' He put the newspaper down. 'Do you think we should go back?'

'Oh, no! Not *we*, Luke, only *you*. I don't give a damn which set of white men wins this war; neither side will do anything for the blacks unless it suits their purposes, but this side of the Atlantic I'm a free man.'

He sat in bed thinking. 'No, I shan't go back, not yet. And that's not only because I'm having such a good time. Here I am, safely in the heart of the British ruling classes. Who knows what I might pick up to take back with me?'

'Well, since you're staying, there's one thing we can be thankful for: you've still got your mine. You can still promise to deliver the gold.'

'Why?'

'Luke, don't you even know your own bloody continent? The Mississippi basin is divided between the French and the Spanish; it won't be involved in the hostilities unless one or other of them decides to join in.'

'True. Have we ever said which side?'

'Don't think so. It'd better be on the west, the Spanish side; there's a chance that the French might join in just for the pleasure of shooting the English. And you can have a bank in New Orleans: that's in Spanish hands now.'

'In fact, it's my main bank; I transferred a small amount of my fortune and extra copies of my papers to the one in Charleston because I thought it was more convenient.'

'So the hostilities are no more than a minor nuisance to you. You'll just write to New Orleans and get more copies and more money.'

'And it'll take another four or five months to get a return!' We looked at each other and smiled. 'Oh, brave, brave boys of Lexington and Concord!'

There was a knock at the door: George Mountford. 'Mr Fitzjames is not at home to visitors, sir. He is unwell.'

'Don't you deny me, you dressed-up ape,' he said, pushing me in the chest with his cane and forcing his way in. 'He'll see me.'

I could have thrown him out there and then, but I thought we ought to find out what he wanted. He sat down, refusing my offer of coffee, and I went into Luke's bedchamber and helped him into his dressing-gown. 'Cautious,' he whispered. 'We'll see what he wants.'

'Get rid of your ape, Fitzjames,' Mountford began.

'Oh, no. I have no secrets from Fortescue. And I'm just a shade reluctant to be alone with you, bandaged up as I am.'

'Very well, then. I agree, he is in on your secrets. That's no doubt why he poured coffee into your lap to stop you betraying one of them.'

'And what might there be to betray?'

'Your sympathies to the cause of the American traitors.'

'What if I have them? It's no crime; Edmund Burke proclaims his in parliament.' Good boy, I thought; at last he was learning some British politics – but of course he was interested in this issue.

'Indeed not, which makes me wonder why it was important to hide them.'

'What do you accuse me of?'

'Sympathies are one thing, Fitzjames. Spying is another. Your arrival is most convenient for such a purpose; you must have left America just as their forces were starting to assemble.'

'You have no proof.'

'Perhaps not. However, I don't think that the head of your family would welcome you, mountain of gold or no, if I laid my suspicions before him.'

'Maybe he wouldn't. But you don't know who he is.'

'Yes, I do. What will you give to stop me telling him?'

'You're bluffing, Mountford.'

'You shouldn't trust your ape so much, Fitzjames. He has a very big mouth when money is waved in front of him.'

'Fortescue?' he asked me.

'He's lying, Mr Fitzjames,' I replied.

'I trust him more than I trust you, Mountford.'

'You'd take the word of a nigger over that of an English gentleman?'

'I'd take the word of a shilling whore with a conviction for forgery over yours, Mountford. Show him out, Fortescue. If he won't go, you have my permission to throw him out.'

I stood over Mountford, who was not a tall man. 'May I show you the door, Mr Mountford?' He saw he had lost that round; he went before he was pushed.

'He'll be back,' I said, after I shut the door behind him. 'And he'll do you harm.'

'I think we've found our ogre.' I was puzzled, so he added, 'Remember? The one that Puss in Boots tricked and ate so the miller's son could have his castle.'

'I don't want to eat the dishonourable George.'

'Let's think. I had thought of forcing a duel on him and shooting him, which would relieve his wife, but it would grieve Lady Mountford: a mother's love, you know.'

'Besides, it wouldn't make you any richer. Take all his money and ruin him.' It would satisfy what I owed both to Luke and to Mountford.

'Hmm. It wouldn't do his wife any good. She's suffered enough already.'

'Well, just take a lot of it.'

'It ought to be something that his wife and his mother don't find out about.'

'Because it's such a dishonourable thing that he'll pay you to keep it quiet.'

'What's dishonourable enough, Josh? As far as I can see, if he has the right connections an English gentleman can get away with beating his wife, forcing his tailor into bankruptcy through not paying his bills, and sodomizing small boys. But there must be something that other English gentlemen won't take.'

'Besides cheating at cards, you mean?'

'Yes, Josh, besides cheating at cards. Do you think he does?'

'Wouldn't put it past him, but I haven't caught him out. I've been more concerned with preventing us being caught out.'

'What else is there that's unforgivable?'

'Betraying his country and showing cowardice in the face of the enemy, that's about all.'

'Could he betray his country or show cowardice in the face of the enemy?' He punched the air with his fist. 'Yes! He could from yesterday! His country's at war, or it will be very soon. Let's get him, Josh, let's get him.'

A couple of days later we were ready; Luke's scald had healed and we'd laid our plans. He sat in front of the mirror practising his expressions of British loyalty. 'What about this? "Our gallant men in red will have those farmers on the run, by God. Then we'll hang every damned rebel!" There, I said it without choking.'

'You're overdoing it. You've been heard to give sympathy to the Americans in the past, so you shouldn't change sides as much as that.'

'How's this? "What a tragedy, that men of English stock have been driven into treason. Is there a chance, even at this late hour, that these rebellious children can be brought back into the arms of their motherland?" Is that right?'

'Perfect.'

He went out to see Lord Winterton and explain that, alas! he must beg for another few months' grace on the loan so that he could get a return from New Orleans. After that, he would go to one of his clubs: the one where George Mountford was most likely to be.

I stayed in our lodgings like a spider in its web, waiting for the fly to walk in. He did. 'Mr Mountford, I regret that Mr Fitzjames is not at home.'

'I know he's not,' he said, pushing his way in as he'd done before. 'I left him playing whist. It's you I want to see, Fortescue.'

'Please leave, Mr Mountford,' I said, allowing a slightly begging tone to creep into my voice.

He took no notice but sat down comfortably and surveyed me. There was a risk that he'd recognize me as Caesar, which would complicate matters though it wouldn't stop them. Fortunately, he was as bad as most Englishmen at telling one black face from another. 'Now, Fortescue, I want some information out of you. And before you tell me that you won't betray your master's trust, remember that you had two guineas out of me to prove yourself corruptible.'

'You gave me two guineas to find out what you could read in the newspapers. Mr Fitzjames allows me to augment my income with that sort of information.'

'So, the price must be higher, eh?' He took a leather purse out and counted out ten golden guineas. 'Who is Fitzjames's father?'

I looked at it scornfully and didn't bother to reply. ('Don't give in to him too easily, Josh; if he pays less than fifty he won't think it's true.')

He added another guinea, then another, until there were twenty on the table. 'That's my last offer, Fortescue. You'd do well to take it.'

'I believe the accepted price of betrayal is thirty pieces, Mr Mountford.'

'No,' he said, sweeping the guineas back into his purse. 'Bribery won't work, but threats will. Fortescue, I know the captain of a slaving ship who'll give me fifty pounds for a big strong nigger like you. If you don't tell me the name of Fitzjames's father, you'll be meeting him very soon.'

He could do it. He would do it. He had done it already though he didn't know it. It was against the law, but who would stop him? I had no need to feign any horror as my legs gave way and. I slumped into a chair. 'Oh, Christ.' We hadn't thought of this. We should have done.

'Who is Fitzjames's father?'

'I don't know.'

'Find out.'

'I've tried!' I wailed. 'Don't you think I've tried to find out all the time I've been with him? All he says is, "My father the duke".'

'Fortescue, you have a problem. You had better try even harder, or one day in the near future you will meet my captain, and you'll regret your omission.'

'Please, Mr Mountford, I can't do it.'

He stood up. 'A pity, for your sake. Not for mine: I'll be fifty pounds richer.'

'Wait!' I cried.

'Changed your mind, eh?'

'I can't find out that, I know I can't. But I'll tell you something else.'

'What?'

'What you said about him being a spy: there's more.'

'Tell me: if it's worth it, you can breathe freely.'

'How do I know that you'll keep your word?'

'I am an English gentleman. You may trust me.'

Oh, yes? 'He's here to buy arms for the rebels,' I said, as if the words were being forced out of me. 'Guns and powder. The British make them better than the Americans.'

'Go on. That's not enough.'

'He's prepared to give half his fortune to the cause. He was devastated when all his money was stolen; he knows that it's important to get the weapons to America soon. He borrowed two thousand guineas from Lord Winterton at a hundred per cent interest over four months just to get something to them; that's how desperate he is. He would have paid two hundred per cent if need be.'

'Did he, now?' he said; he was interested in the bait. 'Tell me more.'

'After I poured coffee over him he told me that he wasn't going to cheer: he was going to curse them for starting too early. He can't get his money out of America now, even though it's for the American cause. He'll have to write to his bank in New Orleans, and that'll take another four or five months. And every month is another month that the Americans don't have the weapons. He can't buy them on credit, because the manufacturers will investigate him and guess what he's doing. But for cash they won't ask too many questions.'

'How rich is he, Fortescue?'

'Richer than you can imagine. He had twenty thousand pounds stolen from him, and he didn't care about the loss, only the delay to his plans. That's why he was outraged at being accused of cheating at cards – it's the last thing he needs to do.'

'Is there anything more you can tell me?'

'Not about that. I can tell you who his mistresses are, if you want.'

'I am not interested in where he puts his cock, only in where he puts his money.' He stood up. 'Fortescue, you may walk the streets freely.'

'Thank you, thank you!' I blubbered. 'You won't tell him I've told you?'

'Of course not. You have my word as an English gentleman.'

Luke came back cheerfully as I was still sitting down recovering. 'My mission's accomplished: Winterton accepted my reason for not paying him. Stupid old fool even lent me another thousand to tide me over. How did yours go, Josh? Did the fly walk into the web?'

'He did.'

'Did it go as planned?'

'Almost exactly.'

'How much did he give you?'

'Nothing.' I looked up at him. 'He threatened to kidnap me and sell me back into slavery.'

'God damn him! The fly turned out to be a wasp, eh?'

'He's convinced. I was very convincing. I really was terrified – I didn't have to pretend.' He poured me out a drink; I took it gratefully. 'I would have told him even if it hadn't been something we wanted him to believe. I'm not going back into slavery. I'd kill myself first, and that's no empty claim.'

He went straight out and came back with a thin parcel. 'Don't you ever tell them in South Carolina that I put this in the hands of a black man, Josh.' I opened it: inside was a long knife, very flat, with a sharp and wicked blade. 'It's designed to be concealed in a boot. You may walk uncomfortably, but you'll sleep a damn sight more comfortably.' While we finished our plans I walked round, adjusting the fit, practising how to pull it out quickly.

'We'll have to play this fish as he wants to be played,' Luke said. 'If he's going to betray his country for money, he won't be any too eager to give us evidence of it. We'll just have to see what he's prepared to risk for the sake of two hundred per cent interest.'

'I've had an idea. What if we don't worry about getting him to sign something, but just find a very credible witness?'

'Oh, come on. He's not going to do this in front of a witness!'

'If he thinks that there isn't a witness he might; if he knows he's out of earshot of everyone.'

'Well, if he's out of earshot, how will the witness know?'

'With a pair of opera glasses she can read lips from a long way off.'

'Lady Verity?' he asked, horrified.

'She'd love it. You said yourself that she doesn't like George. And she might even add something ingenious to our plans. I can't count the number of times I was beaten as a boy because I'd followed her into a scheme.'

'That was just girlish high spirits. She's a woman, now. A beautiful woman.'

I couldn't tell him that she hadn't changed; I couldn't tell him about her glee at her secret knowledge of what he was doing, or at her cleverness at contriving ways for us to be alone together. I certainly couldn't tell him that she'd be most annoyed to be left out.

'Josh, I forbid you to suggest it again. I'm appalled that you'd involve that pure and noble lady in our scheme! How could you think of asking her? She's an angel!'

I loved Althea. I loved her with my heart, my mind, my spirit, and I wanted only to love her with my body. No man would ever love her more. But I would never call her an angel. Adorable and Absurd Althea, certainly. Angelic, no.

He paced around the room, agitated. 'Josh, you didn't tell me about women like her. I thought that they were all horse-faced or bitch-tempered like the Winterton daughters, or lustful ladies with dull husbands. But she – she—'

'She's married. She's faithful. She's not for you.'

'Oh, God, I know that! You wouldn't believe how much it hurts to know that, seeing her with that donkey of a husband, knowing that he can kiss her, he can hold her in his arms, and I can't!'

118

I would believe it very well. 'Keep away from her, Luke. You could only bring her harm.' I seemed to have heard this conversation before.

'I wouldn't harm her. I wouldn't defile her purity. I'm not worthy to touch the hem of her clothes. But just to be in the room with her! Oh, it's not just the fact that she's married that keeps her apart from me: how could I tell her that I'm nothing but a poor boy from South Carolina, a high-born lady like she is? What would she think of me if she knew how basely I'd deceived her?'

Here he was, a man who had fornicated his way round South Carolina and was currently fornicating his way round London, now talking like the virtuous hero in a bad play.

'She's so good, Josh, so honourable and brave and fine. She makes me ashamed of all the women I've had: all the whores, all the slave women, all the bored English ladies, all the Charleston virgins—'

I interrupted him before he went through the entire catalogue. 'In plain words, Luke, you're in love with her.'

He stood for a moment dumbfounded, as if the idea had just occurred to him. Then he slumped into a chair, put his head in his hands, and said, 'Yes, I'm in love with her.'

Chapter 8

W E had a visitor, David Macleod. 'I've been told to deliver these in person,' he said, handing us each an invitation, written in a careful childish hand, to A Boating Party and Pique-Nique on the Occasion of Miss Janet Macleod's Tenth Birthday. We would be happy to come, we said.

'It'll be the circus if the weather doesn't hold, but she's set her heart on this, and on you two coming; she'll be delighted to know you've accepted. Especially you, Mr Fitzjames: I think I should be asking you about your intentions.'

'Hmm, maybe I should seize my advantage now, Mr Macleod. You'll be fighting her admirers off in a few years – Janet will break hearts.'

Even an austere Presbyterian minister likes to hear praise of his children, and he almost blushed with pride. 'Can you both ride and row?'

'I can ride,' said Luke, 'and both of us can row.' South Carolina swamps make it a useful means of transport. 'But I've seen Josh ride, and he's lucky if he stays on the horse.'

'There's one place in the carriage, Joshua; you can have that.'

'Carriage?' I said. 'My word, we are going in grand style.'

'Althea – Lady Verity's. She's a favourite of Janet's; the two of them cooked up the plan between them.'

Luke cheered loudly after he left. 'It's a sign, Josh! To agree to go on an innocent boating party with a Presbyterian minister

120

and his family, and then to learn that she'll be there! It must be a sign!'

'What of?'

'Oh, that – that – that my love is pure!'

'You can't be in love with a married woman and call it pure.'

'Watch me, Josh. I shall behave towards her exactly as I do to Janet, my second favourite woman. Stop looking so prim and miserable. It will be a wonderful day, and we'll all have a jolly time.'

I must try to be Jolly, not Jealous.

Only the Macleods could do this: only they would invite a black manservant and a baronet's wife to a child's birthday treat and know that everyone would get on together happily.

They even had the weather on their side, since it turned out to be perfect: sunny, with just enough breeze to be refreshing. We set off in high spirits, all dressed plainly since we knew what boating could do to clothes. Althea, Luke and David rode, while Fiona and I squeezed in with the children. Four of them, in fact, since Janet's best friend was invited too, a girl of her own age who was at first inclined to look at me with awe as if I had a tail tucked into my breeches, but soon joined in everyone else's easy gaiety on our way to what Janet said would be, 'A day of luxury and dippi— dispi— dissipation!' We bowed and gave her our gifts: an elegant box of finely made playing cards and counters from Luke, and *Gulliver's Travels* from me.

I could have been very jealous, stuck in the carriage with Fiona and the children while Althea and Luke rode together, but I became much more jolly when I saw the complete failure of his attempts at conversation with her. Horseback is not the best situation for carrying out a flirtation with a deaf woman, especially when chaperoned by a Presbyterian minister.

Fiona had a stock of games to keep children amused, including many she'd taught me long ago. We arrived in Hammersmith, a village west of London, almost joined to it now by houses and shops beside the road, and the boys and I were acclaimed as victors in the game of Legs. We left the horses, the carriage and the coachman at The Dove and walked to the boathouse where our two boats awaited us on the Thames, cleaner here before it became London's main sewer. Luke and I kept the children in high spirits as we rowed with stories of alligators until we arrived at our chosen pique-nique spot, where we spread our provisions on the grass under a tree and fought off ants until we'd had enough to eat.

Luke was almost as good as his word. In general his attentions to Althea were well-mannered and amusing, as they were to everyone, and when he did pay her something more, I was happy to see by her pleasant but slightly blank smile that she hadn't picked it up. He didn't know how to speak clearly to her, and I was not going to give him any lessons.

Only one small thing happened to spoil the occasion: Janet's best friend let out a cry when she trod on a thorn that went right through her shoe into her foot. But I picked her up and carried her to a tree stump, and made her giggle about keeping watch for the Indians among the trees while I gently pulled the thorn out. A minute's work bandaging her foot and she was off playing with the rest. Children heal very quickly.

More games followed; I wondered how the children could keep it up until I recalled how Althea and I had been at the same age. She and Fiona gave up early and sat under a tree, while the rest of us went down to the river to race the boats. There was some dispute about fair distribution of crew and craft, and I seized my chance. 'One man and two children in each boat; that's fair. Luke, you keep your eye open for alligators, and I'll go and protect the ladies from Indians.'

I left them debating and walked over to the shade of the tree. 'Janet's so much like you were, Althea,' I said as I sat down. 'You could be sisters.'

'We are, in a way: we were brought up by the same person. Did we have as much energy when we were young, Fiona?'

'You did, the pair of you.' For a while the three of us sat remembering how we used to be, and mourning Pompey; he would have loved this expedition.

'You look tired, Althea,' I said, noticing her drawn expression.

'I am. The children, the strain of reading lips – your husband's a fine man, Fiona, but he has such a strong accent. And Mr Fitzjames's moustache! You're the only people I never have a struggle to understand, you two and Bertrand.' She looked at Fiona. 'I know you think I could have done better, but he suits me.'

'I didn't say that! All I said was that you should wait a year or two, instead of marrying the first passable man who offered for you when you were so young.'

'I wasn't certain that I'd live that long. I never told you this, Fiona; perhaps I should have, but it was such a horrible thing to say. I was very aware that if I died before I was married, my fortune would go to my nearest relations.'

'That's a wicked and unjust thing to suspect!' Fiona protested. 'If Lord and Lady Mountford had wanted you dead, they wouldn't have looked after you so carefully when – when you were so ill, instead of begging me to come back to London to look after you.'

'I don't mean them; they did what they thought was best for me. But George – well, I knew he was thinking of my money, and he was wondering whether murder or marriage was more distasteful to him as a way to acquire it.'

'Now why should he think marriage to you was distasteful?' Fiona cried.

Althea flushed and bit her lip angrily. 'He said—' She broke off.

'Something about not wanting a nigger's leavings?' I suggested.

Fiona was shocked at my crudity, but Althea nodded. 'How well you remember him, Joshua. Those were his exact words.' That's why he'd beaten me so brutally; it was not merely that I'd joined his cousin in an irresponsible adventure. In his mind, my touch had defiled his intended bride.

She leant forward and took Fiona's hand. 'You're always reasonable, Fiona; you always give me reasonable advice, and

I'm grateful. But consider this: if Joshua and I had been reason-able all those years ago, by now I'd be Mrs George Mountford. Sometimes it isn't reasonable to do the reasonable thing.'

She didn't look at me; she didn't need to. Her words had their effect. A mighty weight of guilt was lifted from my shoulders at the misery our adventure had caused her. I had been thanking providence for whatever had saved her from that fate, and now I discovered that I had.

'You don't know the ironic thing about all this, Joshua,' she continued, now looking at me. 'George could have had my fortune with all my good wishes, as soon as I discovered where it came from. I didn't want it. I still don't want it; I'd get rid of it if Bertrand would let me.' She turned to Fiona. 'I must tell him.'

'Yes, he has a right to know.'

'We never wondered about it when we were children, did we? I only found out when the settlements were being prepared for my marriage. My father made his money in the slave trade.'

I burst out laughing. All the years I'd cursed the slave trade; all the years I'd loved a slave trader's daughter! And his name – Freeman!

'I thought you'd be shocked,' said Fiona.

'I didn't,' said Althea. 'Joshua wouldn't visit the sins of the father on the daughter.'

'No, I wouldn't,' I said, calm now. I looked at her. 'It doesn't change my feelings for you in the slightest.' Did she catch my meaning? I didn't know. Had I intended her to? I didn't know that either.

She looked away from me, yawned and stretched. 'And now I'm going to take a rest, if you'll excuse me. I can trust you not to talk about me while my eyes are closed.' She rolled a rug into a pillow, lay down, and soon she was asleep. Her hair was as unpowdered and golden as it had been on the pillow in the room in Gretna Green, and her breathing was as soft as it had been then, at the moment that I looked at her in her sleep and realized that the knot in my gut was love.

'Well,' said Fiona, breaking into my thoughts. 'Since she's just put a stop to us talking about what we most want to, we'd better find something else. In any case, your face as you watched her go to sleep has answered one of my questions.'

'Is it obvious, Fiona? I try not to let it show.'

'You've been very good. It's only in your unguarded moments that I see it, and only because I know you well. Be more on your guard, won't you?'

'I'll try harder. What do you want to talk about instead?'

'I suppose as your godmother I should inquire about your faith.'

'I've a confession: it's gone.'

'Then what you said about the Bible being your comfort these past ten years was a lie? I'm disappointed in you.'

'No, it was no lie. I'd have had a flogging if I'd been found with any other book in my possession, but there was a chance that my God-fearing owner might spare the whip if he caught me reading that. Test me on my knowledge of Scripture and you won't be disappointed. I can recite whole books by heart: the gospels, Genesis, Kings – even those tedious lists of laws. When I said it was my comfort, perhaps I was misleading you. But you misled me, Fiona. You made me believe that Christians were all like you. But now I know what Christians do to their fellows. It wears away your faith if you're owned by a man who holds the Bible in one hand and a whip in the other.'

'Don't disbelieve Christianity just because bad men believe it; you might as well disbelieve Pythagoras's theorem for the same reason. But did your owner's faith make him a better or a worse man?'

I had to admit it. 'A better. He avoided fornication with the slave women, and if he swore an oath on the Bible we could trust him to keep it.'

'Well, then. Blame slavery, not Christianity.' We heard the sounds of the end of the boat race. 'Haven't we been good, discussing theology?' Fiona said as Luke, Janet and the best friend came whooping towards us, claiming their victory.

Luke saw Althea stretched out asleep. 'Shh, everyone. We'd

better be quiet so we don't wake – Oh, we don't need to worry, do we?'

'Why?' asked the best friend.

'She's deaf,' said Fiona. 'She can sleep with a thunderstorm overhead.'

'I wish I could,' said the best friend. 'Isn't she lucky?'

After our innocent pastoral expedition, we returned to less scrupulous matters the next day, when the fly didn't merely walk into the web; he forced his way in.

'Mr Fitzjames is not at home, Mr Mountford,' I said. 'He says that he will never be at home to you.' I closed the door in his face, ensuring that I was doing it slowly enough that he could thrust his cane in the gap and stop me.

'He'll want to hear me, Fortescue. Trust me.'

'Fortescue, is that that dastard Mountford?' I heard Luke's voice behind me. 'I order you to throw him out with as much violence as you can.'

'You should hear what I have to say, Fitzjames. You'll regret it otherwise.'

'Oh, very well. Let him in, Fortescue,' Luke sighed. 'But I must warn you, Mountford, that Fortescue has told me what you threatened him with, and what you forced him to tell you. I consider that the act of an unspeakable scoundrel. I bear him no malice, but I bear a lot for you.'

'Frankly, Fitzjames, you are not my favourite person yourself,' Mountford said, taking a seat without being invited. 'Since our antipathy is mutual, we may be able to do business on equal terms.'

'Business with you? I'd sooner do it with a rattlesnake!'

'One of your colonial animals, I believe. Fitzjames, I know why you're in England, and you know that I know. And, since I am not a fool, my lawyer will also know when he opens a sealed letter in the event of my sudden death.'

'You will find it hard to prove any charge against me, Mountford, for the simple reason that I haven't done anything.'

126

'Yet. But you want to. You are desperate for money immediately. I can oblige you – for a suitable return, of course.'

'You'd betray your country for money?' Luke asked, apparently shocked.

'It's my country. I'll do what I want with it. What has it to do with you?'

'It's no matter to me that you have the morals of a whore. No, I'm wrong – you don't have the morals of a whore.'

'I am indifferent to your opinion of me; you may continue your jibes if it gives you amusement. What do you say, Fitzjames? Are you willing to come to terms if we can agree on them?' Luke rubbed his moustache in apparent thought, and said nothing. 'Oh, come, you won't let your dislike of me get in the way of your American patriotism, will you?'

'No,' Luke said slowly, 'I shan't. Your behaviour has only confirmed my view that we must at all costs seek our independence from the likes of you. How much are you prepared to lend me?'

'Five thousand at once. I can get you another fifteen within the week. You will pay me four times that when your money comes in.'

'Double.'

'Triple, then. And an additional ten thousand for my silence. Fifty thousand pounds in four months' time, as well as my original twenty.'

'It doesn't take account of any reverses; I've had two already, or I wouldn't be accepting your offer. Whenever my money arrives; you'll know when it does, I assure you. Now, what security do you want? You aren't going to accept my word as a gentleman, I presume.'

'No, but I'll accept your signature, witnessed and dated, promising me seventy thousand to be paid at an appropriate date.'

'That's not good enough. It gives you too much of a hold on me. There'd be nothing to stop you denouncing me after you get your money – even before, come to think about it, and then claiming it from my estate after I'm hanged. I want a hold on you too. We make two copies, and we say what the money is for. Then we each keep one.'

'A good attempt, Fitzjames. You know I wouldn't dare produce mine if it said what the loan was for.'

'Then the deal's off. I'm not a fool either, Mountford. I am simply not prepared to give you fifty thousand pounds of my money and leave you with a hand on my throat unless I have a hand on yours.' Mountford hesitated. 'Show Mr Mountford out, Fortescue.'

Mountford – rich, greedy and stupid – said after a moment, 'On my copy it doesn't say what the money is for – but I agree, on yours it does. You might hate me, but not enough to sacrifice your neck merely for the pleasure of my company on the scaffold. But I want one more hold on you, just so that you don't take my money and run with it. I want your father's name.'

Luke hesitated. 'No, I shan't give it to you; I don't trust you with it. But I'm prepared to leave a certified copy of my baptismal record with any lawyer whom we can both trust, with instructions to give it to you if I disappear. It's not enough to prove my identity, or I'd have used it. But it's enough for you to know my father's name; I'm sure you could find a use for it with my family if I did disappear – I'm not planning to, by the way, which is why I'm letting it go.'

'I'm sure you aren't; you will be in much too snug a position for your spying once your family accepts you.'

'And you're prepared to let me do so?'

'For a consideration, of course; nothing that you can't afford when your money arrives. I suggest we leave that until later.'

It took an hour to sort out the details: dates, the lawyer who would hold the baptismal record and the like. But both knew that they would come to terms, and did not let such matters stand in the way of an agreement. They didn't shake hands on it.

I showed Mountford out and closed the door. Then I opened

it again to check that he wasn't eavesdropping. He was. 'Anything further you require, Mr Mountford?' I asked. He said nothing, but turned and walked rapidly away.

Then Luke and I collapsed in so much laughter that our sides began to ache. 'Twenty thousand, Josh! I thought we'd be lucky to get ten!'

'He was practically forcing it down your throat!'

'Oh, I wish I could be there when he finds out that my father is Ezekiel Smith of Jamestown, South Carolina.'

'He's going into debt to raise that fifteen, you know.'

'Will he be ruined, Josh?'

'No. He'll inherit far more than that when his father dies; that's why it'll be easy for him to raise the extra money. But he'll be seriously inconvenienced.'

A week later, Mountford walked away with a promissory note, witnessed by me and the lawyer who was holding the baptismal record, for seventy thousand pounds, as innocent as it would turn out to be useless to him; and Luke walked away with twenty thousand pounds, and a piece of paper, witnessed by me alone, that could hang all three of us.

'I've no more need to cheat at cards,' Luke said as we celebrated that night. 'I can play like the English gentleman I pretend to be.'

'You've no more need to play the English gentleman, either. Why don't you go back to America?'

'Now that I'm ready to snap up what tasty morsels the British ruling classes may let fall? Not me.'

'That's an excuse and you know it. You'd do just as much good for your cause on your own side of the Atlantic.'

'You're not accusing me of cowardice, I hope.'

'No. I'm accusing you of wanting to dishonour Lady Verity.'

'I wouldn't dishonour her.' He sighed. 'But you're right. She's the reason I'm staying.'

'What for? Hoping her husband dies? That's not very honourable either.'

'No! That's not it at all. I've no hope, I know that. But – Josh,

I couldn't bear to have the Atlantic between us. You don't know how I feel.'

Luke and I were walking home late one night – or early one morning – from a satisfactory dinner party as far as he was concerned, though it was less so from my point of view, as he had been seated next to Althea. He was feeling full of love and food, while I was trying to convince myself that she had shown only good manners towards him. Otherwise we'd have been more wary, walking through the dark empty streets. After all, our whole success had depended on the knowledge that it was very easy to be attacked and robbed in London.

I just had time to hear footsteps behind me, and to see out of the corner of my eye a cudgel descending on Luke's head. I ducked and reached for the knife in my boot, and the cudgel intended for my own head fell on my back; it hurt, but I'd had far worse pain on my back and it didn't even wind me. Coming out of my crouch I took two steps to get my back to the railings and stood up; now I could see the enemy forces.

Four of them; not big men, they'd have been no match for us if Luke had been upright instead of lying on the pavement groaning, and they were armed only with cudgels, nothing as vicious as the knife I held out ready to thrust in a belly. But four against one was enough to make me seek reinforcements, and I glanced up and down the street. No other walkers, but there was a carriage about a hundred yards away, and there were houses with people in them who might be wakened, and perhaps the watch might be just around the corner.

'Yah!' I snarled, ferociously brandishing the knife. 'The first one who tries will regret it.' I thrust my other hand behind me between the railings and hammered on them as loudly as I could with my clenched fist. 'Help! Help! My master, Mr Fitzjames, is being attacked!'

They could have taken me if they'd worked together, but a big fierce black man with a wicked knife is enough to put fear into the heart of any London footpad. 'Which one of you, eh? Come on, try me! Who wants to carry his guts home in his hands?' I kept snarling and shouting for help, trying to distract them so they wouldn't think of two of them dragging Luke away while the other two held me at bay, pleading silently for that coward of a coachman down the street to come to my aid. At last, from the other direction, a watchman came; he saw what was happening and swung his rattle in a cacophonous racket that seemed like sweet music to me. That was enough to bring people to their doors; and that was enough for the footpads to flee away from him.

As people gathered around us to help, I saw the coach down the street turn away and drive off, and I began to wonder about it. I gave a description of the four footpads to the watchman, while people were practically fighting each other for the honour of bringing Mr Fitzjames into their house. One of them, a cousin of Sir Bertrand's, had almost as loud a voice; he won the prize, and Luke was supported in by two of his servants. 'Well done, Fortescue! Your master will be grateful to you for this,' Mr Verity boomed as he clapped me on the back.

A doctor was summoned; he studied Luke's wound as he sat on the sofa groaning, and pronounced him well enough to be driven home. 'And your manservant?' he asked. 'Is he wounded at all?'

Luke only waved in my direction.

'No, just a bruise. Nothing that needs your attention, sir,' I said to the doctor, addressing him directly to show I could speak. In fact, now I had leisure to feel I ached abominably, but there was no symptom of a broken rib, and I didn't want to provoke comment on the old lash scars on my back. Mr Verity offered a choice of a bed or his carriage; since Luke was capable only of moans I chose the latter. 'I think that Mr Fitzjames will recover sooner in his own bed.' He might say something that he shouldn't when he could speak.

He was capable of nothing as we went home, and I put him into bed except a low, 'Thanks, Josh.' By noon next day, however, he was sitting up in bed looking more healthy. 'The real thing, eh, Josh? I thought you'd hit me hard, but you were going easy on me compared with those devils.'

'They were waiting for us.' I told him about the coach that had driven off when it was clear that the attack had failed.

'The dishonourable George?' Luke asked.

'That was my first thought, but I can't see why. Surely he wants you alive until your money comes in.'

'So I may have more than one enemy? That's an alarming notion. We'd best take more care.'

'I'm glad you gave me that knife.'

'I think of everything, Fortescue.'

'You do your best, sir.'

He wasn't capable of much for the next day or so, and I could take time from the exhausting round of someone else's pleasure to catch up on the reading that Fiona had given me. When that became dull and signs jumbled together in my head, I had hours of idleness reading a book for my own enjoyment.

The newspapers were full of the story – Luke couldn't scratch his bum without it appearing as an item of gossip. I was transformed from a Sinister Sable Servitor to a Devoted Blackamoor: 'Well done, thou good and faithful servant,' they said.

I went back to reading *Robinson Crusoe*. I wondered how the story would appear from Man Friday's point of view.

Chapter 9

LUKE was fit apart from a lump on his head, and was leafing through invitations to that evening's entertainments when we had a caller. 'Are you in?' I asked.

'Depends who it is. Just say the name loudly enough for me to hear.'

I didn't need to; it was Sir Bertrand. 'Well done, thou good and faithful servant,' he boomed as if he'd thought of it himself. 'My cousin told me about your battle. Fought off four of 'em, eh? Is your master at home?'

'Yes, I'm at home, Sir Bertrand,' Luke called out. 'Come in.'

After a few moments talk about the weather, and inquiry as to Luke's health, Sir Bertrand said, 'Called in to see whether you'd care to join Lady Verity and myself in a small party at Ranelagh Gardens tonight. Just a few people – my cousin says he'd like to meet you again in better circumstances.'

'I'd be delighted to,' Luke said, tossing his other invitations into the fireplace. 'I'd like to express my gratitude to Mr Verity for what he did for me.'

'Bring your man, of course. Now we all know why you never go anywhere without him.' As he took his leave, he turned back and said, 'Just had a thought, Fitzjames. You might be at a loose end when the season's over. Would you care to come and stay at Galbury Hall? Show me how you can shoot in the field, eh?'

'Of course; I'd love to,' Luke said, real enthusiasm in his voice.

'That would be most kind indeed, if you're sure that I would be no imposition.'

'Wouldn't have asked you if you were. We'll be rather quiet; just our country neighbours. Lady Verity likes it at the Hall after the strain of the season.'

I showed him out, wishing I'd shown him out five minutes earlier. An evening in Ranelagh Gardens I could endure and even enjoy now; but in the country together, with so few distractions—

'Yes!' Luke cried.

'No!' I cried louder. 'Living under the same roof, seeing her every day—'

'Yes, yes, yes!'

'Cool down before I throw a bucket of water over you. Just stop and picture it. You'll be there in her company hour after hour. Perhaps she'll be so close you could reach out and touch her. You won't just be dining with dozens of others; you'll be going for walks, listening to music, sleeping under the same roof.'

'It sounds like heaven.'

'No, it's a heaven that you'll be locked out of; one that you can see over the wall but isn't for you. Will you be able to stop yourself reaching out and touching her? Will you be able to keep your feelings to yourself when you're alone together? Will you?'

'Yes. You underestimate me, Josh. I'll prove that I'm worthy of her.'

'Who are you proving it to? Her? You want her to love you too, don't you?'

'No!' Then he sighed. 'Yes, of course I do.'

'And if she did? That would make it even harder. To pass by her bedroom every day, knowing that she's in there, that you'd only have to open the door and you'd see her. Could you stop yourself? And what would you feel when you knew Sir Bertrand was in there with her?'

'Why are you so strong against it, Josh? Oh, that's right, you knew her when she was only a girl. Do you still have a regard for her?'

'Yes, I still have a regard for her. And for you too. Do you think I want to read the filth that would appear in the papers about you? I don't want to see her branded as an adulteress and you as a seducer. I don't want to see her shamed, scorned, divorced by her husband, for *you*. You don't have a mountain of gold; do you think you could do as well by her as Sir Bertrand, fool though he is? Why should she leave her comfortable home, sacrifice everything, just for you? Do you really think that you'll ever be worthy of that?'

'I'm not worthy of her, I know that. But my love is. Leave it, Josh, you aren't going to talk me out of this. We're going, and that's it.'

Oh, no, Luke, I thought. Not *we*. Only *you*. I had enough time to find an excuse; perhaps I'd be forced to break my word to him and leave him before the end of August. He thought that he could take it; I knew that I couldn't.

Ranelagh Gardens will cheer all but the most gloomy. Painted, carved, gilded, lit by hundreds of lamps that shone so brightly that Althea had no difficulty reading lips, crowded with rich and not so rich, ugly and beautiful, all with one aim in mind, to enjoy themselves. In the grand Rotunda an orchestra played, and tiers of boxes all around held Londoners from all walks of life who could afford the entrance fee; higher than Vauxhall Gardens, but still low enough that any workman could bring his girl in their best clothes to celebrate their engagement.

Mr and Mrs Verity were basking in the glory of having helped Mr Fitzjames. They had a daughter, a prettyish young woman; while nobody would have done anything so vulgar as throw her in Luke's way, it was clear that they wouldn't mind if she should happen to catch his eye. She had the loud voice of all her relations, and was a welcome friend to Althea though I could see that Luke winced slightly; she caught his ear far too much to catch his eye. I wondered if there was an eligible deaf bachelor for her somewhere.

Althea was dressed even more absurdly than when I'd

laughed at her clambering out of a sedan chair months ago; the panniers were wider, the heels were higher, and the head-dress was adorned with ostrich feather plumes. But there were even more ridiculous costumes, and not only among the ladies; the macaronis were on parade (I heard Luke humming *Yankee doodle*). I fetched and carried, and was told yet again that I was a good and faithful servant. Sir Bertrand's party had one of the lower boxes; Althea and Miss Verity went up to one of the higher ones to greet some acquaintance they'd met.

They started to come down the stairs to return to our box. Suddenly Althea missed her footing; she tumbled down the steps too quickly for anyone to catch her. We all rushed out of our box to her; several others got there first. She was lying in an ungainly heap like a shot pheasant, the panniers awry like wounded wings. 'Leave me be!' I heard her cry, almost desperate.

'Thank God!' I heard Sir Bertrand's gasp of relief; Luke echoed it – he wasn't as good at suppressing his feelings as I was. Sir Bertrand exerted his husbandly rights and dispersed the crowd that was trying to help but only made her worse. 'She hates fuss,' he said, showing the understanding of her that was one of his redeeming features. 'Let her have air.' Soon there was only our party around her. He didn't waste his breath asking if she was all right when she plainly wasn't; he merely knelt beside her and waited until she was ready to talk.

She lifted herself up slightly so she could see his face; I could see her wince with pain. 'I'll go home,' she said. 'Stay here; I don't want to break up the party.'

'Are you sure?' he asked.

'Yes. Take me to the carriage; I'll have the doctor called, and then I'll go to bed. There's nothing you can do, Bertrand. Please stay.'

There was a rising in her tone that meant that she could bear no argument; he gave her none. 'Fitzjames,' he said. 'May I borrow your man to carry Lady Verity to our carriage?'

'Of course,' Luke said, eager to do what he could. 'Fortescue, stay with Sir Bertrand and Lady Verity as long as they need your services.'

I had dreamt of this moment for more than ten years, the moment when I would take her in my arms. I hadn't dreamt of a monstrous headdress and ostrich feather plumes that waved in my eyes, nor of panniers that got in my way and had to be tucked round her so I could pick her up. I had dreamt of a smile on her face, not gritted teeth; of her eyes closed in passion, not pain; of her hands in my hair, not clenching her fists. I had dreamt of kissing those freckles on her nose and cheeks, but I couldn't even see them under the layers of powder. And I certainly hadn't dreamt of her husband walking beside me, bellowing his approval of what I was doing. 'Good man, Fortescue. Can you carry her easily?'

'Lady Verity is not heavy.' I wished I could tell myself that she was light as a feather, but she wasn't: she lay in my arms like an ornamented sack of potatoes.

'Absurd fashion the ladies insist on nowadays.' For once I agreed with him.

We reached the carriage; the coachman jumped down when he saw what was happening and opened the door for me to put her in as gently as I could. She opened her eyes and smiled bravely at her husband. 'I don't think I'll even call the doctor, Bertrand. It's only a sprain, see,' she said, turning her foot in a circle to show she could move it easily. 'The rest is only a few bruises. I'll have a cold compress and get it bound up, then I'll have a cordial and go to bed. I'll be perfectly well by tomorrow morning. You've no need to worry about me. Go and enjoy the rest of the evening and come home in your cousin's carriage.'

'I won't enjoy it unless I know you're safe. Fortescue will accompany you.' He held up his hand to stop her protest. 'I insist on it, Althea.' Then he turned to me. 'Fortescue, stay with her until I return. You're a good man, I know I can trust my wife to you.' He might have seen my expression of dismay; he certainly misinterpreted it. 'Don't worry about your master. I shan't let him walk home alone. We'll let him down right outside his door and make sure he enters it safely. In you get, now. Make sure Lady Verity has everything she needs.'

There was no help for it. Without any doing from either of us, even against our protests, we were once more alone together. She said nothing all the way home, and kept her eyes closed so I could say nothing to her. I could only sit at the opposite corner of the carriage, futilely wishing I could take her pain on me. She opened her eyes only when we arrived at the front of her house, where we organized the bustle of servants that emerged.

I made ready to carry her in; she held out her arms for me to pick her up. It was the same gesture that she'd used all those years ago, when we knew that we loved each other. At that moment – when I remembered, she remembered, and we each saw that the other remembered – we knew that we loved each other still.

But we'd had months of practice at concealing our feelings; to all appearance there was nothing more out of the ordinary than Lady Verity with a sprained ankle carried to the sofa by a conveniently strong servant. I stood motionless though my emotions were roiling as she was attended to. After about half an hour everything was sorted out; she sat with her injured foot on a stool, sipping a cordial. Her high-heeled shoes and her ostrich feather plumes were removed, but otherwise she was still the fashionable lady who had started out the evening.

Only Jenny, her maid, remained in the room with us. 'I'll stay with you, ma'am, shall I?' she asked.

Althea could have – should have – accepted; she shouldn't have said, 'No, I'll rest here until Sir Bertrand comes back if he's not too late. You go off to bed now, Jenny.'

Jenny turned to me and said, 'Mr Fortescue, there's a bite to eat and a drink of beer in the kitchen if you'd like to come with me.'

I could have – should have – accepted; I shouldn't have said, 'Thank you, but Sir Bertrand instructed me to stay with Lady Verity until his return.'

And that was all the contrivance we'd done since she fell down the steps.

'Very well,' said Jenny, leaving. 'If you're tired of waiting up, ma'am, I know that Mr Fortescue can take you to bed.' I was glad of black skin and white powder, equally effective in concealing blushes.

The door closed behind Jenny; we were alone. 'Joshua, will you close the curtains so nobody can see in?'

'I don't think that's a very good idea, Althea.'

'Perhaps you're right. But if you pull up a stool and sit here,' she said, pointing to a place by her injured ankle, 'you'll seem like an attentive servant.' I didn't move. 'Please, Joshua. I've something to ask you.'

I did what she asked. For a moment we sat unspeaking, maintaining a respectful distance between us that we both knew could be closed in a second, and might well have been had it not been for the uncurtained window. There was a light on my face, but my back was to the window, and her face was in relative darkness. Someone outside even as proficient as she was at reading lips couldn't understand what we would say.

'Before I begin, Joshua, will you take that silly wig off? It makes you look ridiculous.'

'I'm ridiculous? What about what you're wearing? At least my clothes don't cause accidents!' I put my wig on the floor by my side, handy in case I needed to put it back on in a hurry. 'What is it you want to ask?'

'When my family burst into the room and pulled me away from you, I know what my last words to you were. But you said something I couldn't catch; everything was so confused. What was it?'

I didn't answer.

'What were your last words to me? I've wondered ever since.'

I still didn't say anything.

'Do you remember what mine were?'

'Yes.'

'It seems hardly fair that you know mine, but I don't know yours.'

'I said, "I'll love you forever too, Althea".'

'Well?'

I turned away.

'Don't hide your face from me; you know I hate it when people do that.'

I turned back. 'Althea, please don't make me say it.'

'I want to know.'

I wanted to tell her. So much that I had to bite my tongue to stop myself.

'Did forever last ten years, Joshua?' she asked gently, and fractured my resolution at last.

'It's more than ten years. It's ten years, eight months and ten days. That's three thousand, nine hundred and three days. And every one of those three thousand, nine hundred and three days I missed you; every one of those three thousand, nine hundred and three nights I dreamt of you. I thought of you when I was knee-deep in mud planting rice with my back aching from bending; I thought of you when my leg was swollen to twice its size with a snake bite. When I was about to be whipped to death, I wouldn't cry out because I knew you would want me to die bravely. Yes, Althea, forever has lasted.'

Then she said, 'Three thousand, nine hundred and five. You must have forgotten the leap years.'

'Sorry. It's not easy to keep track of time on a plantation.'

'It's been easy for me to keep track of time. There's been nothing to fill it. When I lost you, it was as if I'd lost my hearing all over again. There was something huge missing for me that other people had. I could see people hearing; I could see people loving. But hearing and loving weren't for me. I can manage; I can even join in sometimes. I can't hear the music but I know the steps. When I learnt that you were alive and in London, it was as if someone had said that there was a cure for my deafness.'

There was an expression on her face that I'd longed to see for three thousand, nine hundred and five days. I couldn't stop myself rising from the stool to do what I'd longed to do for three thousand, nine hundred and five nights. But I managed to turn away from her. I stood with my back to her, shielding her face from the window. I did not want anyone else to see that expression; I dared not look at it myself.

She didn't chide me for hiding my face from her, but said only, 'Joshua, I can hear the music again now.'

I turned back to her. 'We can't dance to it. You know that.'

'Yes, I know.' The expression vanished. 'We must carry on behaving well. Lady Mountford has congratulated me on my behaviour, by the way.'

'Fiona has congratulated me, and you know how critical she can be.'

I thought the moment of danger had passed; but suddenly she put her face in her hands and cried, 'Oh, Joshua, how can we endure it?' Just before my control crumbled and I would have taken her in my arms to comfort her, watchers or no, she lifted her head and said firmly, 'But we shall endure it.'

'Yes. We're good at endurance. We've both had a lot of practice.' I sat down; it seemed safe to do so. 'Are you glad or sorry that you know how I feel?'

'Glad, I think,' she said after a moment's reflection. 'And you?'

'About equal. To know that you love me as I love you— Oh, if I could only put it into words!'

'You don't need to; I feel the same.'

'But then the fear of what could happen, if this rigid control snapped – it nearly did just now; please don't weep in front of me again.'

'I'll try not to.' We seemed calm again now; to any watcher we could have been talking about the weather. 'How do you control it? How have you managed these past months? I have my duty to Bertrand to keep me on the straight and narrow path; what do you have?'

'It's something very unpleasant; I don't want to show you.'

'Now you've told me that it's unpleasant I shan't stop wondering what it is. If you think it will help me manage too, then show me.'

I left her and went to the writing table, where I copied from

141

memory that filthy little item of gossip that I'd composed to stiffen my resolve. I handed it to her, and watched her face contort with revulsion as she read it. ' "Lovely woman of high station . . . stooped so far nor shown such folly . . . her choice of paramour; the sinister sable servant . . . Deaf alike to the voices of honour, prudence, wisdom, morality and nature . . . the gross clasps of a lascivious Moor". Oh, burn it, Joshua, burn it at once! It's vile! Who wrote it?'

I put it in the fire and used the poker to ensure that it was nothing but unreadable ashes, then took my place by her side again. 'I did.'

'I know you did; I just saw you. I mean, who composed it? Who's saying such horrible things about us? Who's read it?'

'I mean I wrote it myself, soon after we met again. You asked me what helped me endure: that does. I burnt that one, but there'd be no burning all the newspapers that would have something like that in them, and worse. Only you and I have read that; there'd be gossip and sneers like that over every dinner table in England if I did what I want to do more than anything else in the world.'

She closed her eyes for a moment. 'Thank you for showing that to me. It will help me too. I watched you, over there at the table, with the candlelight glowing on you, and that intent look on your face that you always have when you're writing or reading, as if words were precious to you and you didn't want to miss any of them. I would have walked over to you and—' She opened her eyes again and smiled. 'It's a good thing that my ankle is sprained.'

'I can't read or write in front of you; you can't weep in front of me – is there anything else we must avoid in each other's presence?' She didn't say anything; I knew what she was thinking. 'Must we avoid each other's presence?'

'What do you want?'

'I want what's best for you. That's what love means. Do you want me to go away?'

'I – sometimes I wonder whether it would be a good thing if I

142

lost what remains of my hearing; it only reminds me of what I'm missing. But then I think, it's not enough, it's not nearly enough, but it's far, far better than nothing at all. No, Joshua, if you can bear it, I don't want you to go away.'

'It's going to be hard, especially when we're living under the same roof.'

'What? When?'

'Didn't Sir Bertrand tell you? He's invited Luke to stay at Galbury Hall once the shooting starts, and Luke's accepted.'

'Oh, God, I wish I'd known!'

'Then you wouldn't have asked me what my last words to you were?'

'Perhaps not. But I'm glad I did. This would have happened sooner or later, wouldn't it? No matter how hard we were trying to behave well.'

'Do you want me to give an excuse to Luke and not go?'

'Are you under an obligation to him?'

'I promised to stay with him until the end of August. He saved my life; he stopped his father whipping me to death, and he was disinherited for it – except for one small item of property. Me.'

'But you aren't his property any more, are you? Not in England.'

'No, but I am grateful to him; that's my obligation.'

'Then fulfil it. We mustn't let what we are together hurt anyone else.'

'Althea, we are nothing together. We never can be. If we were, we would hurt many other people: your husband, Luke, Fiona, to name just three.'

'You're right. Even if I were a widow there'd still be the same sort of filth written about us.'

'I must count my blessings: I'm not tempted to wish your husband dead. I can be happy that he makes you comfortable.'

'He does. That's what he promised me. I warned him before we married that I was in love with another man; he accepted it when I said that I thought the man was dead – it's hardly his fault that you're not. He married me for my fortune, an heir and

143

a respectable marriage. I haven't been able to give him an heir, but I must give him something. He's kept his side of the bargain.'

As if on cue, I heard the sound of his return. 'He's back,' I mouthed silently as I grabbed my wig and put it on. One thing to be said for him as a potential cuckolded husband, I reflected. I would always know when he was coming.

'Our first test, Joshua. We shall pass it.'

We did, though it was a big one. By the time he entered the room, I was standing composedly as if I'd been there all the time. She put down a glass of cordial that she'd just picked up for the purpose and greeted him as a wife should.

'Ah, Fortescue,' he boomed. 'Thank you for taking good care of my wife. Your master's in the carriage. It let my cousin's family down at their house and will take you both home before it returns.' I was about to go when he said, 'Before you leave, Fortescue, carry my wife up to her bedchamber. Your master knows, so there's no need to worry that you're keeping him waiting.'

'Yes, Sir Bertrand,' I said, the perfect servant.

And she was the perfect wife as I did so, merely chiding him gently as she put her head round my shoulder to look at him and said, 'Oh, Bertrand, Fortescue has told me that you've invited Mr Fitzjames to Galbury Hall at the end of the season. I must say that I'd rather have had it from your lips than his.'

As I carried her up the stairs, nobody could have guessed what it meant to me and to her. When I set her gently on her bed, nobody could have known how much I wanted to stay there with her. And when she said, 'Thank you, Fortescue, I feel most obliged', nobody could have dreamt that she felt anything more.

I climbed into the carriage and tried to reassure Luke. 'It's not a bad sprain. She'll be walking with a stick for a week, but that's about all.'

'Thank God!'

'Will you excuse me if I don't talk? I'm exhausted.'

'You must be, carrying her like that.' I hoped that this would be the end of his talk, but it wasn't. 'Congratulate me, Josh. I didn't push you out of the way and volunteer to carry her myself.'

'Congratulations.'

'What is it about the English that you could carry her and I couldn't?'

'I'm a servant. We don't have feelings.'

'Josh, that was the first time ever I've wanted to be in your skin. When Sir Bertrand asked if I'd let you carry her upstairs to bed, I agreed just so that I could have the pleasure of imagining myself in your place.'

'I hope you enjoyed it more than I did.'

'Why? I thought you had a regard for her.'

'It was a strain. A very great strain. I'm bloody tired, so will you shut up?'

'Oh, but it wouldn't hurt you to talk.' *Yes, it would.* 'What did you talk about?' *Oh, no!* 'Did she say anything about me?' I blessed his self-centredness.

'Sir Bertrand hadn't told her that he'd invited you to stay. I happened to mention it; it was the first she knew.'

'Does she mind?'

'She told him you were an agreeable young man and she had no objection.'

'An agreeable young man, eh?' he said, enraptured by this small praise.

'She had to say it: the invitation had been given and accepted. Luke, I'm in duty bound to warn you, though I don't think it'll do any good. From what I've seen and heard tonight, I must tell you that you don't have the slightest chance of winning her affection.'

'No more chance than you'd have, eh?' he said, crestfallen. But even that couldn't keep him quiet. He cheered up and said, 'Well, that relieves my mind. I'm glad you told me. I can love her without feeling guilty that I might be bringing her harm.'

I couldn't shut him up. Even when I closed my eyes and said nothing, he did not need me to reply, just to be there, while he kept on and on, almost every word having a significance to me that he couldn't understand. I was no more able to silence him than I'd been able to stop the flies irritating the whip wound on my back when I'd hung all day at their mercy. With just as little intention, but causing just as much pain, he kept on digging into me. He was a very lucky man to get out of that carriage alive.

Exhausted though I was in both spirit and body, I lay awake for hours that night, passionately embracing a pillow and whispering to it the words that I wanted to tell her; it was even deafer than she was and made no objection.

Between us were the barriers of her marriage, my skin, and – greatest of all in English eyes – our different ranks in society: the gulf between a baronet's wife and a servingman. If I'd been the Prince of Timbuctoo or she'd been a housemaid, we'd have had no more to worry about than some puritanical raised eyebrows and a few jokes about Othello and Desdemona. But all three together—

She was probably lying awake, too: she had a sprained ankle to add to her causes for sleeplessness. Perhaps she was even embracing her pillow at that moment, feeling the same joy and the same pain as I was. Knowing that we were united in spirit, and that we always would be – it would have been overwhelming had it not been matched by knowing that we were parted in body, and that we always would be.

The season was ending and Parliament would soon finish. The fact that Britain was about to engage in a desperate struggle to keep its most important colony would not stop its rulers from hunting, shooting and fishing. Parents were celebrating their daughter's success and planning her wedding, or warning her that if she carried on this way she'd never find a husband, or wringing their hands and saying, 'But he's so unsuitable!' Londoners of the lower orders could not escape the heat and were continuing their usual enjoyments such as cockfighting, the theatre, and an occasional hanging.

Althea and I continued to behave just as we'd been doing for months. If I were in attendance where she was a guest, I carefully did not let my eye rest on her any longer than it should have done. She'd greet me with a, 'Good evening, Fortescue, I trust you are well.' But it was hard, much harder than before, now I knew that she was as conscious of my presence as I was of hers, that she was exerting the same iron control, and that she knew the same of me.

Luke had been chaste for a month, inspired by the purity of his devotion. But he couldn't keep it up – or rather, keep it down. I spent a frantic night after a dinner when he disappeared while I was having my own in the servants' hall. He finally returned late next morning, to my mingled relief and fury.

'Thank God you're safe! Where the hell have you been?'

'None of your business, Josh.'

'Of course it's my business! I've been out all night looking for you!'

'It may have escaped your notice, but you aren't my wife or my father.'

'No, but I am supposed to keep you from being murdered! It's bloody irresponsible of you going off without even telling me where you were going.'

'I don't think you'd have been welcome.' He held up his hands. 'Oh, all right, I'm sorry, I should have let you know. But the lady was very pressing.'

'And what happened to that shame you felt about all your other women?'

'You're sounding more like my wife or my father every minute. You have no right to question me about my morals.'

'No, but I do have the right – the duty, even – to ensure your safety.'

'Do you want to come with me, Josh? To wait outside the door while I finish my pleasure? Because that's the only thing that I'll agree to.'

It was a horrible picture, but I couldn't see any other choice. So I'd find a place to wait, knowing what was happening on the other side of the wall, sometimes even hearing it. I'd agreed to it partly because I'd thought that it could not possibly make me feel any more frustrated than I already was: I was wrong. The visit to the quiet of Galbury Hall was much more attractive than it had been.

'How do you do it, Josh?' he asked one day. 'To my knowledge you haven't had any since last Christmas.'

It was longer than that, but I saw no reason to tell him. 'Why are you surprised? Do you think that because you're a lecher every other man must be?'

'Well, you know what they say about black men.'

'It's a lie. The same as all the other lies they say about black men, such as being happy in slavery and not being able to feel pain. It's you that puzzles me, Luke. I know you're in love with her – I can't shut you up about how pure and wonderful she is – but you still go on rutting like a rabbit.'

'That's it, Josh. She is pure and wonderful, and so is my love for her. I didn't understand for a few weeks, until you told me that I had no chance with her. And then I realized that I didn't want to have any chance with her. Oh, I'd had my dreams – but now I feel ashamed of them, as if I'd defiled her even by dreaming about her. Can't you understand that?'

'Not in the slightest.'

'There's love, and there's lust. They're different. Can you understand *that*?'

'I think what you're saying is that on the one hand there's her, and on the other there's every other woman in the world.'

'That's it! You understand!'

I did indeed.

The day before we set off for Galbury Hall, Luke and I called on the Macleods to bid farewell. The door was opened by Fiona. 'Have you had the measles, Mr Fitzjames?' she asked; she looked slightly harassed. 'I know you have, Joshua; you gave them to me.'

'Who's ill?'

'Only Janet at the moment, but I expect the boys to go down at any time.'

'I haven't had measles,' said Luke. 'Only smallpox.'

She looked at him. 'It didn't leave any scars. You were lucky.'

'In one sense. But it killed my mother.'

While they stood on the doorstep comparing measles and smallpox, and saying how much better it was to have them while young, I recalled that hellish time when smallpox had hit the plantation; it wasn't a memory I cherished. Old man Smith was far too concerned with his sick sons and his dying wife to take any care for us; most people were infected, and with the conditions we had many of them died. It was another of those cross-roads where I've wondered, 'What would life have been like if I'd made another choice?' I could easily have escaped: many of the healthy slaves did. Nobody pursued them; nobody even knew they'd escaped – they'd been counted among the dead. But somebody had to look after the sick, somebody had to dig the graves or the corpses would have rotted in the heat for weeks, and I was by far the strongest person left standing. I'd heard Fiona's voice almost as clearly as I did now on her doorstep, saying, 'If you run, these people will die. If you stay, they will live.' That was one reason why old man Smith trusted me: I'd helped to preserve his property. In the seven years of tribulation that followed, the fact that I'd acted righteously was little comfort when I'd thought that I could be living in one of the maroon communities of escaped slaves. But now I knew that I would still be living there, not standing here as a free man, with two good friends comfortably chatting, and knowing that I was loved by the woman I loved. Now I had no regrets.

'I'll come back in half an hour, Josh, if you want to go and visit the sick.'

The boys were kept at home; healthy but confined, they explained Fiona's harassment. I stayed only a few moments with Janet, who was lying in bed looking miserable. 'I hope you'll all be better when I come back,' I said. 'Luke's going away too; he sends his best wishes for your recovery, and is sad that he won't be able to bid you goodbye properly.'

She looked disappointed, so Fiona explained, 'He hasn't had

the measles, Janet. You wouldn't want to give them to him, would you?'

'Where are you both going?' Janet asked me.

'Luke's been invited to Galbury Hall, and I'm going with him.'

'Lady Verity invited us to go too, but we can't, because of the measles,' she said sadly. I silently lamented it as much as Janet did, and no doubt Althea did too: it would have been a lot safer for us together at the Hall with the Macleods present. 'But she says that when we're all feeling better we can go, perhaps at Christmas. Isn't she nice?'

'Yes, she's very nice.' Janet was looking tired, so I left her in peace. 'Fiona, I'll take the boys for a walk on the common if you like; get them off your hands and use up some of that energy.'

She looked even more harassed. 'No, Joshua, I want to talk to you for a few moments in private.' She sent the boys off to the common by themselves, with a parcel of food and strict instructions not to go near anyone else.

'What is it, Fiona? You look very concerned.'

'I am. When Althea called to see Janet she didn't mention that you'd be at Galbury Hall with her. It's not wise, Joshua, it's not wise.'

'What could we do? Sir Bertrand invited Luke and he accepted without either of them consulting us, or we'd have stopped them. I tried to talk Luke out of it, but he wouldn't agree.'

'Must you go with him?'

'I've promised to stay with him until the end of August. Do you want me to break my word? I thought about it, I did indeed.'

'I don't know.' Her face was creased in perplexity. 'I suppose you'd better go. But keep a close guard, Joshua. She knows you as well as I do – better, of course. She'll understand what that look on your face means.'

I didn't say anything.

'Oh, God help you!' It was a prayer, not a blasphemy. 'You've told her already.'

I nodded.

'How could you do such a foolish, wicked thing?' Then she sighed. 'She wrung it out of you. She always could.'

'I'm no more capable now than I was then of resisting her or lying to her.'

'And since she's not the sort of woman who'd do that to a man just for the gratification of it, she loves you too. Oh, God help both of you!'

'Fiona, I wish you weren't so perceptive.'

'I thought there was something strained about her; she always looks forward to going at the end of the season, but she seemed as if she were dreading it. So do you, now I look at you.'

'We are dreading it. Fiona, we aren't planning to commit adultery. We're as aware as you are of how wrong it would be. But we love each other, and there's no doing anything about it. If it lasted for ten years when she thought I was dead and I thought I'd never see her again, it's not going to disappear now.'

'Oh, I wish I didn't feel so responsible! I worried about the two of you, when you were turning into a man and a woman. I should have warned you.'

'I don't think we'd have listened. But you are responsible in part, Fiona. You encouraged us in the outlandish and seditious notion that all God's children are equal in His sight. You even went so far as to suggest that they should be treated that way on Earth. You should have chided her and beaten me when we showed you that it didn't matter to us that she was an heiress and I was a slave.'

'It shouldn't matter, but it does. It matters a great deal to you now: you're not children any more.'

'We are both well aware of that.'

'I'll pray for you. I'll pray for both of you.'

'Won't do any good. I don't believe in God.'

'Yes, but He believes in you, and that's rather more to the point. Joshua, will you—' But we were interrupted. Luke returned bearing gifts; games and puzzles that could be played by a child in bed, and a posy of flowers for Janet.

Fiona ushered me out, but stopped on the threshold. 'Mr Fitzjames, if you'll pardon me giving my godson a piece of spiritual advice before he goes?'

'Of course, ma'am. It may do me some good too.'

'Joshua, I know you're an unbeliever, but will you say just one line of the Lord's Prayer? To yourself, if you like: God will overhear. You know the line I mean.'

I did. *Lead us not into temptation.*

Chapter 10

Early in the morning, the Veritys came to collect us to go to Galbury Hall for the visit that I both desired and dreaded. Luke stepped into their comfortable carriage in the lead, while I travelled in a great lumbering coach with the luggage and Althea's maid, Jenny. *Miss* Jenny, I should say: Lady Verity's maid was one step above Mr Fitzjames's manservant, and she was very conscious of it at first, as well as of the fact that she would spend all day alone with a man who might be disposed to take advantage of the situation.

But I'd learnt enough from Luke to know how to be agreeable to women without being flirtatious, and she unbent after half an hour or so. Fortunately, this part of our journey held no memories for me; when we'd fled, Althea and I had laid a false trail by starting out in the direction of Bristol, where she had some relations on her father's side. (Now I knew why her father's cousins lived in Bristol: it was a slave-trading port.)

Miss Jenny was an agreeable young woman, with a clear voice (of course), and considerably attached to Althea. Though we talked of our employers, as servants always do, she was as discreet about anything that mattered as I was. I traded tales of alligators and Indians for the knowledge of where Althea bought her clothes and how long it took to prepare her fashionable appearance. The most important thing I learnt was that my picture of her in bed was wrong: those absurd headdresses took

153

so long to create that she'd sleep in them for a week at a time, propped up in bed with a board.

The conversation found its way round to Pompey: this was the first time the journey had been made without him. 'We all dreaded what would happen when he died,' she said. 'She was so attached to him, and we knew it wouldn't be long. But luckily he was killed in an accident, and it was all very quick, so she wasn't distressed at all.' She looked at me inquiringly. 'Hampton said it was because he ran over the road to greet someone he knew; an old friend, he said. A Negro. That wouldn't have been you, by any chance, would it?'

I confessed. 'Yes. I used to be Lady Mountford's page; looking after Pompey was one of my duties.'

'Oh, you should have said, Mr Fortescue!' All at once I became part of the family, and she was much more friendly. I diverted the conversation to Pompey's misdeeds; there were enough to keep the conversation going for some time. We agreed that it was little short of miraculous that he'd lived as long as he had.

She produced a pack of cards, and I proceeded to lose money to her; small though the stakes were, I ended the journey more than thirty shillings to the worse. It wasn't only my usual lack of skill at cards: the latter part of our journey was the one Althea and I had travelled all those years ago. I knew she would be remembering it; even though she'd travelled it many times and this was my first return, she had to be thinking, as I was thinking, *here*'s the place where we joined the road, *here*'s where we stopped for refreshments, *here*'s where we hid from a carriage that looked like the Mountfords' but wasn't.

There were many changes: the roads had been improved beyond all recognition, which was why this journey was taking only one day, rather than the two that would have been needed before (it had taken us even longer, but we'd not come the direct route). With the improvement in roads had come more traffic, and with that, more people to serve the needs of travellers. Small hamlets were now substantial villages, with toll-booths, stables and inns.

It was dark well before the end of our journey, so the memories were not so vividly presented to me, and I even won some of my money back. Eventually Miss Jenny informed me that we were approaching Galston, the village of which Galbury Hall was the chief estate. 'All this land on the right here belongs to Sir Bertrand,' she said. 'My lady brought a sizeable fortune to him, and they've purchased a lot in the past few years.'

We approached the main posting inn of the village, the Royal Oak. I remembered it; we'd decided not to stay there but to seek more unobtrusive shelter in a barn – as unobtrusive as a very young lady, a black youth and a noisy spaniel could be, that is. It was too dark for me to see the barn now, but I resolved to visit it – to revisit it – as soon as I could. I didn't know who it belonged to now, any more than we had then, but the worst that could happen if I was found there was that I'd be warned off so long as I wasn't poaching or stealing.

Turning off past the Royal Oak, we drove about a mile before we reached the Hall. Everything had been made ready; the servants were lined up to welcome the master and mistress. Miss Jenny and I got out and stretched, while a footman came forward to the carriage in front of us. Althea stepped out, and no more than she'd done before did she look at me as she accepted the footman's arm; she now walked without a stick, but she still limped.

Everyone was tired, and Miss Jenny and I were considerately sent off for supper in the servants' hall. Black faces are far more rare in the country than in London, and I was the object of some curiosity; many of the servants said that I was the first Negro they'd spoken to. I tried to take it all in good part and not regard it as impertinent: 'Yes, I'm the same colour all over, and no, it doesn't wash off.' Miss Jenny came to my aid, and told them about the way Pompey died; this won me approval. Curiosity was, after all, better than the hostility I'd been shown at the Wintertons'. So when I went to bed I didn't much resent the inquisitive glances of the under butler (only two to a room – the Veritys were better employers than the Wintertons), and merely turned my back on him as I used the chamber pot to foil his desire to find out whether it was true what they say about black men.

Luke groaned when I woke him in the morning, and groaned even louder when I told him the time. 'Country hours, Luke. You're set for a full day's slaughtering of bird life today, and you start early.'

He sat up in bed, and took a first gulp from the cup I handed him. 'What's this, Josh?' he asked in distaste.

'They called it coffee.'

'They lied.'

'You should drink tea. It's much better here.'

'*Tea?*' he exclaimed with outraged American patriotism. 'Throw it into Boston harbour – that's all tea's good for.' He looked at me with his eyebrows raised. 'You seemed to be getting on very well yesterday with what's-her-name, Lady Verity's maid. Attractive young woman, that.'

'Her name's Jenny. Luke, I hope you'll think that Lady Verity's purity extends to her household. It really is not the thing for a guest to hump the housemaids.'

'No, no. If I feel the urge I'll make an excuse to go into town to the nearest good brothel. You wouldn't know where that is, would you?'

'I'll find out.'

'I was thinking that she might suit you.' I was surprised. 'See, Josh, haven't I made progress in the past few months, actually suggesting that you might be interested in a white woman?'

'Well done, Luke, but I'm not.'

'You can't go on living like a monk all your life.'

I feared all too much that I'd have to. 'You aren't going to need me when you're out shooting, are you? Sir Bertrand's loader will look after you.'

'Why, what do you want to do?'

'Go for a walk. Perhaps have a mug of beer at the Royal Oak. Stroll about as a free man in the English countryside. It's beautiful round here.'

'Have you been here before?'

'Well, that's what they say,' I said to cover my slip. 'And I like country air; Lord Mountford has a big estate about thirty miles north of London, and I'd often take Pompey out for a walk.' With Althea.

'Of course; once you've seen me off, the rest of the day's yours until dinner. I hope you enjoy your innocent country pleasures as much as I shall showing Sir Bertrand what American shooting can do.'

It was indeed good to walk as a free man in the English countryside. In ordinary clothes, no longer in my gaudy livery and stupid wig – though I kept the boots in case of brambles – I strolled happily down the drive to the Royal Oak. The English summer sun was about the same as a South Carolina winter, but that was all the similarity there was between now and my condition last Christmas. The woodlands smelled different from the plantation, the leaves were a different green, and the birds sang a different tune. Of course it would be a strain, living under the same roof, but I could manage it, and I knew she could too, my brave, good Althea. We'd managed it for months; we'd continue to do so.

Word of my existence had already spread to the Royal Oak, and these people, who worked on a well-travelled road, had seen black faces before. So they were sociable rather than inquisitive; a few stories of alligators and Indians went down as well among them as my beer was going down me. A bite of good country bread and cheese also went down well, and I succumbed to the temptation of another mug before bidding a cheerful farewell.

The Royal Oak, Galbury Hall and the barn I remembered so well formed a triangle; it would be half a mile to the barn, then another mile back to the Hall, though this time across fields and pastures rather than made-up road; I would be glad of the boots.

A few yards beyond the inn was the shop from which, all those years ago, we'd bought a seed cake for our supper. It was irresistible. I pushed open the door, jangling the bell that I'd

157

forgotten until now, and bought a large slice of a cake that was obviously made to the same recipe; I'd eat it at the barn.

As I walked along the muddy path to the barn, memories flooded over me: memories that I'd often recalled, and memories that had been stored away until that moment. I relieved myself of some of the beer against the same oak, and I remembered Althea's voice envying such a male ability.

If I could wind back the clockwork of time, and have those two children do the sensible thing of asking Fiona Macleod for help instead of running away together so we'd never discovered that we loved each other, would I?

No. Despite all the pain of the past and the strain of the future, the woman I loved with all my being loved me in return, and that made up for everything. Besides, she'd have married George Mountford if we hadn't, instead of the stupid, decent man who gave her a comfortable life.

The barn came into view; smaller than in my imagination, of course. But one change was not the result of my imagination; a chimney had been added, an unusual feature in a barn. As I walked closer I saw that otherwise the barn had changed little from the outside – if anything, it was in better repair than before. I opened the wooden door and went in.

Here, almost all had changed. There was still hay, but much less of it, and now piled neatly in bales to serve as decoration more than storage. In its place in the middle of the room was a small wooden table, with two rocking chairs either side. At one side was a cupboard, at the other was the fireplace.

But there was no change in one matter: a matter of overwhelming importance.

Althea.

She stood looking out of the window at the other end of the barn from me. She hadn't seen me arrive, nor had she heard me come in. I could leave and she'd never know I was here.

Get out, I heard Fiona's voice in my head. *Joshua, get out now. Lead us not into temptation.* But I could not leave. I saw her, my love, in a plain walking dress, her hair unpowdered and tied in a knot, the light forming a halo as it had done before, and I could not leave.

But I did not move towards her to take her in my arms and love her as my body cried out for me to do. I stood in the doorway, pulled between conscience and desire, and I did not move.

And then it was too late. She turned round, and smiled as if she'd been expecting me: perhaps she was.

'Do you like the changes I've had made?' she asked. 'I think it's much more comfortable. It's my property; I bought this and the field around it when I was first married. I come here almost every day when Bertrand's out with the guns. He knows I come here; if I'm not back in time for dinner he'll send a servant to collect me.' She was gabbling. She always gabbled when she was nervous; much easier for her than trying to catch what other people were saying. 'He doesn't approve of me going for walks on my own, but he's used to it now. This is the first time I've come without Pompey – though he was hardly much protection in his last few years. Everyone wondered why I loved him so, but it was for your sake, not his; he was all I had left of you. Poor Pompey: I couldn't mourn him as he deserved, not when I heard that he'd died in your arms.'

I hadn't moved; I couldn't speak.

'There's a draught, Joshua; come in and close the door behind you.'

I did; I could never resist her. But I could, just, resist doing anything more.

'Is that seed cake you've brought? I brought it too, the first time I came. But I don't need seed cake to remind me, so now I bring something else. The tea's here; so is some wood if we want to make a fire. Everyone knows that they must make this place ready for me when I come home at the end of the season. See how tidy everything is?' She walked around the barn, pointing to the improvements. 'The chairs and table are old things that I found, but I had them repaired and they're comfortable. Usually

I'm on my own, but sometimes I have a visitor. I'll need the stick to walk home with; Bertrand was concerned about my ankle, but walking is good exercise if it's not too far. The place is still used as a barn if there's a good crop of hay; I had another barn built and this is just used if there's an excess. I had the fireplace put in the first winter; it gets icy in here in December, and I need to wrap myself in a blanket until I get the fire going.'

Now she was standing in front of me, an arm's length away. I held my arms rigidly at my side to stop myself reaching out for her. 'Why don't you say something, Joshua, instead of standing there without moving a muscle?'

'You know what I want to say. You know what I want to do.'

'Then say it and do it.' Still I didn't move. 'You said that we were nothing together. I know that we are nothing apart.'

And my love was in my embrace, and her lips were on mine, and her arms were round me. And then there were the little impediments of buttons and boots and laces before we stood again embracing skin to skin. And then we lay together on a blanket spread out upon the hay, and our bodies were as united as our spirits.

This is it, I thought; the peak of the mountain. Life cannot possibly hold anything more wonderful than this. I lay on my back, one arm round her as she lay by my side with her head on my shoulder, stroking her hair that draped across my chest. My own words were inadequate to describe my bliss, so I used Shakespeare's:

'If it were now to die
'Twere now to be most happy, for I fear
My soul hath her content so absolute
That not another comfort like to this
Succeeds in unknown fate.'

'What are you saying? I can feel your voice but I can't understand the words.' She propped her head up on one hand so she

160

could see my lips. It took several repetitions before she understood Shakespeare's complicated language, which rather lost the magic.

'What's all this nonsense about dying?' she said. 'Where does it come from, anyway?'

'*Othello*.'

'That's a very bad choice of play, Joshua. Othello and Desdemona were a silly couple. We're not.'

'No, but we are an adulterous couple.'

'I'm an adulteress. You're merely a fornicator. You aren't even a seducer. You left all the seducing to me, which was very ungentlemanly of you.'

'I didn't make you do much work, did I?'

'More than you know. More than I knew, until I turned round and saw you in the doorway and thought, "Well, at least I put up a struggle". I think, looking back on it, that I've been trying to seduce you since we met in Bond Street.'

'Were you expecting me today?'

'I don't know. I set out for my walk, just as I'd normally do, and I think I was leaving it up to you.'

'I wasn't expecting you to be here. I wouldn't have come if I'd thought you might be.'

'Are you glad or sorry that you did?'

I pulled her to me and expressed myself in a way that left her in no doubt of my gladness. 'Is anyone else likely to come in?' I asked when I let her go.

'Probably not.'

'If you'll excuse me for a moment,' I said as I hastily got up. I wedged the door shut with a chair, then moved the cupboard so that we couldn't be seen from the window. It made the barn so dark that she'd have difficulty reading my lips unless I was very close to her, which was no hardship.

When I returned to her, she said, 'Lie face down, Joshua.'

'Then you won't be able to see my lips.'

'Doesn't matter; just shake or nod your head. I want to see your back more closely.' I let her, conscious of every lash scar. 'It's not very good, is it?'

I shook my head.

'Do you want me to kiss it better?'

I nodded energetically.

Her lips brushed the old scars from my first years when I was useless both to myself and my owner, and the few from the seven years when I was forced to use the whip rather than have it used on me, and the ugliest one, not yet a year old, which the flies had infested as I hung on the post. They'd all healed physically, even the most recent, but I hadn't realized how much they'd scarred my spirit until she kissed all the bitterness away. I wanted to tell her that if I'd known she'd do this I'd have asked for more lashes, but that would have meant turning over and stopping her, so I let her carry on healing me.

'Better?' she asked. I turned on my side and held her close; she knew how much better it was.

I kissed her ear. 'I wish I could kiss this better too,' I said, then pulled back so she could read my lips when I said it again.

But before I could repeat the words, she put her fingers on my lips and stopped me. Her face was filled with wonder. 'I think you just did.'

'What?'

'Did you just say, "I wish I could kiss this better too"?'

'You heard me!'

'Yes! Those are the first words I've understood without seeing the person's lips since I was nine years old! Say something else.'

I spoke more deliberately this time. 'I love you, Althea.'

'I love you too, Joshua, but that was a bit obvious. Say something that I couldn't guess.'

'In the beginning was the word.'

'Something about the beginning of the world?'

'In the beginning was the word,' I said, moving so she could see my lips.

'It's not perfect, but it still seems something like a miracle!'

'If God has miraculously given you back your hearing as a reward for adultery, then I think that I've misunderstood His holy writ.'

162

'Of course not. It must be because nobody with a deep voice like yours has spoken so clearly so close to my ear before now.' That told me more about her marriage than she knew she'd revealed. Her husband's voice wasn't as deep as mine, but it was certainly louder; he'd never done the natural, loving thing.

We experimented with her hearing; we stood up, as lying down made it awkward for me to move around her head. We found the best distance away from her ear, the best level of sound and depth of voice, and which ear was stronger (the left). 'So this is the best?' I said, the best distance away from her left ear in the best tone.

'Yes. That's it.'

We stood for a moment looking at each other in joy, loving each other even more for what we'd brought to each other this day. Then I leant forward to the right place and said, 'I want to make love with you again.'

'I can see that,' she chuckled. 'It's not only your lips moving, Joshua.'

This time, when there was all the passion of before and none of the urgency, when I felt her hands on my newly healed back, when I said words of love that I knew she could hear, when her ecstasy matched mine, I found that life held something more wonderful still.

Chapter 11

WE walked back to the Hall, to all appearances Lady Verity, with a weary ankle, accepting the arm of a chance-met servant. Even our conversation could have been overheard. There wasn't much; she could never read lips and walk at the same time unless the ground underfoot was much smoother than this muddy track. I felt her lean heavily on me, so I stopped. 'Shall I carry you, Lady Verity?'

'No, I can walk, Fortescue, but thank you.'

'I'm relieved. I've been somewhat worn out by my exertions today.'

'Could you undertake similar exertions tomorrow, Fortescue?'

'Nothing would give me greater pleasure, my lady.'

We returned to the Hall, where we behaved exactly as we'd done before. Guilt replaced strain, that was the only difference. No exchange of glances, no inward chuckle at their innocent words that had extra meaning for us – we were betraying them enough without laughing at them.

I served at dinner, attentive manservant, and she listened to Luke and Sir Bertrand's talk of the day's bag as a faithful wife and agreeable hostess should; even when their account palled, her eyes were raised to the ceiling, not to me. Luke at last began to realize that details of every single dead bird might not interest someone who hadn't been there. 'My apologies, Lady Verity. Please forgive my enthusiasm for your husband's fine coverts.'

'Not at all, Mr Fitzjames. I'm so glad you enjoyed your day.'

'And how was yours, my dear?' asked Sir Bertrand. 'Did you go for your walk as usual?'

'Yes. It wearied my ankle, but luckily I met Fortescue and took his arm.'

'My dear, I don't like you walking alone like that, now you don't even have Pompey. What if you should fall and hurt your ankle again?'

'Perhaps you're right, Bertrand. At least for the present I should have a servant to attend me.' She turned to Luke. 'Mr Fitzjames, would it be too much to ask if Fortescue might accompany me? I was very glad of his arm on the way back today, and he speaks much more clearly than our Warwickshire servants. Only when you're out with Bertrand, of course.'

'Of course, Lady Verity. Make use of his services as much as you like.'

'Thank you, I shall.'

'I must say, my dear, the exercise does seem to have done you good. You're positively glowing with health. You've been looking a little strained of late.'

'I feel better, Bertrand. It must be this country air. You know, I think I'll have a lock put on the door of the barn; it would stop vagabonds wandering in.'

'A good idea. Fortescue can fit it for you tomorrow.'

She turned to Luke. 'I have my own private barn about a mile away from here; it's a good distance for a walk, and I like to stay there in peace for an hour or so. You'd be most welcome to come and see it if you'll just tell me the day before so that I can make sure everything's ready to receive a visitor. I sometimes feel awkward when people call in suddenly, because it's not prepared for them.'

'I'd be delighted to.'

'Another thing, Bertrand: I might have curtains or shutters put up on the window, to give me more privacy.'

'It seems that Fortescue will have a busy day tomorrow.'

As I was readying him for bed, Luke asked, 'You don't mind accompanying Lady Verity, do you, Josh?'

'No, no, not at all. You know I've always held her in some regard.'

'I wanted to ask you, but it would have been a little out of place.'

'You did just the right thing.'

'Did you enjoy your country walk?'

'Yes, thank you, I did.'

It was all so easy. The very things that had kept us apart were now the things that made it inconceivable to everyone else that there could be anything other than innocence in our behaviour; they would almost as soon have suspected Pompey.

Next day I set off respectfully following her since she had no need of my arm on the way out, with a bag of tools and materials over my back, glad that I'd held out for not wearing livery on such walks. We arrived at the barn. 'First, I'm going to do what I've been told to do, which is to put a lock on the door and a curtain rod up on the window.'

'I'll make a fire and get some water from the spring so we can boil up a kettle for some tea.' By the time the kettle was on the hearth I'd fixed the rod so she could put up the curtain, made of material so fine that it let in light enough for her to read my lips but prevented prying eyes peering in. Then she sat down to wait until I finished the lock. It was all very domestic.

'You know, Joshua, I think before we have our tea, after you've locked the door, what I might do is take off your waistcoat, then undo your shirt from the top very slowly, so that I can kiss your chest all the way down as I do it . . .' And she sat there demurely and described in great detail exactly what she planned. The kettle started steaming as it came to the boil; I knew how it felt. Still talking, she stood up and took it off the fire. '. . . And then we'll have a cup of tea.'

I turned the key. 'Sorry, Althea? I was concentrating on the lock and I missed what you were saying. You'll have to show me.'

It was the honeymoon after a wedding that had been torn away from us. We couldn't go there every day: sometimes a downpour made a walk implausible; sometimes visitors to the Hall made it impossible. But on most days, while her husband and my friend were out shooting, fishing or riding, we set off as usual.

Outside, in the rest of the world, for the rest of the time, there was guilt at our betrayal, and knowledge of the appalling scandal that would erupt if anyone found out. But once we'd locked the door behind us we were free; freer than either of us had ever been in our lives. We were free to make love, to talk about whatever we wanted to, or simply to sit quietly reading books, drinking tea and eating cake, the other's presence bringing happiness enough. We explored each other's bodies, finding out what gave most pleasure; we explored each other's minds, finding out what changes the years had made.

'I love my love with an A because she is Adorable. Very adorable. I hate her because she is Absurd. That too. She eats Apples – here's one – and her name is Althea.'

'I love my love with a J because he is Jolly. I hate him because he is Jealous. He eats Jam – we don't have any, the ants get into it – and his name is Jeremy.'

'Thank you, Arabella.'

'Are you jealous, Joshua?'

'A bit. Mostly I'm jolly. I'm very jolly right now. I know you haven't shared with him what you've shared with me.'

'I don't like to talk about him – as if I could betray him any more than I'm doing already – but I want you to know something so you can be more jolly and less jealous. He – well, somehow he seems to make it all a chore that we have to go through to produce an heir. He asks, and if I say I don't want to, he doesn't insist. I haven't wanted to since I knew you were back.'

'Have you thought – oh, you must have – have you thought that you might not be the only one committing adultery?'

'I don't think so. I've never seen any evidence. I think that he doesn't – well, he's just not very lascivious. I wondered about it, but I wasn't certain until you showed me something different.'

167

'Because I am?' I laughed. 'Oh, yes, with you I'm very lascivious.'

'What a coincidence! I'm only lascivious with you.'

We spent some time demonstrating most magnificently how lascivious we were with each other, and then she said, 'It's your turn. Should I be jealous?'

'Are you sure you want to know?'

'Yes. How many women have you made love with?'

'I've *made love* with only one woman in my life, and I've just made love with her, and I'll make love with her again as soon as I get my lasciviousness back. But I've *fornicated* with six others.' She didn't say anything. 'Do you mind them?'

'A little. It's more lascivious of you than I'd have liked. Do you have any children?'

'I don't know.'

'You don't know?'

'Sometimes a woman was to be sold away from the plantation, perhaps so far away that she'd never see her friends or family again. And some of those women – five of them, in fact – came to me before they had to leave, and said it was their last chance with me, or would I cheer them up, or something like that. I was the chief slave for seven years: that was my attraction. Well, it would be ungentlemanly to refuse, wouldn't it? It almost became part of the ritual of being sold; she'd pack her belongings, she'd get into my bed, she'd say farewell to her family, and she'd be gone. I have no idea whether those unions bore fruit.'

'Five times in seven years? That isn't very lascivious at all.'

'Five nights, rather: I can be very lascivious in the right circumstances.'

'Why only those women?'

I wished she hadn't asked that question. I sat up: there seemed to be a chill draught on my back that hadn't been there before.

'Surely not just so that you wouldn't have to look after any children?'

I couldn't let her think that. 'It was – well, it was because they were the only women that I wouldn't be ordered to whip one day. I said I was chief slave because I was trying to soften it for you. I was the slave-driver: whipping was part of my duties. I did it because if I didn't then someone else would do it worse, and I'd get whipped too. And with whipping it's much better to give than to receive.'

She was silent for a moment. 'That's rather horrible, isn't it?'

'Yes, it is.'

'I wasn't shocked by the scars on your back; I've been an Abolitionist long enough to know what happens. But to know that you did it—'

'Althea, please try not to hold it against me. I—'

'Oh, God, Joshua!' She knelt up and pulled me to her, my face between her beautiful breasts. 'Don't ever think that I could. I know what that must have done to you; how much you hated it. You don't have to tell me.'

I stayed there gaining comfort from her, then I moved so she could see my face. 'I'm glad you don't hold that against me. Much better that you hold these against me,' I said, cupping her breasts in my hands.

'That's one of the things I love about you, Joshua: the way you laugh at things that ought to make you weep.'

'Why weep about things if you can manage to laugh at them?'

'Do you mind talking about it? What you had to do? What you had done to you?'

'I don't mind here, now, with you.'

'Did you ever have to—? Oh, the sixth woman.'

'The first, rather.' I stopped stroking her and wrapped my arms around my knees: to caress one woman while talking about another seemed like disloyalty to both of them. 'I learnt my lesson after that. I'd just been made driver, so I hadn't yet learnt how to make it look worse than it was. I didn't love her, but I cared for her and I admired her. There'd been an outbreak of smallpox; she and I stayed to look after the sick – it was comfort we sought together as much as anything else. She was a fine woman. She still is, I hope. She chose my friend Olakunde after me; she was the woman he tried to escape with.' I'd told Althea the story.

169

'You helped them for her sake as well as his?'

'Yes, but mainly I helped them because they reminded me of us. There's no need for you to feel any jealousy about Sarah: I'd never have stopped loving you. But I'll admit that, perhaps, in time, with her I could have become reconciled to losing you. I don't know. I'll never know – I wasn't given the chance. When the order came, Sarah insisted that I carry it out rather than refuse and have us both whipped worse by our owner, but that was the end of anything between us. To have to do that to a body that I'd known in such another way – it was the only time that it wasn't better to give than receive.'

Althea began to blink. I put my hand to her cheek to wipe away her tears for my pain that caused me even more pain. 'My love, don't feel sorry for me. In some ways your lot is worse than mine. My tribulation lasted ten years and it's over now, but you'll never get your hearing back.'

'You're feeling sorry for me now, and soon we'll start feeling sorry for ourselves, and that's even worse.' She sniffed. 'There must be something better we can do.' We kissed and caressed each other, but too many memories had revived for me to be lascivious so soon after the last time. She stroked me gently: 'Oh, well, if you can't make love, make tea.'

I did so, and we sat in front of the hearth drinking it. 'See,' I said ruefully as I set my cup down so I could hold her again. 'I'm afraid it's not true what they say about black men.'

'Well, I don't know,' she said, apparently deep in thought. 'On the evidence of my admittedly limited experience – one black and one white – I would say that it is. Though I'd better not say so in public.'

I felt more jolly. I kissed the freckles on her nose, then her cheeks, and worked my way round to her ear. 'I wish you could,' I said, and sat back so she could see my lips. 'It would save me some embarrassment if only it was possible for you to tell people. And who Luke's father is, come to think about it.'

'That's an odd combination of secrets. Why?'

'You wouldn't believe the number of women who – er – want

to find the answer to those two questions in my bed. It's hard to be chaste – spelt "-te" – when you're chased – spelt "-ed".'

She burst out laughing. I was surprised: it was a very feeble joke. 'Oh, I love you, Joshua! You really don't know, do you?'

'What?'

'Women don't chase you out of curiosity. And if black women on the plantation are anything like Englishwomen in society, they didn't chase you because of your authority.' She put her finger to my chest. 'Women chase you because you're a very attractive man.'

'I hate to disillusion you about such an important matter.' I brought her finger to my lips and kissed the tip. 'But I think that you might be a little bit prejudiced in my favour.'

'No, I'm not. Well, of course I am, but that's beside the point. Have you noticed how women's heads turn towards you when you follow Mr Fitzjames into the room?'

'Yes, but surely—'

'I'll wager you think that they're all looking at him, don't you?'

'You mean – me?' I sat back in surprise.

She patted my thigh. 'One of the things we ladies discuss with much animation when we leave the gentlemen alone with the port is whether we'd prefer to be shipwrecked on an uninhabited island with you or Mr Fitzjames. Robinson Crusoe is in the lead, but that's only because there are many who can recommend him. I'll have to keep quiet about Man Friday's talent, but I might have a discreet chuckle to myself next time the other ladies speculate about it.'

'You know, you're not a very respectable woman, Lady Verity.'

She nodded. 'I'm sitting here stark naked in the embrace of an equally naked black servingman while my husband is out fishing, and you've worked out that I'm not a respectable woman. There's no hiding things from you, is there?'

'I'm quick like that.'

'I wonder.' She was suddenly mischievous. 'Joshua, why did we run away together?'

'Absent-minded, ageing Althea,' I said, stroking her forehead. 'Getting so old that she's losing her memory.'

'Go on, tell me why you think we did it.'

'Well, it was to save Pompey, and to stop me being sold, and so you wouldn't have to be the Mountfords' ward and be forced to marry George.'

'Nothing to do with being in love with each other?'

'Not when we started out. It was only at the inn, when you woke up and saw me by your bedside that we realized it.'

'I thought so,' she said, laughing. 'The best part of eleven years, and it hasn't dawned on you. There might have been other ways to do all those things, but it was the only way that I could think of to marry you.'

'What? Oh, that's abominable, Althea!'

'Yes, but very amorous.'

'Artful – and appalling – and atrocious – and – and—'

'Angry-making?'

'No.' I held her close and spoke in her ear while she shook with laughter in my arms. 'Amazing – and amusing – and attractive – and—' because laughter renewed my lasciviousness when tears had not '—above all, Althea, absolutely and astonishingly arousing!'

It was last thing at night on the thirty-first of August. 'Well, Josh, you can walk out with a clear conscience tomorrow,' Luke said. 'I hope you'll stay, but you don't have to.'

'I'll stay while we're here. After we get back to London – well, I don't know.'

'Even though you're now obliged by Royal Proclamation to "disclose and make known all treasons and traitorous conspiracies"?'

'What's that?'

He laughed. 'For once I know more about British politics than you do!' I'd had other matters on my mind. 'King goddamn George has just issued a decree commanding all loyal citizens to denounce anyone who supports the American rebellion. You have to choose between me and your country.'

'I don't have a country.'

'I thought you were English?'

'I grew up in England – perhaps I was born here, I don't know. It's made me a free man. But it also enslaved me in the first place; it still has the biggest slaving fleet in the world; its prosperity is built on black backs. Between England and you? Well, I'm not choosing England.'

He patted me on the shoulder. 'Thanks, Josh. I knew I could trust you not to betray me.' *Not in that way, no.* 'You like it here, don't you?'

'A lot more than I liked it in America.'

'No, I meant right here, staying in Galbury Hall.'

'I like it very much indeed.'

'I can see the difference in you. You seem – freer.'

'I feel freer.'

'It's her, isn't it? Lady Verity.'

'What do you mean?' I asked cautiously.

'You know what you said on the first morning we were here, about her purity extending to her household? It does, doesn't it? Everything about the place seems fresh and stainless.'

That day, she had done things to me that would have had a whore thrown out of a brothel for obscenity, and laughed triumphantly at her power to reduce me to helpless pleading ecstasy. 'It's certainly a pleasant place,' I said, 'and I agree that she has much to do with it.'

'You feel it, I feel it – Josh, I haven't gone into town to find a good brothel, and nor have I humped a housemaid.'

'Well done.'

'The servants look so much healthier than in London. Even Sir Bertrand's voice doesn't sound too bad in the open air, especially when I've just had a gun blasting in my ear. She's—'

'Ear plugs,' I said, grabbing the chance to divert the conversation into channels that caused me less guilt. 'You should have your ears covered when you go shooting. Very loud sounds can make you go deaf.'

'I'd look strange.'

'Better to look strange than lose your hearing.'

'She seems happy.'

Something snapped in me. 'How dare you say that? That's as stupid and wicked as saying that slaves are happy! I bet you thought I was happy as your father's driver. If you knew how much it costs her to seem happy, to manage in a world where hardly anyone gives her any consideration, how much joy it gives her to find a miserable scrap more hearing than she thought she had—' I forced myself to be quiet before I betrayed myself further.

'All I said was that she seemed happy. Why are you so angry about it?'

'Well, I do know how much it costs her,' I said more calmly. 'I know how hard she and Fiona worked to stop her being shut off from other people. Her husband is one of the very few who'll take the trouble to ensure she can understand him; he's much better than you are, Luke. But what about the people who can't afford someone like Fiona as a governess? They can't hear, they can't understand, they're lucky if they've learnt to speak. That's why I want to learn how to help them. If I had to choose between being a slave with my hearing or free and deaf, I'd think long and hard before I made up my mind.'

'I'm sorry; I didn't understand. All the same, she does seem happy. No, she seems more than happy; it's as though she's the sun and she's spreading the light of happiness around to us all. She's been getting more beautiful with every day since we arrived; haven't you noticed?'

I had indeed, but I'd thought it was only in my eyes. I must warn her to be a little less radiant. 'Must be the fresh country air and exercise.'

'What does she do when she goes to her barn, Josh?'

'It's her private place. I don't think she'd want me to tell you.'

'Sometimes I've been tempted to go in and see her. Only today Sir Bertrand and I were passing and we heard her laugh. I

174

wondered what gave her such pleasure, but he said that she wouldn't like it if we called unexpectedly.'

There are advantages in a black skin, or he'd have seen the blood rush into my face as I recalled what had made her laugh; it had given me a lot of pleasure, too. To think that Luke and her husband were so close they could hear her, so near to coming in— We'd have had no warning before they knocked on the door, because she wouldn't have heard them and I'd been somewhat preoccupied. The blood rushed out of my face as I pictured what could have happened.

After that we were more careful: the rest of the world wasn't as shut out as we'd thought. But nothing could stop her looking beautiful.

At dinner one evening, Sir Bertrand said, 'My dear, I'm afraid I have some news for you that you'll find rather disagreeable.'

'What is it, Bertrand?'

'Your cousin George has invited himself and Charlotte to stay for a few days.'

'Oh, no!' she groaned. 'When's he coming?'

'This Friday.' He turned to Luke. 'As you can tell, George Mountford is not a favourite with my wife.'

'I confess that he's not much of a favourite with me, Sir Bertrand. Would it be easier for you if I left?'

'No!' she cried. 'Above all, don't desert us. In fact, I'll invite as many visitors and guests as possible to dilute the poison.'

'We'll take him out shooting as much as we can.'

'Don't bring him back.'

For the next few days, both she and I were too busy to go for a walk, as in our separate ways we made the preparations for a lot of visitors; she sent invitations to people who were surprised and honoured to receive such flattering attentions from Sir Bertrand and Lady Verity, even at short notice, while I helped the rest of the staff with cleaning and polishing.

But the morning before Mountford and his wife arrived, Althea had had enough. 'Bertrand, I'm going for a walk. I'll need as much fresh air as possible to get through the next few days.'

'Even in paradise there was a serpent,' I said when we arrived at the barn.

'I could never be tempted by George to eat an apple. Every time I see Charlotte I think, "That could have been me", and I'm very kind to her.'

'Is there anything I can do to help?'

'Stay out of his way as much as you can, and wear that silly wig. He might recognize you if he sees you in my company.'

'He hasn't recognized me so far, and he's seen me close up without a wig.'

She put her head on one side. 'Have you been up to something with him by way of taking your revenge?'

'Yes.'

'And you didn't ask me? I'm rather put out about that.'

'I suggested it, but Luke flatly refused. He called you an angel.'

She almost wept with laughter. 'Is he in love with me?'

'His secret, not mine.'

'I think he is. Would it hurt him to know about us?'

'I can't think of anything that would hurt him more.'

She sighed. 'We bring our own serpents into paradise, don't we?'

Perhaps it was our lovemaking just before Mountford arrived and the knowledge of how much it would infuriate him if he knew about it, but something cheered her up. She was almost civil to him, and she took Charlotte off for a good cosy gossip as soon as she could.

I was kept busy for the next few days, as were all the servants at the Hall, since it was full to the roof all the time. Shooting parties were arranged every day, which meant that Althea didn't have to endure Mountford's company except in the evenings, and his wife didn't have to spend all day watching to ensure she had his approval; I even heard her laugh once.

Luke was a great success with the visitors. He was liked in any company, and these farmers and their families were the closest he'd met in England to his own kind. English farmers don't keep slaves – though the life of a farm labourer isn't much better – but they have the same concerns as a rice planter about pests, weather and prices. I overheard him giving some very sound advice to a farming couple lamenting the activities of their wastrel son.

My only concern was that he let his guard slip. He'd been very controlled when he was the only guest – after all, you can't go moon-eyed over a woman while her husband is by your side. But here, where there were plenty of other people to attract Sir Bertrand's attention, I sometimes saw him looking at her with a worshipful expression that made me feel slightly ill.

Finally it was time for Mountford to go. Althea and Sir Bertrand saw him and Charlotte into their carriage to go back to London. 'Thank you for your hospitality, Sir Bertrand. It has all been most agreeable.'

'Not at all, not at all. We've had some fine days' shooting, eh?'

'Althea, I shall let you return to your country pleasures. They seem to be doing you good.'

'Thank you, George. My country pleasures are doing me a great deal of good. All this exercise, you know.' I saw the slight twitch of a smile – she had no objection to laughing at George. I hoped that he didn't see it too.

There was a feeling of relief over the whole household. The servants didn't have to work so hard, and at dinner Luke and the Veritys were in high good humour. A footman came in, bearing an important and official-looking letter.

'Wonder what it is,' Sir Bertrand said as he opened it. It obviously gave him great pleasure. 'My dear!' he cried, and if they didn't hear him in the Royal Oak they were having a very noisy time. 'What an honour! Read it for yourself!'

She took it, and for a moment there was a flash of dismay in her face, but her husband was too excited to notice it; I hoped Luke didn't. 'Oh, such splendid news, Bertrand! May I share our good fortune with our guest?' She turned to Luke. 'Bertrand has just been appointed as Under Secretary for the American Colonies!'

Luke expressed his congratulations. 'Well done, Sir Bertrand. I'm sure you'll treat those American rebels just as they deserve. If you are the Under Secretary, may I ask who the Secretary is?'

'Lord George Sackville Germain; his is a new appointment too.' He frowned. 'The only thing I regret is that I must go to London; I'm afraid this is the end of your visit, Fitzjames.'

'Oh, of course. I wouldn't dream of standing in your way, believe me. The sooner the American colonies are in your hands, the better that suits me.'

'My dear, will you stay here, or will you accompany me?'

'Of course I'll go with you, Bertrand. I wouldn't miss your triumph. When must we go?'

Sir Bertrand rubbed his chin. 'Well, I suppose we should set out tomorrow. But I confess that I was looking forward to another day's shooting in peace now our visitors have gone.'

'Do you think that the American colonies can wait another day for your attention, Bertrand?'

'I think they can. We'll start out first thing the day after tomorrow.'

So, this was the end. I must be grateful that we'd be allowed one last day together in our small private world. London would not allow such meetings.

Luke was suppressing whoops of delight as I readied him for bed that night. 'With him as the Under Secretary, our independence is assured! Didn't you admire my sincere congratulations? I'll be sorry to leave here, but the sacrifice is all worth while.'

'You're right to celebrate, but for the wrong reason. Sir Bertrand's a fool, but Britain can manage perfectly well with fools in command – it's used to it. The man who should really make you happy is the Secretary, Sackville Germain. He's the best news you could wish for.'

'Why? Do you know him?'

'I know of him; everyone in England knows of him. But I've never seen him, because Lord and Lady Mountford wouldn't have him in the house when I was a page. Imagine the dishonourable George in thirty years time, with an infamous reputation for cowardice on top of that.'

'What did he do?'

'The Battle of Minden, nearly twenty years ago. He was in command of the cavalry. The infantry had taken fierce fighting, but they'd succeeded in breaking French lines. He was given a direct order to lead the charge to finish the French off, repeated several times. Not only did he refuse to charge himself, but he also stopped his second-in-command from doing so. It was a scandal – cowardice in the face of the enemy of the worst sort. He was court-martialled and disgraced.'

'Then why has he been appointed Secretary?'

'I've no idea. It must be that he has good connections – he's the son of a duke. Perhaps a few bribes smoothed his path. But if that's the sort of man the British government sees fit to put in charge of the action against the Americans, then you've won your fight already.'

We made love slowly and sweetly. The poignancy of knowing that it was our last time here, and perhaps for ever, made it beautiful and memorable; we might have to remember it for the rest of our lives.

Afterwards she rested on my body, and I held her in silence, not wanting to let her go, ever, but knowing that I'd have to. Her ear was so close to my mouth that she could hear me without needing to read my lips.

'Joshua, I only want to make love with you.'

'I'm glad to hear it.'

'No, you shouldn't be. I mean that I won't be satisfied with anything less. We shan't be able to do this in London; it would be a sneaky, nasty thing, not like we've had here. Do you mind?'

'I love you. I want what's best for you. You know that.'

'Yes, I do, which is why I can ask you. If we do it again, it must be no secret.'

I didn't say anything.

'Are you asking something like *when*, Joshua? Because you should speak up if you are.'

'I'm not asking.'

She sat up and looked at my face. 'Why not?'

'Because I would be asking you to leave all your fortune and your husband who treats you well to come and live in poverty with me and face the filth that would be thrown at you. I can't ask you to do that. But you only have to lift your finger to ask me.'

'I – I'm not lifting my finger. I don't know if I ever shall. It's not the poverty I mind. But to hurt Bertrand – to face the filth – I'm sorry, but I'm a coward.'

'Althea, you're the bravest woman I've ever known, and I'd believe that even if I didn't love you so much.'

'There's something I must find out; perhaps I'll lift my finger when I know the answer.'

Again I said nothing.

'You don't ask what it is?'

'If you want me to know, you'll tell me. I won't distress you by asking.'

'Oh, Joshua, you're the kindest man I've ever known, and I'd believe that even if I didn't love you so much.'

'I love you; of course I want to be kind to you.'

'You didn't love me when I was sobbing so bitterly for the loss of my parents and my hearing. Lots of people must have heard me, but you were the only one who came in and tried to help. You didn't love Janet's best friend when she had a thorn in her foot and you made her laugh while you drew it out.'

'I don't like to see people suffering.'

'I know, and that's why it was so wicked to make you a slave-driver. Did any of the other slave-drivers refuse to take their pleasure with women they might have to whip?'

'No. Some of them even used the threat of the whip to force the women.'

'You came through seven years of that with your kindness still whole. If I didn't love you already, I'd fall in love with you all

180

over again.' She bent over me and kissed me; I didn't protest.

'I had an idea last night,' I said when she let go of me. 'It's nothing to do with us, except that it might make me feel a little less guilty about cuckolding your husband. It's such a good idea that someone else is bound to think of it sooner or later, and I'd like him to get the credit for it now he's Under Secretary.'

'What is it?'

'If the British in America issued a proclamation offering freedom to any slave who ran away from his owner and joined the British Army, they'd gain a lot of recruits very cheaply.'

'I'll suggest it to him in such a way that he thinks he's had the idea himself – that's one of the first skills that a wife has to learn.'

'And it'll give a lot of slaves a chance of freedom, which is something I care about far more than which side wins the war.'

'I'll be serving my country, my husband, and the cause of freeing the slaves, which will make me feel much more virtuous than I've done for some time.'

'Do you feel guilty? No, that's a bad question; of course you feel guilty. But is it so much guilt that, later on, you're going to regret what we've done?'

'No. I'll never regret what we've done. I would if we did it furtively, as we'd have to do in London.'

'You don't think this is furtive?' It had seemed furtive enough to me.

'Not really. We've walked out together openly; we've come back often arm in arm. Why don't people suspect us? They would if I did that with someone like Luke Fitzjames; perhaps even with an English manservant unless he was sixty and half-witted. But it's literally unthinkable to them that someone like me could love someone like you.'

'You and I – we have to shift around and find space in a world made for people with white skins and good ears. They've left us a small space, and we've used it.'

'We've used it well.' She kissed me, and it had its effect on my body. 'Do you want to make love again?'

'No. That wouldn't be making love. It'd be indulging my lust.

Leave me with the memory of the last time; it may have to satisfy me for the rest of my life, so I'd prefer it to be a good one.'

'I love you so much, Joshua; you're such a lovable man.'

'Now, stop kissing me or you'll make me change my mind – and I would regret that.'

We dressed, and tidied the place so that there were no signs of us. We stood together by the door, unwilling to open it and go back to the world.

I held her hands in both of mine, perhaps for the last time. 'Before we leave, my love, there's something I must tell you. You will decide whether to stay with your husband or come with me. It'll be a hard decision for you, and I shan't reproach you if you choose him. But so you don't feel guilty about hurting me, I want you to know that if I have your love, and he has everything else of you except your love, then I wouldn't change places with him, not with his baronetcy and his Under Secretaryship thrown in.'

'Joshua, I'll love you forever.'

'I'll love you forever too, Althea.'

Chapter 12

'ARE you staying, Josh?' Luke asked once we were back in Bond Street.

'For the moment. I might have to give you very short notice – perhaps just pack my bags and leave a note – but if that's all right by you, I'll stay.'

'I'm glad. Are you going to follow me when I pursue the lusts of the flesh?'

'No. Get your throat cut by all means. But tell me so I don't worry.'

'I'll start now. I'm going to Covent Garden to see how many whores I can hump in one night. Purity is all very well, but pleasure has its attractions.'

He was brought home in a sedan chair in the middle of next morning; he could barely walk up the stairs, and he fell into bed with only the energy to gasp, 'Six, Josh, six!' before he was asleep.

I left him in peace and wondered at the difference between us. Now I knew the incomparable difference between indulging lust and making love, it would be Althea or nobody. That wasn't a vow of eternal fidelity; it was a prediction – I wouldn't enjoy it with anyone else. I'd been tempted before, but I wouldn't be so again. What he'd done seemed as stupid to me as taking pride in being able to piss six times in one night. I had enough male vanity to have been very pleased with myself when I'd managed three times in a couple of hours, but she'd had just as much pleasure as I had – we could match his total between us. He was right that there was a difference between lust and love, but he was wrong to think that you couldn't feel them for the same woman. I did, and I wouldn't have changed places with him either, even if he had been a duke's bastard with a gold mine.

'Now I've satisfied the needs of the flesh,' he said when he woke up, 'I'm going to satisfy the needs of the spirit. Let's go and visit the Macleods; they should all have recovered from the measles by now.'

Fiona was almost as good as Althea at wringing the truth out of me; I wouldn't hold out for five minutes. 'I don't think I'll go, Luke,' I said, trying to find a plausible excuse without success.

'Why not? Hey, you're looking guilty. What have you done?' He wagged his finger at me in mock reproof. 'You haven't followed your godmother's spiritual advice, have you?' He was no mean wringer himself. 'Now, which line of the Lord's Prayer didn't you follow? Let me think – it's the only bit of the Bible I remember; Pa beat it into me when I was very young. "Our Father which art in heaven. Hallowed be thy name—" '

'That's the one; you guessed it. I haven't hallowed His name. It's a bad thing for a good Christian woman to be godmother to an unbeliever, and I'm rather embarrassed about it. You go, and give my love to everyone, and find some excuse for me, will you? You're a much better liar than I am.'

'You're a strange man. You don't believe in God, yet you know the Bible backwards and you live like a monk. Now I do believe in God, yet the only reason I haven't committed sloth is because I've been too busy with the other six sins.'

'We're different. Leave it at that.'

'Oh, all right. I'll go and lie to your godmother for you. Josh, I wouldn't have your conscience for a gold mine. It must make life very difficult for you.'

'It does. Believe me, it does.'

Sir Bertrand and Lady Verity requested the pleasure of Mr Luke

Fitzjames's company at a dinner to mark his appointment as Under Secretary of the American Colonies.

'Sounds good, Josh. With luck, Sackville Germain will be there. Just watch me butter him up! You never know what hints he'll drop over the port.'

Perhaps I should have made an excuse not to go, but I did want to see her again. It would be a strain, with guilt and memory added to what had been a strain before, but I could hide it, and I had no doubt that she could too.

She did, of course; she was the perfect hostess in her new part as wife of an Under Secretary. I overheard comments like, 'She's deaf, you know, but you wouldn't guess, would you? Isn't she marvellous?' The only sign she gave – and I doubted that anyone else noticed – was when she expressed a shade too genuine a regret to Luke over the sudden end to his visit to Galbury Hall. Lady Mountford watched her far more closely than I did, and occasionally sent a glance in my direction too, but I was confident that neither of us revealed more than there should have been. Unfortunately, family civility also dictated that George Mountford was invited, which was a trial to several of us present.

Luke made himself agreeable to Sackville Germain; he was fully prepared to have his advice asked about the Americans and their new General Washington. He picked up a lot of useful information, and gave it too; his was so useful, indeed, that it could have been discovered in any newspaper or book of reference.

'Delighted to have Sir Bertrand with me!' said Sackville Germain at one point. 'Sound man. Came up with a damned good idea. If we promise freedom to any slave who runs away from his rebel master and joins the British army, we'll have a whole regiment of niggers on our side! Won't have to pay 'em a penny beyond their keep, and they'll fight like the devil for us. Good notion, what?'

'Sir Bertrand's idea, ha!' said Luke when we got home. 'His wife's, I'll bet. Maybe he even thinks it's his idea.'

'I wouldn't be surprised.'

'She's the perfect wife, isn't she? Beautiful, charming, giving him ideas and letting him think they're his own— What a woman!'

'It gives me some amusement, the notion of slave owners fighting for liberty and the tyrants offering freedom,' I said before he could start to praise her fidelity. 'I've decided: I hope the British win.'

'No!' he cried, as outraged as if I'd made an immoral suggestion about his mother. 'You heard Sackville Germain; he has no interest in freeing the slaves for their own sake. It just happens to suit British interests at the moment.'

'Yes, but it does suit British interests. And I'm a free man in this country.'

'Josh, I know that slavery's a problem. But it's a problem that Americans must solve, not the British.'

'Do you think that the likes of your father will ever get round to solving it unless they're forced to?'

'Their sons might. My father's son will try. You know what you've done to me, you rat? You've turned me into an Abolitionist, and that's a wicked thing to do to a South Carolina man.'

A letter came from Lady Mountford; it was addressed to *Mr* Fortescue.

> I have made enquiries about your parentage and birth, as I believe you have a right to know such matters. Unfortunately, so many years later, the records have gone. All I have is the enclosed document. Please accept it in the spirit with which it is sent, as a token of our mutual forgiveness.

The yellowing sheet of paper was a receipt for the purchase, about twenty years before, of a Negro Boy, for the sum of Five Pounds. I could have felt chagrin at such a low price, but when

I looked at the signature of the seller, I realized that this was a family rate, paid by Lady Mountford to her brother-in-law, Mr Charles Freeman of Bristol. Althea's father.

Sometimes I wish I believed in an afterlife, so that he could know what his daughter had done, and that he'd brought us together. One day I would visit his grave just to hear the sound of him turning in it.

A few days later I accompanied Luke to an engagement, but I knew I would not be accompanying him home as soon as I saw how well he was getting on with a comely lady in her mid thirties whose husband was already snoring on the sofa. Luke barely needed to wink at me. I set off home out of the servants' door.

I don't remember anything after that.

Head; viciously aching head. There was nothing else in the world apart from my headache for a few moments, and then I became aware of a blanket. I was lying on it. Beneath that, a hard stone floor.

What had happened between the servants' door and here? There was no trace of a memory. And where was here? That could be answered better if I knew more of the place than the blanket and the floor. Groaning slightly, I turned over.

'Fortescue, there is a pistol aimed straight at your belly.' Those were not the words I wanted to hear. Nor was the voice: George Mountford's.

'There is a bottle of water on your left if you want to drink. There is a bucket on your right if you want to vomit. If you move farther off the blanket than you need to get those, I shall shoot you in the belly and leave you to die in agony.'

I didn't move; I wanted my head to clear before I did anything. I was wearing nothing but my shirt; I was already stiff and cold from lying on the floor with only the blanket beneath me. I was in a small stone room with very little in it. Mountford was sitting on a three-legged stool, and there was a table beside him; I couldn't see what was on it from this angle. Apart from the bottle, the blanket and the bucket, that was all. I was tempted to use the bucket, but I didn't know when I'd next get any food to replace it, so I fought down my nausea and took a swallow from the bottle. Then I sat up, looking as cowed and abject as possible; ten years on the plantation had given me a lot of practice.

'Fortescue, it is very important that you understand me. If you have any questions, ask them, and I may answer. If you are still dazed from the blow to your head, I shall wait until you recover.'

'Why am I here?'

'A good start. You are here because I want you to write a statement describing the adulterous relationship between your master and Lady Verity.'

'That's a lie.'

'I expected you to say that. I have patience. I'll wait until you're ready to write it – perhaps.'

'I shan't do it.'

'You prefer to die rather than betray your master? How touching. I might even believe you. You fought off four men to defend him rather than run away; it was you I wanted, not him, but you didn't know that. The threat of slavery is one that you fear far more. So, Fortescue, one of these days – it may be tomorrow, or it may be in a month – I shall arrive with enough men to take you in chains to that slaving captain we discussed last time.'

I began to despair. If he'd chosen any other woman but Althea – and there were plenty to choose from – I might have given in to his threat. I no longer needed to pretend to be abject and cowed. 'Why do you want me to do this?'

'He has a hold on me; I have a hold on him. I want one more hold to give me the advantage. I'm not a fool, Fortescue; I know the signs of a man besotted with a woman – and I know the signs of a woman who's getting a thoroughly good humping, too. He will not want your statement to be made public.'

'It's not true. There isn't anything between them.' He ignored me; he had decided that there was, and he had good reason, as I

188

knew all too well. It would be easy for me to create a lying statement that would convince Mountford; even though it was untrue, Luke wouldn't want it to be made public.

'You'll be a tougher nut to crack than I expected after you gibbered in fear and betrayed him last time; I didn't expect you to stand and fight for him. That's why I prepared this place. You won't escape from it; I've had two acquaintances test it for a wager, and they couldn't get out between them. It is possible that you will find a way to kill yourself; I've tried to remove all ways of doing so, but you may be more desperate than I. In that case, I shall forge a statement from you; I have a copy of your signature. I shall also forge it on the day my patience runs out and I decide to sell you to recover the expense of preparing this prison for you.'

'Where are we?' I asked, not expecting an answer.

'On my property, in a very lonely spot; nobody will hear you call for help. And in the unlikely event that someone passes, they will know better than to come to your aid.' He stood up. 'On this table is bread, paper, pen and ink. You have enough food and water to last until I return. It will not be comfortable for you, but you know far better than I do that it is much more comfortable than the hold of a slaving ship.' He backed towards the door, still pointing the pistol at me, and opened it behind him. I caught a glimpse of trees outside. 'I bid you good day, Fortescue. Perhaps next time I shall come with the slavers; perhaps not.'

I sat and listened to him leave to gain any more clues about outside; a key being turned, two depressingly loud beams drawn across the door, a man getting on a horse, and receding hoofbeats on what sounded like forest floor. When I thought he couldn't hear me, I stood up and swore, long and loudly, and then I began to think.

What were my choices? Slavery: I'd rather die. Betraying Althea: again I'd rather die, though if it had only been Luke I was betraying I'd have considered it. Escape, then: I had no reason to trust Mountford's word that I couldn't.

There were no guards, and I wondered why until I realized

that there was nobody he could trust that much. Hiring a set of footpads to set upon someone was one thing, but guarding a prisoner was a different matter – especially a prisoner whom he believed to be the valued servant of an unimaginably wealthy man who could offer an enormous bribe.

I spent the rest of the light exploring my prison, yelling when there was a sound outside, but I got no help from the birds or rabbits that had caused it. The walls of its single room were solid stone; there were signs of fresh mortar. The slabs of the floor were newly laid; I guessed it had been an earth floor which I might have dug my way out of, given time and fingernails enough. Once there had been a fireplace, but it was bricked over. The window had no glass, and four iron bars were newly set in place; outside I could see nothing but oak woodland. The door was heavy timber, and I could see marks of someone's failed attempts to break it down – he'd probably told the truth about having had it tested.

The roof was made up of wooden planks laid side by side, and seemed to hold promise, despite more marks of failure. I stood on the table, and pushed with all my strength against one of the planks, but he must have weighted it down in some way from outside. The only result of my effort was that the table collapsed beneath me and I fell down cursing; I was lucky to escape with only bruises. I pulled a leg off the table to use as a tool and tried again, but with only the stool or the floor to stand on, all I did was add more dents in the wooden planks above me.

Inside there was bread and water enough for two days; three if he didn't mind me going without for the third. The bottle and the bucket were both of tough leather; no sharp edges or tools for digging and scraping. There was an ink bottle, a quill pen, and three sheets of paper. No matter how hard I tried, I couldn't think of a use for them besides writing with, and nor could I see much help in the blanket apart from keeping me warm – it wasn't as though I needed to tear it into strips and climb out, since I was at ground level anyway. The table and stool were jointed and glued; no convenient nails. There was no lamp or means of lighting a flame; I'd be in the dark half the time.

Once dusk fell, I took a portion of bread and another swallow of water, moved the bucket to the far corner and pissed in it, then sat down on the stool. I began to feel very gloomy; I could see no way of escape. I couldn't even see a way of killing myself, other than to tear my shirt into strips to make a small rope to tie round the bar of the window, jump off the stool, and hope I had resolution enough not to pull myself up again before I passed out. If I'd been imprisoned for years, I might have been able to wear away the mortar, but how much time did I have? A month?

It was possible that Luke might find me. He would probably assume that I'd been taken rather than left him voluntarily; I'd said I'd leave him a note. He'd certainly pick Mountford as the likely kidnapper. But then what? Mountford had plenty of time to think of this; he would take precautions against Luke trying to throttle the information out of him. But I had just enough hope not to kill myself today; I'd leave it until the last moment I dared. I didn't think that Mountford would bring the slavers next time; he would put more pressure on me first. Besides, I might find a better way than slowly strangling myself.

There are few things so depressing as sitting in the dark trying to think of ways of killing yourself. I was good at cheering myself up in the depths of tribulation: I'd had ten years of practice. So I made love to Althea in my mind, which helped a lot, and then I stood by the window watching what I could of the woodland night, occasionally stretching my legs by walking round the room in the dark until I felt tired enough to sleep. I folded the blanket in two, wrapped it round me leaving my legs sticking out, and put my head on the three sheets of paper as a pillow. I will not break under his pressure, I thought. I have endured far worse than this for far longer. Althea comforted me until I fell asleep.

I woke up, discovering that there was one way in which this imprisonment was worse than South Carolina: one lowering, spirit-sapping way – it was cold. One blanket, one shirt and three pieces of paper don't do much to keep out the chill of a stone floor on an autumn night. I walked around to try to get the ice out of my bones; it helped a little, but not much. I kept on walking, though I was tired and the pain in my head returned. I must not despair, I told myself. I shall not despair. But I couldn't help it. Even Althea couldn't cheer me; I thought of her grief at losing me a second time, and I couldn't bear it. I was nearly at the point of thinking that slowly strangling myself now might be preferable to waiting it out.

Then Fiona's voice in my head said, *Pray.* Why not? I thought. It couldn't do any harm. I might not believe in Him, but He might believe in me. I knelt down and recited the Lord's Prayer to start, then I said: 'Oh, Lord, Thou knowest that I am a sinner. I am a fornicator, and Thou knowest that I do not repent, and wish only to continue my fornication. But Thy mercy is infinite. Thou knowest that I would kill myself rather than be taken into slavery or betray my love. Please, Lord, show me a way to avoid the sin of self-murder.'

A voice – it might have been God's, but it sounded like Fiona's – said, *You are not afraid of death. Why fear his weapon?*

'Thank you Lord,' I said – Fiona wouldn't mind me giving Him the credit – and I stood up again and walked about the room. Mountford just could not threaten me with his pistol; it was no threat to a man who'd been thinking seriously of slow strangulation. So, next time he came, I would attack him. I would do my best to beat him and avoid the bullet, but if I couldn't, so be it. I'd prefer not to die slowly with a bullet in the belly, but it was worth the risk. All sorts of other things could happen: I might be killed more or less instantly, or I might merely be wounded, or he might even miss – I'd do my best to ensure that he did. Although I was contemplating the serious possibility of a slow and painful death, I felt very cheerful: the despair had gone. I might even be able to go back to sleep again; it would be a good idea to rest, and there was nothing I could do until dawn when I could see.

I lay down again, wrapping the blanket as much round me as I could. It didn't seem the right thing to contemplate fornication with Althea at that moment, so I recited the Bible, starting with Matthew Chapter 1, Verse 1.

The book of the generation of Jesus Christ, the son of David, the son of Abraham. Abraham begat Isaac; and Isaac begat Jacob; and Jacob begat Judas and his brethren; and Judas begat Phares and Zara of Thamar . . .

It didn't provide much in the way of spiritual sustenance, but it was a very good way to get off to sleep.

As soon as there was light to see I got up, ate, drank and used the bucket again, then surveyed my stock of armaments. The bottle or the bucket were favourite, if he ask me to fill one or empty the other. The ink bottle might do, if he wanted me to write. I might get close enough to the stool to pick it up and throw it. A table leg might serve as club, but it was so obvious that it was unlikely that he'd let me use it. I couldn't think of a way to use a loaf of bread, three sheets of paper, a quill pen, a shirt or a blanket in any way for which the opportunity might arise.

Then I practised movements; if he were standing *here* and wanted me to go *there*, I could pick up *this* and throw it *that* way. That gave me some useful exercise, and I celebrated with another drink of water. After that, I just sat and waited for more ideas to come to me.

I might be wounded and need a bandage, so I tore up my shirt, leaving only enough for a makeshift loincloth; I'd be colder tonight if he didn't come today. I might also need a splint, so I arranged the table legs to look like a futile attempt at attack rather than what they were really for; I also rearranged the bandages to look like an abandoned attempt at killing myself. Perhaps he would take his eyes off me for a moment to read something written on the paper, so I composed some scurrilous verses about him; not great poetry, but I enjoyed writing them.

Behold an English gentleman of birth!
He waits impatient till his father dies.
What mounts, what fords he'll own upon this earth.
Corrupt, corrupting, cowardly, unwise.

That was all I could think of, so I had nothing to do but wait, take some more exercise, eat some more bread, drink some more water, have another piss, and, on one momentous occasion, have a shit. It was not an exciting passage of time. However, it was endurable, which is more than the hold of a slave ship is.

I tried to get into George Mountford's mind. It was probably futile; on the plantation we'd never been able to guess what our owners were likely to do, but if you can't control your life, at least you want to understand it. I had no idea when he would return; if I had to make a wager, I would put it early tomorrow morning, after a second cold night on the stone, with my food and water exhausted or nearly so, and the bucket stinking and nearly overflowing.

One thing was sure; he still didn't recognize me as Caesar, even though I'd been in much the same position lying at his feet at the wharf in Liverpool. The other thing was that he'd made his first attack on me before he'd gone to Galbury Hall and seen those revealing – if misleading – looks on Althea's and Luke's faces. Perhaps he was simply searching for any hold on Luke; if he hadn't come up with that one, he'd have found something else.

I recited a lot of the Bible; this seemed appropriate. I tried not to think of a wound to the belly, and on the whole succeeded; I'd had plenty of practice at not thinking about pain ahead of me. I also tried not to think of Althea, in case God really did exist and would disapprove. This was much harder, since I'd spent ten years thinking of her as a way of not thinking about pain ahead. I compromised and recited the Song of Solomon.

Let him kiss me with the kisses of his mouth; for thy love is better than wine. Because of the savour of thy good ointments thy name is as ointment poured forth; therefore do the virgins love thee. Draw me; we will run after thee: the king hath brought me into his chambers: we will be glad and rejoice in thee, we will remember thy love more than of wine: the upright love thee.

I am black, but comely, O ye daughters of Jerusalem . . .

Chapter 13

DAWN of the third day. I rose, stretched, finished the last of the bread, didn't finish the water, filled the bucket almost to overflow, and knelt down to pray. 'Oh, Lord, I thank Thee for the blessings Thou hast given me in my life, particularly the one Thou most disapprovest of. If I die today I pray Thee to forgive my sins, even the one I don't repent. I beg for mercy on my soul, and if Thou couldst spare a little mercy for my body, I'd welcome it greatly.' I finished with the twenty-third psalm; the part about walking through the valley of the shadow of death seemed more likely to appeal to His taste than my feeble attempt.

Some more exercise to limber myself up, and another check round the room to see if there was anything more could do. I took the scurrilous verses, crumpled up the paper as if I'd written something and regretted it, and put it carefully in place so that if he asked me to pick it up and give it to him, I'd be in a good position to spring at him if he went where I most expected him to stand: close to the window so the light was shining from behind him and he could get fresh air. I also put the blanket there, in case there was a chance I could pull it from under his feet.

I was gratified to hear hoofbeats; I was right in my guess about when he'd come. There was a faint possibility that it wasn't him, so I yelled out of the window for help. I could feel my nerves and muscles in just the right state; jumpy and alert, but not panicking.

'Fortescue, there's no point in appealing for help from me,' came his voice from outside the door. 'Now, listen very carefully. You will place the blanket in the position in which it was when you regained consciousness. You will sit on it with your legs folded and your hands on your head. When you are ready, you will tell me, and I shall open the door. If you are not in that position, I shall close the door again and leave you without food and water for another day or so.'

I did what he commanded and took an abject position. 'I'm ready!'

The bolts were moved, the key was turned, the door opened slowly; he stood outside where he could see me, his pistol at the ready. Satisfied, he came in and surveyed me and the room. 'Pah!' he said, his nose wrinkling at the stench from the bucket. 'This room reeks of your nigger filth. And back to the savage state,' he said as he saw me clad only in a loincloth. He looked around at the wreck of the table and the remains of my shirt. 'No escape, as I said.' He took the position I expected him to; I was pleased, even though I'd had to move the blanket.

'Get rid of this stink first, Fortescue. You will stand up, you will pick up the bucket of your filth, you will go to the door and empty it outside on your left; don't throw it on the path where I'll have to walk in it. You may stand on the threshold for a moment if you wish, looking out at the freedom you can have for just one page of writing, but if you put one foot beyond the threshold I shall shoot you in the back and leave you to die.'

Thank you, Lord, Oh, thank you! This was the one I'd hoped for above all. Slowly I got to my feet, still looking abject, while I rehearsed in my mind what I'd do. When I got to the point closest to him, I'd hurl the contents of the bucket at his chest, jump one step sideways to spoil his aim, then run towards him and grab him by the throat. Hurl, jump, run, grab, I repeated as I went to the bucket, picked it up in the best position to throw, and started towards the door, conscious of his weapon pointing at my belly. Hurl, jump, run, grab. Lord, give me Thy mercy. One step more and I'd be there. Lord, help me.

Hurl! With all my strength I threw the filthy contents straight at him.

Jump! There was a flash, a bang, and an impact. Thank God, it's only my leg.

Run! I couldn't; I could only hobble, fighting the agony from the bullet wound. I don't have time to feel pain, Lord; give it back to me tenfold when I do.

Grab! He could have escaped me easily, but he was crying out with disgust at the filth that covered him, trying to brush off my shit from his chest; it gave me just enough time to fall towards him, my hands around his neck. My weight bore him down; he was fighting back, but I was much heavier and much more desperate. I battered his head on the stone floor, once, twice, three times; and then he was still.

And the Lord gave me back the pain tenfold. It was so agonizing that it went to my belly, and so did the enormous relief that I felt; I added my vomit to the rest of the filth that covered him.

Thank You, Lord, for Your mercy. I do not ask that You take away the pain, but please, give me strength to endure it so I can stop myself bleeding to death.

I crawled to the stool on two hands and one knee leaving a wide trail of blood. I dragged myself onto it, then wiped my hands clean of my filth with one of the bandages and some of the water I'd left. I examined the wound. On the outside of my upper thigh; a little one way and I'd have escaped, a little the other and it would have shattered the bone. It looked almost as ghastly as it felt: my flesh was torn and bleeding, but there was no bright red pulse that meant that I'd bleed to death in minutes. The pain was almost – but not quite – unendurable. I could survive this. Thank You, Lord. It could have been worse.

I put a pad on the wound and bandaged it on, then I drank the last of the water. I looked at Mountford where he lay in my filth; I could see his chest rise and fall. He was still alive.

Shall I kill him? I asked myself. There were plenty of precedents in the Old Testament for smiting the enemy. I literally had

him at my mercy: would I show it? If he recovered, he'd tell a
story far different from the truth: it would be his word against
mine, and I knew whose would be believed. He'd be no loss to
the world – even his wife wouldn't grieve for him. He was such
a scoundrel that only a mother could love him.

And his mother did. I remembered Lady Mountford and her
token of our mutual forgiveness. I remembered Althea's words:
'Do what you like to George, so long as it isn't anything that will
bring much grief to his mother.'

I remembered some other words: 'Joshua, you're the kindest
man I've ever known.' I didn't feel very kind towards the man
on the floor. He'd beaten me savagely while I was helpless, he'd
sold me into slavery, he'd taken me prisoner and threatened my
friend and my love, and he had given me the appalling pain I felt
now. Even apart from the wisdom of stopping him lying about
me, I had every reason to take my revenge on him. I had hated
him for ten years. But during those ten years I had done something far more important: I had loved Althea. I could not appear
before her as a murderer.

Lord, I shall show mercy. But please have mercy upon me, and
let me be believed when I tell the truth. Forgive me my tres-
passes, and I shall forgive him who has trespassed against me –
or at least I shan't kill him.

Using one of the table legs as a stick to support me, I stood up
and walked a few steps; the pain was bearable, which was the best
I could hope for. I went to Mountford and dragged him out of the
worst of the filth, then turned him on his side so he wouldn't choke
if he swallowed his tongue or vomited in his unconsciousness, and
put the blanket over him to keep him warmer.

Now to go and find help. I hobbled outside and looked
around. Oak woods in all directions; no way of telling which
way to go. Outside the door was a notice above Mountford's
signature: 'Savage madman. Keep away.' I looked at the roof to
see what had kept the planks on: it had been thatched over. But
it was very old thatch. No, it wasn't thatched over: it was
planked under, to keep me from forcing a way through.

Suddenly I knew where I was. I'd have fallen to my knees in thanks if only I'd been able to get up again. Mountford was stretching the truth when he said it was his property: it wasn't his yet, but his father's. We were on Lord Mountford's estate, about thirty miles from London. I'd often taken shelter in this building with Althea and Pompey if we'd been caught in the rain on one of our walks. About two miles away was the church of St Luke's: I hoped it was a good sign. The incumbent eleven years ago was a fox-hunting parson little interested in saving souls, but he had once stood up to Lord Mountford and George – admittedly it was over a matter of cubbing rather than worship, but he might be willing to give me a hearing if he was still there. Two miles, with one useless leg. But there were four very good legs standing right by me.

I don't like horses; teeth at one end and kicks at the other. As Luke said, I'm lucky if I can stay on them. I thought I could stay on this one; well-trained and with enough exercise in getting here not to be skittish and jumpy. Getting on it was the problem. I was a stranger – a very strange-smelling stranger. I'd have to undo the reins so that it was free of its tether and hope it didn't run away. I'd have to get it to stay still while I mounted. I'd have to use my bad leg either to stand on bearing my weight or to put in the stirrup and lift myself up.

I looked in the saddle bags to see if there was anything useful. In the first were my clothes; I wondered whether to put them on, but it was far too much effort. In the other were more bread and a large bottle of water; he'd have kept me there for another two days. I filled my empty stomach, and felt a little less bad for it. Then I had an idea: I searched in the first bag more thoroughly and found – Thank You, Lord – my knife. Now I wouldn't have to undo the tether before I mounted: I could cut the reins once I was on.

Now to get on that bloody horse. I said calming words to it as I patted its nose. So far so good. I thought that it would be better – less awful – to stand on my bad leg and mount with the other, so I tried it. I could – just – endure the pain. But the horse didn't

200

like it; I was mounting from the wrong side. It stamped and snorted and refused to stay still. I gave up the attempt; it'd have to be the other side. More horse-calming words – or at least a horse-calming tone of voice: 'Stand still, you brute, and let me get on you, there's a good, kind horse.'

A prayer. Stand on one leg. Lift the other leg up and ease my foot gently into the stirrup, hold onto the saddle. A deep breath, then I took my weight on my arms and my bad leg and threw myself over in one agonizing movement. I fell on top of the horse and grabbed its neck, willing it not to throw me while I gasped and got over the pain.

I was on! I put my good leg into the other stirrup, reached for my knife and cut the tether, and urged the horse to move. I couldn't ride properly, so I sat in the saddle like a sack, gripping what was left of the reins, and let the horse take its own pace; if it went in the right direction, that was enough for me. I was comfortable compared with before, now I could use somebody else's legs. The pain was as bad, but I didn't have to spend all my mental energy keeping it at bay; I was able to think.

A near-naked, filthy, wounded black man on George Mountford's horse was not going to be believed if he told the implausible truth; I'd be lucky if they even listened to me before locking me up. So I'd present myself as heroically riding to Mountford's rescue to summon help for him; that would get me shelter and a doctor for the wound, and they'd send a message to Luke to come urgently. I'd decide when I knew more about the people how much of the rest of the truth to tell before he arrived to vouch for me. A good thing that I'd shown mercy.

The steeple of St Luke's church came into view. I rode up to the vicarage, and, raising my voice as loudly as I could, cried out the words: 'Help! Help! Your master, the Honourable George Mountford, has been assaulted!'

'I thank Thee, Lord, for these blessings.' The blessings were many. I was in a comfortable bed with soft pillows propping me up. I'd had a chance to wash the filth off, and I'd been lent a nightshirt by the fox-hunting vicar of St Luke's – cleanliness and clothing add a lot to credibility in English eyes. The bullet had been taken out (not pleasant) and the wound had been dressed by a doctor. A message was on its way to Luke; I'd told the story that Mountford and I had been attacked (which was true, in a sense), then moaned in agony if they wanted to ask more and said that I should tell Mr Fitzjames first. Best of all, Mountford, the last I heard, was still unconscious; he'd been carried to Mountford Park for attention.

Yet another blessing appeared: a possible ally. The door opened and the housekeeper entered bearing a pot of tea and some cake – I knew her. 'It's Martha Jones, isn't it?' I asked. 'You were kitchen maid at Lord and Lady Mountford's eleven years ago.' She'd disliked Mountford as much as the rest of us had, in the days before *noblesse oblige* had turned him into a passably good employer.

She looked at me for a moment. 'Caesar?'

'That's right. But I'm called Fortescue now; I'm a free man in the service of Mr Fitzjames.'

'I wouldn't have recognized you. My, how you've changed!'

A few reminiscences later, I thought she viewed me favourably enough and Mountford badly enough for me to give her part of the truth. 'I haven't told anyone how all this happened, and I'd prefer not to until Mr Fitzjames appears. But it's something that reflects badly on Mr George; if he recovers he might tell a different story, and I'll be locked up. If that happens, can you make sure that Mr Fitzjames knows where I am so he can come and get me out?'

'Course I will, Caes— Mr Fortescue. Though if you want to tell me anything that reflects badly on Mr George, I promise I'll believe you.'

'I'll wait till Mr Fitzjames arrives, but thanks. Please don't tell Mr George that I used to be Caesar; he hasn't recognized me, and I don't want him to know.'

'I won't. But what happened to you after you ran off with Miss Althea? What have you been doing since?'

'What did you hear?'

'They said that they'd sold you for not stopping Miss Althea running away with Pompey like that, but we all thought that was hard on you. We knew that she just had to lift her finger and you'd come running.'

I still would. 'Yes, that was about the truth.'

'She's Lady Verity now, did you know?'

'Yes, I've heard.'

'What was the place like where you were sold? Not too bad, I hope.'

'It could have been worse.'

A few more exchanges beginning 'Do you remember—' and 'Whatever happened to—', and she left me to rest. With the knowledge that I would at least get a hearing, I fell solidly asleep.

It was dark when I was woken by the welcome sound of Luke's entry, with the fox-hunting parson. 'Here's your man, Fitzjames. The hero of the hour. Got on Mountford's horse though he was badly wounded himself, then rode to fetch help. The doctor says Mountford wouldn't have lasted much longer without attention. Your man's gallantry saved Mountford's life, no question about it.' Then he turned to me and said exactly what I knew he'd say: 'Well done, thou good and faithful servant.'

When he left us alone, Luke said, 'I'm very glad to see you, Josh; I've been searching all over for you. But what the devil were you thinking of, saving the dishonourable George's life?'

I told him the story, leaving out the possible divine intervention and what Mountford saw in Althea to make him think she was committing adultery. Though Luke had the impression that I'd done it for him rather than Althea, I didn't say so in as many words. When I finished, he put his hand on my shoulder. 'Josh, you—' I could see that I was about to get some undue thanks.

'Luke, if you say, "Well done, thou good and faithful servant", I swear I'll get out of bed and throttle you.'

'Well, I'm grateful, that's all I'll say. And Lady Verity will be grateful too, when she hears.'

'I'd rather she didn't know.' Because she'd know why I'd done it. I'd be saying to her: *See what a hero I am, Althea; what dragons I slay for your sake.*

'Doesn't she have the right to know that Mountford is her enemy?'

'She already does. But think what a position it would put her in. She'd be bound to tell her husband; you know what she's like. And though he'd say that he believed she was innocent, there might always be the nagging doubt in his mind. "No smoke without fire", that sort of thing.'

'Hmm. But we'll have to tell the truth to defend you if Mountford wakes up and starts telling lies, or wants to bring charges against you. In any case, I'm reluctant to let him get away with it. It's got my dander up; not only what he did to you, and wanted to do to me, but to bring her into it—'

'He might want to keep the story as quiet as he can. I've been thinking: no matter what he says, there are two things that he can't deny, and that he'll hate to have known more than they must be. He was found covered in a black man's blood, piss, shit and vomit; and the aforesaid black man gallantly rode off and saved his life – and it was bloody gallant, though I say so myself. You know what I feel about horses.'

He gave a burst of laughter. 'Oh, if only I could have been there to see him! I can think of only two of your bodily products that you didn't dump on him!'

'Well, excuse me, I'm very fastidious about where I put one of them.'

'I'm not fastidious at all, but even I wouldn't dump that on the dishonourable George. But the other— It gives me an idea, Josh: wait till you can walk and I've had time to think it over and I'll tell you. You'll like it, I promise you. In the meantime, I've been offered a bed, supper, and an interminable discussion about fox-hunting; we'll go home in the morning.'

'Luke, think up some suitable lie to stop them asking questions, will you? I've had to scream in agony every time they asked just to shut them up.'

'I don't need to lie at all. I shall stand there looking noble, and I shall say that you've told me everything, and that you've done just the right thing, and that I don't want to say any more because it would besmirch the fair name of an innocent lady – all of which is perfectly true.'

I heal quickly. Within a few days I could walk without much of a limp, though it tired me, and I still preferred to spend a lot of time in bed – of course I did: Luke had to do the work while I could read all day and look heroic.

Luke came into my room and spoke quietly. 'Fiona Macleod's here to visit the sick, with Janet as her small chaperone. Are you too ill to see her?'

'No; I'd welcome her with open arms. I need her spiritual advice.' We had enough to discuss that I could avoid talking about Althea, and I could always wince to cover any guilt in my expression.

'I'll send her in and leave you two together while Janet beats me at Piquet. By the way, you had a bad cold when I went on my own to see them.'

I told Fiona the story of my imprisonment and escape, concentrating on matters spiritual and avoiding anything that she'd disapprove of. 'What do you think, Fiona? Did God speak to me? Did He deliver me from evil?'

'What do you think, Joshua? That's more important.'

'I'm sorry if this distresses you, but I think that everything that happened can be explained without invoking God. I think that I was so desperate for help that when there wasn't any around I invented it. But I'm not quite sure; that's why I'm asking you.'

'It doesn't distress me. It relieves me. I thought for a moment that you'd become superstitious, not religious.'

'You surprise me. I was ready with arguments – I think to convince myself.'

205

'Joshua, I'm very happy that you're willing to listen. But I assure you that if God speaks to you, He'll use His own voice, not mine. I also think that He might find something other than a bucket of your own waste to deliver you.'

'Thanks, Fiona. I can rest more easily in my unbelief. No, I'm not an unbeliever any more, I'm a don't-knower; is there such a word?'

'There should be. I think you had great courage, quick wits and mercy, and a bit of luck. You did it for Althea, didn't you?'

'Of course. Luke thinks I did it for him; don't disillusion him. And please don't tell her about it; I don't want to seem to be showing off.'

Suddenly her face crumpled and she burst into tears.

'What's the matter, Fiona?' I asked as I put my arms round her and patted her. 'Did I say something that distressed you?'

'It wasn't you, Joshua,' she sobbed. 'It was me. I caught myself wishing that Sir Bertrand would die so you two could marry, and it's terrible to wish death on a decent man.' She blew her nose. 'If you're looking for divine intervention, think of it if you ever find a way to live with her without sin and without his death.'

'I don't wish him dead, Fiona. I know he treats her well,' I said, comforting her as she mourned for my sorrows. 'The woman I love loves me. That's more than a lot of people have, isn't it?'

'Oh, stop being so good about it. You'll only make me weep more.'

Rodney Winterton called; he was very much an admirer of Luke's since the affair with the Ace of Hearts.

'Fitzjames, you asked me to tell you when Mountford's back in town. Can I ask what you want to know for?'

'Can I ask you first what you think of him? I know he's your brother-in-law.'

'Much to my regret. I'm sorry my sister ever married him. We thought she'd done well for herself, Mountford title and all that.

But now— You wouldn't believe it, but she used to be a very taking girl before she married him.' Brotherly affection is a fine thing; I couldn't remember her ever being taking.

'So you'd be my second if I called him out? No family scruples?'

'None at all. But he won't accept your challenge, you know.'

'Yes, he will. I'll do it in such a way that he can't in all honour refuse.'

'Not certain that he has much honour. You know what they say of him? "Corrupt, corrupting, cowardly, unwise".' (Oh! I'd forgotten to remove those scurrilous verses.) 'It was he who put me up to making my disgraceful accusation against you, you know.'

'Yes, I did know. That's why I wanted you to escape with honour and skin both intact.'

'But why do you want to call him out?'

'He has done a despicable thing, and tried to besmirch the name of an innocent lady. You'll understand why I don't want to tell you any more. 'I'd be grateful if you wouldn't even reveal that to anyone else, if you can avoid it.'

'Very well, Fitzjames. He's at White's right now.'

'Thank you. Fortescue, are you ready?'

'Yes, sir.' This was Luke's revenge, not mine, but I had no objection to playing my part.

'I say, you can't take Fortescue into White's!'

'I must. Will you back me up, Winterton?'

'Of course.'

I had a feeling of having done this before as Luke brushed aside the porter's objection to my presence. He was far more polite than the barman in Jamestown, and White's was as far away in social distance as in physical. But the porter's 'Excuse me, Mr Fitzjames, but I regret that your manservant—' meant much the same as the barman's 'No niggers allowed in here'. Inside, the lush furniture, thick carpets and elegant wallpaper were also a world away from the spittoons and smoke of the Jamestown tavern. But the carefully expressionless faces of the gamblers were the same though they played for hundreds of pounds, not tens of dollars; the cards were the same though the games were different; and they turned in surprise at Luke's action of bringing me in as they had in Jamestown.

Luke ignored everyone except Mountford. He strode over to him where he sat playing whist, Winterton and I following. Then he raised his voice, though he didn't need to; everyone was waiting to see what he'd do. One hand pointing dramatically at Mountford, the other indicating that he was addressing me, he said, 'Fortescue, I am going to give you a command which you will obey instantly and without question. I take the entire responsibility for this. Fortescue, I order you to spit in this man's face.'

My aim was perfect. Mountford sat, a gobbet of my spittle dripping slowly down his left cheek, saying nothing, so shocked was he.

There was an outcry. 'Fitzjames, what the devil did you do that for?'

'He knows,' said Luke. 'I'm waiting for his reply.'

There was only one reply that Mountford could give and keep any shred of his honour in the eyes of English gentlemen. It was the ultimate insult: Luke hadn't even bothered to do it himself, but had ordered his black servant to do it.

'Well, George?' asked Winterton quietly once the first outcry died down to an expectant silence. 'Do you demand satisfaction?'

'Give him time,' said Luke. 'He knows what I'm capable of with a pistol. He's wondering if I'm as good with a sword. Believe me, Mountford, I'd be delighted to show you. *Delighted.*'

Luke, the master bluffer. He knew only one thing about sword-fighting: that in a duel it's more deadly than pistols. Against even the best shot you stand a chance of survival: a pistol may misfire or the single shot may go awry. But if you are up against a better swordsman who wants to kill you, you're dead.

Mountford took a handkerchief and wiped my spittle off his

face, then stood up. 'It would give me no satisfaction to teach a bastard good manners.' He walked out. It wasn't a bad reply in the circumstances, but it was nothing like enough. He had refused the challenge; he had allowed himself to be publicly spat on by a black servant; he had shown cowardice in the face of the enemy.

Perhaps in a few years it would be forgotten – Sackville Germain had shown that it could be. But in the foreseeable future, he would be turned away from the houses of the English gentry and nobility, he would be excluded from every club, and nobody would blame his wife if she left him. I was sorry for his mother, but mothers will forgive anything in their sons. He could take no revenge on Luke by denouncing him; his own neck was just as much at risk. It was the end of him.

Or so we thought.

Chapter 14

THERE was a message for Luke; would he come to the Veritys' house urgently on a matter of great delicacy? 'You're coming with me, and you're staying, Josh. If it's a matter of great delicacy I'm going to need you.'

We were ushered into the room where Althea and I had made known our love for each other. She wasn't there, but her husband was. And so was George Mountford. 'Get rid of your man, Fitzjames,' said Sir Bertrand. 'This isn't a matter a servant should hear.'

'I'd prefer to keep a man I can trust at my back. Mountford will serve me an ill turn if he can; I'm sure you've heard how he refused my challenge.'

'I'm afraid I must insist, Fitzjames.'

'Oh, very well. Stand outside and wait for me, Fortescue.'

I was excluded. I could make a good guess about what was going on; Mountford, out of nothing but spite, had told Sir Bertrand of his suspicions. I tried to hear what was happening, but the house was solidly built and the door was thick. I could hear nothing but the low rumble of Sir Bertrand's voice. Servants were coming and going in the hall, so I couldn't put my ear to the door; instead I stood with my back against the wall. I could still make out nothing until I defied convention by taking my wig off and pressing the back of my bare head on the wall. Now I could understand Sir Bertrand, but nobody else. I knew now why she had stayed with him: the blessing of being able to hear him! 'Most unpleasant allegation – unwilling to believe it – give you the chance to deny it.'

A footman came in answer to a summons: 'Ask Lady Verity if she would be so good as to join us here.' So she would be asked to face the charge too: she was innocent of adultery with Luke, but could she deny adultery?

She arrived at the top of the stairs and paused looking down at me in her high hair and wide dress. Looking up at her I suddenly understood why she wore these clothes that had seemed so ridiculous. They were her flag of defiance, declaring that she could be as fashionable and as absurd as any woman in a hearing world. She needed nobody's pity.

She placed her hand deliberately on the banister rail, making sure I could see it. Then she lifted one finger.

There was nothing and nobody in the world except her at that moment. My love was coming to me! I would have run up the stairs and carried her off then and there, but she raised her hand in a slight gesture to stop me. I must let her leave here in the way that she wanted to. She came down the stairs, not looking at me but watching her footing; she would not risk another sprained ankle. But when she reached the bottom she stopped for a moment. I did not need her skill at reading lips to understand the one word she said silently: 'Tomorrow.'

She swept by me into the room. I had no chance to warn her of the charge ahead of her; she would have to face this alone and unprepared. Once more I pressed the back of my head against the wall, straining for every sound and straining harder for the meaning. All her life she had to go through this.

I heard her husband: 'I hate to put you through this, my dear – you'd want to face your accuser – no, I don't believe him – kidnapped Fitzjames's man – threatened with slavery – unarmed – yes, my dear, very brave indeed – rode for help and saved his life – no, I don't know why, either – reason for the challenge – coward refused – still claims to be true – prove the scoundrel is lying – swear on the Bible.'

And then her voice, the first I'd been able to hear apart from her husband's, ringing out her declaration: 'I swear by God that I have never committed adultery with Mr Fitzjames.'

There was a crash, and Luke's voice raised in alarm: 'My God, she's fainted!'

I couldn't stop myself. I rushed into the room to see her lying in a heap on the floor, a table overturned beside her. I had just enough self-control in the few steps I needed to reach her to convert myself into an attentive – over-attentive – servant. 'I heard the noise, Sir Bertrand,' I said as I knelt beside her. 'Shall I carry Lady Verity to her room?'

'Yes, do so, Fortescue,' he said, his voice breaking. 'Oh, God, I pray that this hasn't harmed her.'

'I notice she said only that she hadn't committed adultery with Fitzjames,' said Mountford. 'She didn't swear that she'd never committed adultery at all.'

'Get out, Mountford!' Sir Bertrand roared. 'Get out before I kill you for what you've made me put my wife through!'

I looked at her in my arms, at her drawn face, her closed eyes. This was no contrived faint. I longed to carry her straight out of the front door, but I knew that she wouldn't want me to; she wanted to leave quietly tomorrow, away from Mountford's sneers. To do so she had sworn an oath on the Bible which, though true in the letter, was false in the spirit. It had cost her too much.

I carried her up the stairs; though the wound in my leg hurt badly with the effort, my anguish over her was far worse. I put her down on her bed, where her maid fussed around and exclaimed over her. 'Jenny, get me a cordial, please,' she asked, and opened her eyes.

While the maid's back was turned I took my chance. 'Ten o'clock,' I said silently. 'I'll come with a hackney.' She nodded. I could trust her to find an excuse so we'd go quietly.

Sir Bertrand came in, full of apologies, and she closed her eyes again. 'Please, Bertrand, leave me alone. All of you leave me alone, except Jenny.'

We left her. I wondered if he felt as badly about this as I did. 'Thank you, Fortescue, for your prompt action. Well done, thou good and faithful servant.'

Luke was waiting for me at the door; Mountford had already gone. I stood by invisibly and barely listened to their embarrassed exchanges – the etiquette books give little guidance as to what to say in such circumstances – but Sir Bertrand's voice boomed into my consciousness: 'It's not like her to faint; this vile allegation must have hurt her badly. I reproach myself; she's not been well lately. She vomited only this morning.'

It was lucky that I was invisible as the thought hit me. A wonderful thought, but not one that I wanted Sir Bertrand to have before I could take her away from him. Oh, why had she not told me earlier? Was I doing the right thing in leaving it until tomorrow? Should I go back now and take her away? I remembered her pale face. No. Let her recover; let her pack, and perhaps leave a letter for him, and above all have a chance to rest. And I had things to prepare too.

Luke was almost weeping with fury as we went home. 'The swine, the scoundrel, the son of a bitch!' he exclaimed, and carried on swearing in good South Carolina style for several minutes. 'You guess what happened, Josh?'

'Mountford told Sir Bertrand that you and she were lovers.'

'Yes! I told Sir Bertrand the story of how the scoundrel kidnapped you and threatened you with slavery unless you lied, and I tried yet again to make him face my challenge. Then I swore on the Bible that it was untrue, but he still convinced her husband to make her do it too. And look what happened!'

'I'm sorry, Luke—' I began, but he interrupted me.

'It's not your fault, for God's sake. It's mine. I should never have let my love for her show.'

'Don't feel guilty.' He had far less reason for guilt than I had. 'But I meant that I'm going to add to your troubles, I'm afraid. I'm leaving you tomorrow.'

That pulled him up short. 'Why so suddenly? Is it something

to do with what just happened?'

'Partly, but I'd rather not tell you why until tomorrow. You'd be in the way.'

'Josh, if you're going to kill Mountford I want to be in on it.'

'No, I'm not planning to. But you can be assured that he won't like it.'

'Very well, I shan't press you. I trust you.'

And Sir Bertrand trusted Althea, and they'd both be bitterly hurt by the truth that we weren't worthy of their trust. But tomorrow we could stop lying at last, and face the scandal in the open.

Her decision had been made for her: there was no way in which my child could be passed off as her husband's, no way to avoid hurting him, no way to avoid the scandal. She must already have known the first signs at our last meeting in Galston: this was what she meant when she'd said she wanted to find out something. She'd had to decide only the moment to leave; knowing her, she'd be rather relieved than dismayed. Yes, I felt guilt; yes, I felt concern. But nothing could compare with my joy.

My next task was to go to Clapham, where I was relieved to find Fiona alone. 'Fiona, Althea and I need your help and advice.'

'I'm glad you have the sense to ask for it this time. What's happened?'

I poured out the truth about us, though I kept Luke's secret – there was no need for me to betray him any more than I had. She was shocked, as I knew she would be, and kept uttering small reproaches, then stifling them. 'Fiona, I think she's with child,' I finished.

'Yours?'

'Well, if the baby's not a beautiful golden brown I'm going to have one or two words with her.'

She put down her cup of tea. 'So, you and Althea are planning to run away together and live in sin, and you're bringing a bastard into the world, and you want me to help you.'

'Yes, we do. If you won't we'll go elsewhere. But you reproached us for not asking you last time.'

She sighed, and put her head in her hands. 'And you want David to help too, a minister of the church.'

'Yes. Tomorrow, I want to collect her quietly and bring her here, where we can have your advice – and David's too – about what to do next.'

'Oh, Joshua, you know what David will advise you to do.'

'Yes, and I want to know what you'll advise us to do once you're convinced that we'll never be parted again. I'll understand if you turn us away from your doorstep tomorrow; we'll sleep in a barn – we've done it before. I'll understand if you think I'm not a fit person to be a teacher; I'll dig ditches to support us – at least I won't be whipped and I'll have her and the child to go home to. There is nothing that you or David can say that will persuade us to leave each other.'

She looked up. 'I can't condone it. But I can't condone turning away a woman with child from my doorstep. Bring her here. At least you can sit quietly drinking tea while David tells you what you won't hear any more than she will.'

'Tell him about the elopement; let him know we served our ten years.'

'Jacob laboured fourteen years for Rachel.'

'True, but they saw each other every day. I think our love's shown that it can pass the test.'

'Do you want me to pray for you?'

'Yes, I'm a believer enough for that.'

'I will, Joshua. I don't know what to do. I only hope that the Lord will see fit to tell me.'

I had just finished packing everything except what I'd need for tomorrow when Luke came in; surprisingly early.

'Josh, you're not the only one who's leaving. The story's over.'

'You're going back to America?'

'The day after tomorrow. I've booked a passage to France, which will be less obvious than a direct passage, and I'll go on a

French ship from there; I don't think either side will stop a neutral flag. You sure you won't come?'

'Quite sure, thanks.'

'I'll miss you. Especially when I'm seasick. I'm not looking forward to that.'

'It's easier the second time. Are you leaving because I am?'

'Partly. Partly it's because I know I ought to go back and fight for our liberty – and before you make any jokes about slave owners, I'm going to be fighting for liberty for all Americans, not just the white ones; I've come a long way since I've known you. Partly it's because I've picked up enough tit-bits that Sackville Germain has let slip over the port that I know will be very welcome to General Washington if I can get them to him as soon as possible. Partly because it's not far off the time that I'd get a return from New Orleans and people will want to see my gold and my parentage. But mainly it's because of what happened today. I thought my love couldn't harm her; now I see that it has. It'll be easier to bear having the Atlantic between us.'

I wondered for a moment whether it would be possible to hide the truth until he'd left, but I dismissed the thought. It would be better for him if he knew; he wouldn't mourn his lost love for years, or at least he wouldn't mourn her purity. But I wouldn't tell him today; I'd leave a note when I left tomorrow morning, breaking the news as gently as I could.

'Right, Josh, grab a piece of paper and a pen, and let's work out what's left over after the debts are paid. Though I warn you that if you want to give any of Mountford's money back, it'll have to come out of your share.'

'My share?'

He looked at my face. 'Josh, you didn't think that I'd run out on my best friend without splitting the profits, did you?'

'Well – I just didn't consider it. I suppose I've always thought of it as yours. I didn't come for the money, you know.'

'Equal partners: you were most insistent on that, I recall. And you did give me two guineas out of the first four you earned. But if you want me to have it all, I shan't argue with you.'

'I want it all right.' Suddenly everything seemed much brighter. I wouldn't be taking her into poverty and digging ditches to support her and our child. It was nothing like her own wealth, but it would give us a life about half-way between her condition and mine, which seemed right. And I was sure that she'd gain as much pleasure from living on money taken from George Mountford as I would – it was cleaner than her own fortune, after all.

'Now,' he continued. 'I'd prefer to behave like an honest man rather than an English gentleman: I want to pay the tradesmen's bills.'

'Yes, but do it discreetly, or everyone will know from such an outrageous action that you're planning to flee the country.'

'What about the money from Lord Winterton?'

'I think we should pay him back the original, but not the interest. And leave him a note saying that he's bloody lucky to get that.'

'I agree. He's produced at least one good son: Rodney Winterton isn't a bad sort.' I did the calculations.

'Luke, that's about twenty-two thousand pounds we have to share!'

'Eleven thousand pounds!' he breathed. 'Over forty thousand dollars!'

'Forty-eight thousand, eight hundred and – oh, forget the leftovers. Sounds good, doesn't it?'

'Sounds beautiful. Will you be safe when I've run off?'

'Of course. If anyone can tell the difference between one black face and another and asks me, I shall lift up my hands in woe and say, "Alas! Mr Fitzjames deceived me as much as anyone!" That should keep me safe.'

'Here's something else,' he said, passing me the document specifying what George Mountford's loan was to be used for, with its incriminating signatures. 'You keep this: it could hang all three of us, but it'll protect you. Give it to a trustworthy lawyer with instructions to pass it to the British government if you suddenly die or disappear, and tell Mountford you've done so. It won't harm me once I'm the other side of the Atlantic – it's more likely to give me a promotion.'

'Thanks, Luke.' It would protect Althea too. If she suddenly died or disappeared, I wouldn't care if I was hanged.

I thought about my new wealth for a moment. Ten thousand pounds of George Mountford's money seemed mine by right: one thousand for every year of slavery he'd condemned me to. But the rest— No, it wasn't mine, but I had a use for it all the same. 'Luke, there are two more people we owe; two more we wouldn't be here without. Take the money out of my share; you'll have to do the work. If I give you a thousand pounds, will you use it, the first thing you do when you get back to America—'

'The third. First I'm going to a whorehouse, and second I'm going to tell General Washington about Sackville Germain's conversation.'

'All right, the third. Find Olakunde and Sarah, buy their freedom – and their baby's, if the poor thing's still alive – and give them the rest to set up a home.'

'Of course, Josh. Thanks for reminding me: I'll spend a thousand of my own doing the same for my children and their mothers. Just one thing; who are Olakunde and Sarah?'

'Don't you remember? They were the two slaves who ran away together. They were caught, and they revealed that I'd helped them. That's why your father wanted to whip me to death. You wouldn't be sitting there with eleven thousand pounds and a headful of useful secrets if it wasn't for them.' I gave him as much detail of where they'd been sold as I could remember; he could find out more from his brothers.

'That was the best thing I ever did in my life, saving you,' he said. 'I don't mean because of what it's brought me; it would have been the best anyway. When I die, and God looks at those six out of seven deadly sins on my score, I can point to that, and maybe He'll let me scrape in.'

'Why did you do it, Luke?'

'It just seemed wrong; I don't think I can put it into words.' He stopped, then nodded. 'Yes, I can: that's another thing I owe to you – I wouldn't have been able to express this before, but I

218

can now. I looked at you, strung up on the cross piece, and I knew what Pa owed to you, staying when the smallpox hit us, and ever since; he'd said so himself often enough. And I thought; This is a man, for God's sake. You shouldn't do this to a man. All my life I'd disobeyed my Pa, but I'd always believed that he was right and I was wrong, but just then I knew that I was right and he was wrong. I gained my freedom at that moment as much as you did when you set foot on English soil. But you, Josh: why did you help Olakunde and Sarah run away? You'd never done that before – or at least, you'd never been caught.'

'No, it was the first time I helped anyone, though I'd looked the other way a lot of times. It was because—' I'd give him a hint; perhaps the news wouldn't come so hard later. 'It was because I saw that they had together what I'd once had with a woman. We tried to run away together too. It didn't work for us either.'

'Did you? You've never said.'

'You've never asked. We were just about to get married when her family tore us apart. That was my brief visit to Gretna Green that I told you about.'

'You eloped? Good God! I thought you were talking about running away with a slave woman.'

'No, no, she's English. I've a confession to make: she's the main reason I wanted to come back. Oh, I did want to show my gratitude to you, and I knew that I'd be a free man on English soil. I also wanted to get my revenge on the people who'd done that to us. But she was what I wanted most.'

'And?' he asked. 'Did you find her? Was she waiting for you? Is she the reason you're leaving? And what about your revenge? Josh, you can't leave a story half told!'

'Yes, she is the reason I'm leaving. I don't want to tell you any more at the moment; you'll know the rest of the story before you leave, I promise.'

'Well, Josh, I hope you'll be very happy together. You deserve to be.' I doubted if he'd say that tomorrow. 'And I hope your revenge is satisfactory.'

'Yes, it is. Very satisfactory.' Not so much on the people I'd once hated – old man Smith, Lord and Lady Mountford, and not even on George, though the prospect of living on his money after I'd covered him with my filth gave me much pleasure. What gave me most satisfaction was my revenge on the rich aristocratic white world that had brought me up and cast me out: I had taken an ignorant South Carolina wastrel and passed him off on them as one of their own.

I looked at my creation, and I saw that he was good.

I couldn't get much sleep that night. Four thousand nights ago, we'd found each other and been torn apart (and I had counted the leap years this time); this was why she'd chosen today. Would something go wrong, as it had before?

I rose early. I dressed in my livery so I would still be the good and faithful servant Fortescue when I collected her, and packed the last of my possessions. Then I sat down to write a note to Luke. It was more difficult than I'd imagined, and there were half a dozen crumpled sheets of paper with little more on them than, 'Dear Luke, I'm afraid I must tell you something that will hurt you.' Perhaps it would be better to keep it from him; it would certainly be easier for me.

It was a hard thing to break the news that the woman he loved was running off with his best friend, that the best friend had been deceiving him all along, and that the woman was not so pure as he'd dreamt. That would be very hard for him to bear; it would be hard for any man. I hoped that this would be what he'd feel, but I feared that though he'd come a long way from South Carolina it wouldn't be far enough, and that what would hurt him the most was the thought of his angel in bed with a black man.

I was trying again when there was a message. I was surprised that it was so early, and appalled when it turned out to be from Sir Bertrand asking Luke to see him again urgently. Slow though his brain was, it seemed to have worked just a few hours too fast.

I shook Luke awake and showed him the message. 'Have you time to get ready while I find a hackney? Because I'm going to get in it whether you're with me or not. I think something bad is happening there.'

'Go! I'll be down in a minute.'

I grabbed my belongings and was just climbing in the hackney when he rushed down the stairs in his breeches, carrying the rest of his clothes. He put them on as we drove. 'What do you think's the matter?'

'I'm not going to tell you: I may be wrong. I hope I am. But make sure the hackney stays waiting; we may need one in a hurry.'

We arrived, and my fears were confirmed when I saw the faces of the servants, fascinated to overhear what was going on. Luke didn't notice, and he followed the footman into the same room as yesterday. Althea was sitting on the sofa, still in her nightgown, her hair undressed and her face unpowdered so her freckles stood out against her white face; she did not look well. Sir Bertrand was stamping around the room raging so fiercely that he didn't even notice me as I moved invisibly to stand close to her. He stopped stamping. 'Mr Fitzjames, I have to inform you that my wife is with child.'

Luke stepped forward, his hand out. 'May I be the first to congratulate you, Sir Bertrand? And you too, Lady Verity.' I was glad I hadn't warned him; even with all his skill in lying he couldn't have managed such innocence.

'What?' exploded Sir Bertrand. 'You have the infernal temerity to congratulate me when it's your child she's carrying? You oath-breaker! You scoundrel! You seducer!'

'My child? Oh, no, Sir Bertrand, on my word as an English gentleman, if you won't take my hand on the Bible!'

I went to the sideboard, poured a glass of brandy and put it on a silver tray. I took it to Althea, knelt down beside her and offered it to her as reverently as if I were offering gold, frankincense and myrrh. We exchanged a speechless, loving smile.

'Fitzjames, what's your man doing with my wife?'

'Lady Verity seemed so unwell, sir; I brought something to restore her.'

'Thank you,' she said, putting the glass back on the tray. 'You have restored me greatly.'

I stood up to take it back to the sideboard. It was a mistake: I was too far away to stop Sir Bertrand as he strode towards her, shouting, 'If it's not him, who is it?' He raised his arm; I ran to grab him, but I couldn't stop the blow as he cracked his hand on her cheek. 'Whore!'

With the whole of my strength and weight behind it, my fist landed on his chin and sent him sprawling across the floor.

'Well done!' said Luke. 'A clean hit.'

I knelt beside Althea; tears from the shock of the blow had sprung to her eyes. 'Let's take her to a place of safety.'

'Good idea. I'll stay here and make sure he doesn't give chase until you have her safely in the hackney.'

I made to pick her up, but she waved me away. 'I want to walk out of here with my head up,' she said, but she swayed dizzily as she stood. 'I would appreciate your arm.'

We walked out into the hall; the entire staff seemed to be watching, mouths open. Jenny came down the stairs carrying some bags. 'Here you are, ma'am.'

'Jenny, you're a treasure. I'll miss you.'

'I'm sorry to see you go, ma'am, and thank you for the money you've given me in place of notice.'

I helped Althea into the hackney, and Luke ran out to join us. But before he could get in, out came Sir Bertrand. A quiet departure was not going to be possible. 'I'll have that man of yours flogged for this, Fitzjames!'

'The only reason he laid you out is that I was too far away to do it first,' said Luke, taking a place protectively between him and us. 'I was taught to believe that an English gentleman never struck a woman. Go!' he shouted to the driver.

'Where?'

'Straight ahead, man! We'll tell you later,' he cried as he swung in, leaving Sir Bertrand roaring his grievances into the street.

As soon as we were out of earshot, I called out to the driver, 'Clapham, as fast as you can.' Then I turned to Althea. 'We're going to the Macleods.'

I wanted to weep to see how ill she looked. 'Joshua, did you say the Macleods?' she asked. I nodded. 'It's so dark in here I find it difficult to read anyone's lips.' It wasn't all that dark, but the strain was too much for her. 'Thank you for your help, Mr Fitzjames,' she said. 'Will you excuse me if I rest? I trust you not to talk about me while my eyes are closed.'

Luke took his head out of his hands. 'Oh, God, you guessed, Josh, didn't you? Fainting and sickness in the morning— I should have guessed too. But I couldn't imagine that such a pure woman—'

'Luke, that pure woman trusts us not to talk about her while her eyes are closed. I'm sure she'll tell you everything that you have a right to know when we get to Clapham and she's had time to recover.' I tried to turn the subject to his voyage to America, but he wouldn't be budged.

'Josh, I can't go. I can't leave her alone, unprotected, abandoned.'

'She isn't alone. You don't think the Macleods will abandon her, do you?'

'They're very good people. If she's bearing another man's child—'

'Especially if she's bearing another man's child. Now, what time do you have to be at the wharf tomorrow?'

'But who'll call to account the scoundrel who seduced her?'

'Listen to her story before you make any assumptions,' I said, and made one last effort to get him to talk of something else. 'Luke, by the way, I've changed my mind about your fight. I hope your side wins.'

It worked. 'You do? I knew you'd come over to the right side. What made you change your mind?'

'It was easy once I asked myself the right question.'

'And that is?'

'Who's more likely to solve American problems: people like

you and Benjamin Franklin, or people like Mountford and Sackville Germain?'

For a good while we talked American independence, and when that began to pall on me, I took out my change of clothes and started to strip off my livery.

'You can't change in here in front of her!' he cried, outraged.

'Yes, I can. She won't mind; her eyes are closed. Oh, all right, I'll keep the shirt and breeches on for the sake of your modesty if not hers. Changing breeches inside a moving hackney carriage isn't too easy anyway.'

I rolled up my silly wig and the rest of my livery into a ball. As soon as we passed a rag seller I threw the bundle out of the window at him; this was his lucky day. 'Farewell, Fortescue, thou good and faithful servant.' I held my feet out. 'Notice that I'm keeping the boots even though the story's over. They're good boots.'

He sighed. 'The miller's son didn't marry the princess, after all.' Then he gave a great laugh, like the one he'd given in victory in the tavern in Jamestown, and the one he'd given in defeat on the London wharf. 'But he had a hell of a fine time, and he learnt a lot, and he took a good bit of the ogre's castle back home with him!'

Chapter 15

The Macleods were waiting for us. Fiona took Althea off to recover, while David stayed with Luke and me. 'We've sent the children to stay with friends,' he said. 'I fear there'll be an ugliness that I don't want them to see. And it leaves two rooms spare,' he added significantly. I understood and was grateful; he'd shelter us, but he wouldn't allow adultery under his roof.

'Josh, you knew this was going to happen!' Luke said. 'That's why you were so secretive yesterday, coming here and making preparations. You're a marvel!'

David raised his eyebrows at me. 'He doesn't know?'

'He will soon enough.'

'What will I know? Mr Macleod, Josh, what are you hiding?'

'We're not hiding anything from you any more, Luke,' I said. 'Just asking you to curb your impatience until she's well enough to tell you.' I turned to David. 'Sir Bertrand guessed. Luke and I managed to get her out, but he won't take long to work out she's here.'

'What did he guess?'

'He knows she's with child. He doesn't know who the father is. He accused Luke again this morning, even though he'd sworn yesterday on the Bible that he'd never sinned with her. It was all very unpleasant.'

'You hit him?' he said, looking at my knuckles.

'He had just hit her.'

'I don't think you should have, but if it was to stop him hitting her again—'

'I didn't wait to ask his intentions.'

Fiona brought Althea down, looking much better. She was dressed plainly and unpowdered, and the colour was back in her cheeks; too much colour in one of them – it was already starting to swell. As she sat drinking tea and eating scones, I thought that she had never looked more beautiful.

'Oh, I'm glad of this,' she said as she ate. 'I was violently ill this morning. That's why he guessed at last. He was shouting and storming at me, and all I could do was vomit. But now I feel better.'

'You look better, Lady Verity,' Luke said.

'Don't call me that. I have no right to it any more. Oh, I know he hurt me, but this is going to hurt him far worse.'

'I don't care what you've done, ma'am, he had no right to hit you. You don't have to tell me anything; I'll always believe that you are the sweetest, finest woman in the world.'

'Oh, I'm not. I'm just a woman in love with a man who isn't her husband and I'm bearing his child. That makes me an adulteress. I will tell you the story: everyone else in the room knows it but you.'

'Are you sure?' I asked. 'I'll tell him if you like.'

'No, it will come better from me. Besides, it's easier for me to talk than read lips.' As she spoke, I quietly moved furniture out of the way in preparation for what I feared I'd have to do if South Carolina proved too strong, and then I took my place standing beside her, ready to move.

'Almost eleven years ago,' she began, closing her eyes so as not to be interrupted, 'I eloped to Scotland with a man. I say a man, but he was hardly more than a boy, and I was hardly more than a girl. We reached Gretna Green, and we found someone to marry us the next day. But less than two hours before the ceremony my family burst into our room. Lord and Lady Mountford took me back to England; George dragged him away. I thought he died – you know George, so you know why I thought that –

226

but I never stopped loving him. Everything was kept quiet and I married Bertrand. But the man I loved wasn't dead, and he never stopped loving me. He endured ten years of terrible suffering, missing me every day, dreaming of me every night, thinking he'd never see me again. And then, earlier this year – at the time you came to England – he found a way to return. He tried to keep away from me because he learnt I was married, but there was a chance meeting in the street; I knew him at once. We behaved very well for months, as if our elopement had never happened. Nobody knew what we were feeling; we didn't even know what the other was feeling. Even after we discovered that we still loved each other, we still carried on behaving well, until – until we found that love was more important than anything else to us. We were going to leave quietly today, but Bertrand guessed too soon.'

She opened her eyes. 'Mr Fitzjames, let me tell you about this man. He didn't tell me this: I found out only after I'd decided to leave with him. He faced almost certain death to protect my reputation. Perhaps that's not unusual: you were prepared to fight for my honour when you challenged George, and I'm grateful to you – though I wish both of you had realized that your lives are worth far more to me than my reputation. I'll forgive you, Mr Fitzjames, because you didn't know any better. He did, and he'll answer to me for it.' She glanced up at me: she didn't appear very fierce. 'But then he did something else, Mr Fitzjames, something I don't think any other man would have done. He had his enemy wounded and helpless at his feet: a man who had done him a grievous wrong in the past, and if he lived would probably do him a grievous wrong again. He had every reason to kill his enemy, yet he let him live: no, more than that – he saved his enemy's life.' She looked up at me: I looked down at her, loving her for the love for me that shone in her face. 'I wonder why he did that.'

'I – he – I think that he – well, he's just not very good at hating.'

'He's very good at loving.' She turned back to Luke, who still

227

hadn't put two and two together, though the equation was on the board in front of his eyes. 'We know that there will be the foulest gossip; there'll be no easy life for us. But together we can bear anything; apart we can bear nothing. We loved each other for ten years without hope; now we have it. Now we have a child on the way. Can you understand us, Mr Fitzjames? Can you forgive us?'

'Ma'am, I understand. I have nothing to forgive. I love you: I've never said so, but you must have known. I believed that you were the sweetest, finest woman in the world: I still believe it. Thank you for telling me your story: it's made it easier for me to bear, knowing that you chose a better man than I could ever be.' He pulled out a handkerchief and blew his nose. 'So you all knew this?' he asked the rest of us.

'Fiona told me about it yesterday evening, after J— after the man came and asked to bring her here today, and there are some questions I have to ask,' David said. He was about to ask them, but thought better of it. 'You're right: he is a good man. If there's any way I can help them I shall – short of condoning adultery.'

'I knew about the elopement soon after it happened,' said Fiona. 'I taught both of them when they were children, and I watched them grow up together. When he came back to England, I was one of the first people he met. I advised him to keep away from her, and I've given him advice since. He doesn't seem to have taken much notice of it, but he keeps asking for more. Perhaps he's right to disregard what I've advised him to do, I don't know. All I know is that I love both of them almost as much as I love my own children.'

'What about you, Josh? When I first told you that I loved her, did you know about it then? Couldn't you have warned me?'

'I had the best of all possible reasons for knowing about it.' I paused, waiting for him to pick it up; he didn't. 'I'm sorry, Luke, I tried to warn you, but—'

'I thought you were talking about her husband. I might have felt differently if I'd known the kind of man I was up against.' He sighed. 'Well, if you'll excuse me, ladies, Mr Macleod, I'll go. I presume that he'll be here soon, and I'd prefer not to meet him. Let's go, Josh.'

'Luke, everyone's been trying to break it gently to you; we've been dropping hints, and lately we've almost been shouting it at you. He's here already.' Then, as his gaze went towards the door and the ceiling, I added, 'He's in this room now.'

His gaze swept round, found no lurking strangers, then fell upon a Presbyterian minister and model of virtuous husbandly love.

'I'm the man.'

'What man?'

'The man she loves. The man who loves her. The father of her child.'

'Oh, Christ!' He covered his face with his hands. When he took them away I saw, not justified anger, but sick revulsion: South Carolina had won the battle. I stepped forward to protect her. 'I thought you were so pure, and all the time you lusted after a nigger's cock!'

I hit him before he could say anything else. He fell neatly into the space I'd made for just this purpose. I was sorry that I needed it.

'Thank you for minding the furniture,' said David. 'All the same, you shouldn't have done it.'

'What did he say?' asked Althea. 'It must have been very bad.'

'Aye, it was,' said David. 'I shan't sully this house by repeating it.'

'It was the sort of thing George would say,' I said, turning to her again. 'But he isn't like George. I know him. I hoped he would take it out on me; he has a right to. After all, I did deceive him.'

As Fiona went to Luke as he lay sprawled out and started to tend him, David said, 'Joshua, you can't hit every man who uses that kind of language to her. I fear that a lot of people will say such things. You must find a better way, for the sake of your knuckles if not of your soul.'

We heard a groan from Luke. 'Oh, God,' he said looking up at

Fiona. 'My memory's a little blank about what happened. Did I say something abominable?' South Carolina had lost the war.

'You did.'

He rolled over and crawled on all fours to Althea, where he rose to a kneel. 'Ma'am, is there any way that I can ask for your forgiveness?'

'Of course, Mr Fitzjames. I didn't hear what you said.'

'I wish nobody else had. Thank you, ma'am.' I gave him a hand to stand up. 'Can I ask you to forget what I said, Josh, and remember only that I was glad that she'd chosen a better man?'

'I can't remember a word you said after that; I was so over-come by your good opinion of me.'

He clasped my hand in both of his. 'Thanks, Josh.'

'Now, I've one or two quest—' David began, but Luke was still speaking.

'And I've more to ask your forgiveness for, ma'am. And you too,' he said to Fiona and David. 'I've deceived you. I'm not really Mr Fitzjames. I'm—'

'The Marquis of Carabas,' said Fiona. 'We've known since the night I was reading the children *Puss in Boots*, and Janet said, "Isn't he just like Joshua?" '

'And I've known since the day after we met,' added Althea.

'Josh told you?'

'As soon as I asked him. We don't tell lies to each other. I must say, I'd be grateful to you even if you hadn't brought Joshua back to me for all the amusement it's given me watching your progress.'

'Now can I ask my questions?' David said, cutting through Luke's expressions of chagrin. 'When you two eloped, you went to Gretna Green with the intention of marriage, you say?'

'Yes,' I said, sitting down next to Althea. I held her hand; David made no objection to this, but I didn't risk his disapproval by putting my arm round her, so we sat holding hands like the children we used to be.

'Were there witnesses that you wanted to marry each other?'

'You think it'd make life easier for us if we could prove that?' I asked.

'It might, it might.'

'Well, there were the people at the inn: they knew why we were there. Oh, and the smithy: we went there first of all to get my collar taken off.'

'The blacksmith was the one who was to perform the ceremony next day – though it cost me my diamond bracelet to get him to agree to it,' Althea added. 'I didn't understand a word he said, so Joshua had to translate everything.'

'Hmm. That's a pity. There'll be witnesses to say that Joshua wanted to marry, but not you.'

'Oh, no, I said so too. The blacksmith asked me clearly whether I wanted to – that was all I did understand, except when he said that he'd marry us.'

'Can you remember his exact words when he said that he would?'

'Of course: he said, "Then I shall marry ye".'

'What did he do after that?'

'I don't know. We weren't looking at him.' She looked at me now, and, almost eleven years later, I recognized the look that she'd given me at the time.

David coughed loudly. I heard him, but Althea didn't. 'David's just coughed to attract our attention,' I told her. 'He can't hit the anvil with the hammer like the smith did.'

We turned back to him: his normally austere manner had slipped. 'And after that?' he asked. 'You shared a room?'

'Yes. David, why all these questions?'

'One more and then I'll tell you, but you must answer me truthfully. Did—'

But just then we heard the sound of the world arriving on the doorstep; I think David suppressed an unministerly curse. Sir Bertrand's voice was loud and demanding as he stormed in, followed by George Mountford. Everybody began shouting at once.

'Oh, Bertrand,' Althea said, mercifully unable to hear the noise. 'Did you have to bring George?'

'Who is he?' Sir Bertrand bellowed. 'If he's not Fitzjames, who is he?' I was still apparently invisible to him though I sat holding hands with his wife.

But Mountford saw. 'Of course, Althea, I should have guessed earlier. You have a taste for black flesh, don't you? Did your brain fever send you mad as well as deaf? First that scum Caesar, now this one.' I felt David's hand on my shoulder, pressing me into my seat. Mountford turned to Sir Bertrand. 'The family should have warned you before you married her. Be grateful you know it now, before she spread her legs for every nigger in England.'

David's high, dry minister's voice cut through the uproar: 'Mr Fitzjames, will you help me pacify Sir Bertrand? We can leave Mr Mountford to Joshua.' His hand lifted from my shoulder.

I leaped towards Mountford; I ignored the noise around me as the others prevented Sir Bertrand from attacking me. I heard only Althea's voice, 'This time I want to see, Joshua.' I grabbed Mountford by the throat with one hand, and with the other forced his arm behind his back, hard enough to let him know that I could force it a lot harder. I stood behind him and turned him round so we were both facing Althea. Everyone else fell silent.

'It's the same nigger, Mountford; I came back,' I said quietly and clearly in his ear. 'Even though you tied me up and beat me, and sold me to the first slaver you met, I came back. I defeated you. And even though you held me an unarmed prisoner with a pistol in your hand, I defeated you. I'll always come back and I'll always defeat you. I spared your life when you were wallowing in my filth because I didn't want to grieve your mother. I'm sparing your life now because I don't want to offend our host. Don't ever believe that you'll be lucky the third time. Now, you will apologize to your cousin for what you just said to her.'

'Sorry, Althea.'

'That's not good enough,' I said, forcing his arm higher up his back.

'Will you accept my most profound and abject apologies for what I just said to you, ma'am?'

'Oh, very well, George,' she said. 'But only because Joshua wants me to.'

'I don't hate you,' I said, and I realized it was true. 'I just want to be rid of you, because you're a bloody nuisance. So you will go away. You will never do anything that harms me or Althea, or the people we love. And you will never see me again. Because, believe me, George, if you cross me once more, I'll be the last thing you'll ever see. Do you agree?'

'Yes.'

'Yes what?'

'Yes, sir.'

I let go of him and watched him walk out, then I sat next to Althea and took her hand again. 'You're right, David. There are much better ways than hitting people.'

'Aye, well, it's not a means that I'd use among my flock, but it's a step in the right direction.'

By this time Sir Bertrand was, if not pacified, at least sitting down; his voice could be heard only in the street rather than all Clapham. The rest of us left him and Althea to talk, making sure only that he couldn't hit her again.

'Why, Althea? Why him of all people?'

'I told you before we married that I loved another man, but I thought he was dead. He isn't, as you can see. We loved each other when we were hardly more than children, and we eloped.'

'You eloped? Good God! Did your family know?'

'Of course. They were the ones who stopped us. They kept it all quiet.'

'So you didn't marry him?'

'Oh, Bertrand, of course I didn't marry him. I wouldn't have married you if I had; I wasn't sure he was dead.'

I saw a movement from David, but he stopped himself and let them talk.

'Althea, there's something I must know. Were you – were you a virgin when I married you? Was he there before me?'

I felt her hand tighten on mine. 'Well—'

'Althea, answer his question,' David said. 'Give him the truth;

233

this is more important than you know. After the blacksmith said he'd marry you, did you engage in sexual relations?'

We looked at each other; her face was scarlet, and I felt the heat in my skin. We had been so young, so fumbling—

'Yes,' she said. 'We did.'

'I'll have the law on you, damn you!' Sir Bertrand roared, standing up. 'I'll sue you and your family for every penny! I'll have him in prison for this, if there's a law in England!'

'Aye, there is a law in England, though I doubt if it gives you all that,' said David. 'But there's a different law in Scotland. Will you sit down again, Sir Bertrand, please? There's something that you need to know before you go spending good money on lawyers.'

He sat down with bad grace. 'Well?'

'These two eloped and reached Scottish soil. There they declared their intent to marry in front of witnesses, who acknowledged their declaration, and they consummated it afterwards. Under Scottish law, that counts as marriage.'

For minutes nobody spoke; all I could hear was the clock ticking as I looked at the astounded, beautiful face of – my wife! Then she said slowly, 'I think I misunderstood you, David. I think you said that Joshua and I were married.'

'Aye. What you called a ceremony is nothing but a public recognition of the union. That blacksmith wasn't promising to marry you the next day: he was actually doing so. That wouldn't have been binding in itself: it's the consummation that matters. You've been husband and wife from the moment you first acted as such.'

'Oh, but that means I've committed bigamy!'

'Is that better or worse than adultery? I don't know. But at least your bigamy was unintentional; I don't think there's a court that would punish you for it.' He turned to Sir Bertrand. 'Any more than there's a court that would punish you for stealing another man's wife. Though of course, it might do so for assaulting another man's wife,' he finished reflectively.

Sir Bertrand stood up. 'I shall consult my lawyer,' he said, very quietly.

'Aye, that would be wise.'

Althea stood up and went to him, holding her hand out. 'Bertrand?'

He refused to take it. 'Goodbye, Althea.' He left; David showed him out.

Althea sat back on the sofa with me. She sighed, then took my hand and smiled at me. She'd known she'd have to hurt Sir Bertrand; it could have been worse.

I exchanged glances with Fiona; she seemed almost as happy as we were. 'Your advice, dearest godmother: divine intervention?'

'Dearest godson, I'm not going to give you any more advice. You're big enough and old enough to make your own decisions. All I shall do is give thanks to the Lord, whether He intervened or not.' She turned to Luke and gave a slight nod towards the door. 'Mr Fitzjames?'

He looked at Althea and me holding hands. 'Oh, yes, of course. I – er – I'll bid you – I'll say— Oh, goddamn it!' he said, forgetting his manners. 'Will you come and see me off at the wharf? Both of you?'

'Of course.'

'I'll see you tomorrow.' Then he and Fiona left us alone.

I held my wife in my arms, and she held her husband in hers. She kissed her husband, and I kissed my wife. And then there was a loud cough outside the door, and my wife and I sat holding hands again, demure but rumpled.

Only David returned. 'Can it be true, that we've been married for almost eleven years without knowing it?' I asked him.

'Well, I put it more strongly to Sir Bertrand than was warranted. You were underage to marry without the consent of your guardians: it could be challenged. On the other hand, there's a child coming that'll proclaim its paternity as soon as it's born: the courts won't make it a bastard if they don't have to.' He was uncomfortable – we were being rewarded for our lustful behaviour. 'If you take my advice, you'll go and live over the border, so the case can go to a Scottish court. And you'll find that blacksmith, or at least another witness of your intent.' He shrugged. 'In the end, it will come down to how good your lawyer is – I'll give you the name of one in Edinburgh – and how hard Sir Bertrand will fight it.'

It seemed a flimsy foundation to support the difference between sinful lust and virtuous matrimony, but I wasn't going to argue with it.

Nor was Althea. 'Bertrand won't fight it at all if he can be free to marry again, so long as he can keep my fortune.'

'Keep your fortune?' cried David, outraged. 'If he's not married to you he has no right to it!'

'I have no right to it either. Neither did my father. If any of us has a right to it, it's Joshua: it was made out of the misery of him and people like him.'

'Then use it,' I said. 'Use a slave trader's fortune to gain us our freedom.'

'I shall. That seems fitting, doesn't it?' She turned to David. 'All the same, it would be very good to know now if we're married, rather than waiting for the court ruling. Will our baby be born a bastard or not?'

'What do you say, David?' I added. 'We'll take your word on it until the court decides.'

'My word, eh? I'll give you more than that; I'll give you my deed.' He blushed. 'You haven't asked where Fiona is. I told her she could go and fetch the children home, because we'll need only one bed tonight for the pair of you.'

Around us was a forest of masts, as ships were making ready to carry cargoes to and from all parts of the world; sugar, tea, cloth, coffee – and guns to trade for slaves. We stood beside the French ship that would carry Luke away to the American war. Althea and I would then take the first stage of our journey to Scotland. We'd travel slowly and comfortably now we had no pursuers; she needed time to get over her sickness in the morning. We wouldn't read any newspapers until we reached Gretna Green; perhaps by then the worst of the scandal would have died down.

Besides, we'd have better things to do than read newspapers.

We were all three very tired: Luke had spent his last night in Covent Garden, and Althea and I had spent our first night in a marital bed – at least, the first time we'd known about it.

Luke held out his hand. 'I give you my very best wishes for your future health and happiness, Mr and Mrs— Mr and Mrs What, Josh? You've been Caesar, Joshua and Fortescue, but no proper surname. You'd better decide on one unless you want to be Mr and Mrs Er-Um all your lives.'

'We have. I'm Joshua Freeman from now on: it was my wife's maiden name.' It felt good to call her *my wife*.

'Very appropriate too. Mrs Freeman, I shan't promise to love you without hope for ten years like he did, but it will take me some time to get over you. Maybe when the war is over I'll come back and marry Janet. I fear that she'll be old enough by then. I only hope I come back before she's a grandmother.'

'I only hope you come back.' She put her arms round him and kissed him.

'Ah!' he said with satisfaction. 'I've wanted to do that for a long time.'

'Not as long as he did.'

He turned to me. 'Josh, I was thinking last night, in between whor— Oh, sorry, Mrs Freeman.'

'I quite understand. You have a long voyage ahead of you.'

'I'm failing, Josh,' he said in an undertone and hardly moving his lips. 'Only four.'

But he'd shaved off his moustache, and Althea was very proficient. We smiled at each other complacently.

'Anyway,' he continued. 'You know we said it was the end of the story, Josh? Well, last night I asked myself, "Whose story?" I thought it was mine – you know, young man sets out for adventure with nothing but his wits and his good and faithful servant. But I suddenly realized it was your story all the time.'

'You should have known. It's not called *The Marquis of Carabas*; it's called *Puss in Boots*.'

One last hug of farewell, then he walked up the gangplank,

turned at the top to wave at us, and disappeared into the ship that would start him on his journey to the west.

I was about to set off on our own journey, but she stopped me. 'Now that he's gone, you can tell me. What did he say that made you hit him?'

'Er—'

'Come on, Joshua. You know I'll get it out of you sooner or later.'

'He said – well, he said that you lusted after a nigger's cock.'

'You shouldn't have hit him. He was only telling the truth.'

'Althea!'

She laughed at my expression. 'Shouldn't I say things like that now we're a respectable married couple?'

'Probably married, never respectable.' I held her hands in mine. 'Oh, my love, I have everything I've ever wanted and more – except for one thing. If only you could have your hearing back.'

'It doesn't matter when I'm with you; I can always understand you. You have beautiful lips.'

I took my cue. It was our first kiss in public, and we made it a good one. Some people would be shocked; some people wouldn't be. We didn't care.

We had freedom in our love.

Author's Notes

FOR dramatic effect, I have exaggerated the differences between American and English language and culture in 1775: these became much more obvious after the American Revolution (though Luke, as an American patriot, would use the unofficial local currency of the dollar rather than the pound).

In particular, it is unlikely that gamblers in a small South Carolina town at that period played a recognizable form of that very American game, poker, which developed on the Mississippi river boats in the first half of the nineteenth century from the eighteenth century French game of Poque.

Techniques for teaching the deaf and Deaf Sign Language were not as widespread as I have indicated: indeed, some of the pioneers in the field tried to keep their methods secret to discourage imitators.

This is not a novel about the Atlantic slave trade. However, it would be wrong to omit reference to the scale of the trade during the eighteenth and early nineteenth century. According to James Walvin, in *Black Ivory* (see Bibliography): 'About 12 million Africans were transported across the Atlantic, but a substantial minority died *en route* (some 10 to 20 per cent). . . . In the years 1700–1810 the British shipped perhaps 3 million.' These figures take no account of the millions who died before, or soon after, the Middle Passage, nor of the millions more who lived and died in slavery to make Britain, America and other Western nations rich.

Bibliography

Brander, M., *The Georgian Gentleman*, (Saxon House, Farnborough, 1973)

Carter, A. (trans.), 'Puss in Boots' in *Perrault's Fairy Tales*, (Jonathan Cape, London 1967)

Equiano, O., *The Interesting Narrative of the Life of Olaudah Equiano* (1789), republished as *The African*, (The X Press, London, 1998), and as *The Interesting Narrative and other writings*, ed. V. Carretta (Penguin, Harmondsworth, 1995)

Fryer, P., *Staying Power: The history of black people in Britain*, (Pluto Press, London 1988)

Gerzina, G., *Black England: Life before emancipation*, (John Murray, London, 1995)

Greene, J.P. (ed.) *Colonies to Nation 1763–1789: A documentary history of the American Revolution*, (W.W. Norton, New York, 1976)

McCrum, R., Cran, W. & MacNeil, R., *The Story of English*, (BBC Books, London, 1986)

Meltzer, M., *Slavery: A world history*, (Da Capo Press, New York 1993)

Miles, B., *British Sign Language: A beginner's guide*, (BBC Books, London, 1988)

Parlett, D., *The Oxford Guide to Card Games*, (Oxford University Press, Oxford, 1990)

Porter, R., *London: A social history*, (Penguin, Harmondsworth, 1996)

Stone, L., *The Family, Sex and Marriage in England 1500–1800*, [abridged edn.], (Penguin, Harmondsworth, 1979)

Walvin, J., *Black Ivory: A history of British slavery*, (Fontana, London, 1993)

Walvin, J., *An African's Life: The life and times of Olaudah Equiano 1745–1797*, (Continuum, London and New York, 1998)